DECKER'S DILEMMA

A SUBIC BAY MYSTERY

JACK AMBRAW

Blank Slate Press | St. Louis, MO

Blank Slate Press
Saint Louis, MO 63110
Copyright © 2015 Jack Ambraw
All rights reserved.

A Subic Bay Mystery

For information, contact:
Blank Slate Press
An imprint of Amphorae Publishing Group
4168 Hartford Street, Saint Louis, MO 63116

Manufactured in the United States of America
Set in Minion Pro and Gill Sans
Interior designed by Elena Makansi
Cover Design by Kristina Blank Makansi
Library of Congress Control Number: 2015950065
ISBN-13: 978-1-943075-06-5

To Lynn

DECKER'S DILEMMA

CHAPTER ONE
2230, MONDAY, DECEMBER 23, 1986

The cruiser sliced through the South China Sea, bearing northwest at eight knots, twenty-three miles from Luzon's west coast. The sailor stepped through the hatch and dogged the watertight door behind him. He stood frozen in his tracks, breathing in the salt air and waiting for his eyes to adjust to the blackness. A third-quarter moon on the horizon, mostly lost in cloud cover, provided the only light.

Elliott Decker smiled. Standing a few feet away, he recognized the familiar posture silhouetted against the water. The five-foot-six frame. Crew cut. Wire rim glasses. Extending an arm, Decker put a hand on the sailor's shoulder. Kippen jumped, his entire body quivering.

"You should've seen your face," Decker laughed.

Kippen seized the lanky, dark-haired sailor by the shirt collar. "Are you nuts? You scared the hell out of me."

Decker took hold of his friend by the wrists and freed himself from clinched fists. "What's got you so jumpy?" He glanced around the deserted main deck passageway. "And what are you doing out here?"

"Hack said you'd be topside." Kippen nodded towards a nearby ladder. "Let's get away from the hatch."

The sailors walked up a level and stood at the aft edge of the helicopter flight deck. Kippen crossed his arms. "I need to talk."

"Good or bad?"

"Depends. It's work related."

Decker laughed and ran his fingers through his thick, neatly combed brown hair. At six-foot-two, he towered over his friend. "You've forgotten more about the naval supply system than I've ever learned. You sure I'm the right person for this?"

"No, but you're the only one I can trust. I've found a problem with our inventory. We're missing a few expensive items. It's like parts are being ordered, but never arrive on board."

"Maybe it's operator error," Decker shrugged.

Kippen glared at his friend. "It's not that. I'm the one who places the orders."

"But you're not the only one who accesses the system. Chief Fray does, too. And he and computers don't exactly get along. He's an errant keystroke away from crashing the whole network every time he logs on."

"That was my initial theory," Kippen admitted. "A computer glitch causing duplicate orders, but I haven't been able to find any proof of that."

"Have you told anyone else? Chief? How about Suppo? He worked at the supply depot before the *Harvey.*"

Kippen shook his head. "Not yet. I want to solve the problem first, so I don't get blamed for it. I *did* call the depot a few days ago, but they were no help."

Even in the dim light, Decker could detect concern in

Kippen's face.

"Has this got you that worried? You're too much of a perfectionist, Kippen. Remember when you thought you lost the message folder? You said your career was ruined. Turned out it was a simple case of misfiling." He studied his friend's expression in the moonlight. "Unless there's something else?"

An eastward swell tipped the ship hard to starboard. The sailors squatted to maintain balance as salt spray hit their faces. Kippen took off his glasses and wiped them clean with his coveralls. "There *is* something else. Claire drove down from Clark yesterday. Said she's transferring and didn't want a long distance relationship."

"Ouch," Decker frowned. "Where's she going?"

"Wichita. McConnell Air Force Base."

"That qualifies as long distance. Sorry to hear that, my friend."

"Thanks," Kippen sighed. He took a handful of papers from his back pocket. "I thought she might be the one."

"You've said that about all your girlfriends."

Kippen disregarded the observation, wadded a sheet of paper, and lobbed it into the ocean. He reached for another. "Letters from Claire," he explained. "Want to toss one?"

Decker shook his head. "They're all yours," he said, peering over the side. "And you'd better put more into it. I think that one blew back on the ship."

Kippen shrugged and threw another paper ball. "How are you and Vega?"

"She mentioned the dreaded F-word the other day."

"Friends?"

"'Fraid so."

"That's not a bad thing," Kippen reasoned. He started to hurl another letter overboard, but paused in mid-delivery. "Let me get your opinion about something. I was in a trike going home the other day—"

The sound of a hatch opening interrupted the conversation. The sailors watched two boiler technicians emerge from the ship's lower level and walk aft towards the fantail.

"What about the other day?" asked Decker.

Kippen waved his hand. "It was nothing." He pitched the last letter and turned to Decker. "I want some time alone to think about things. Thanks for coming out here. I needed to talk to someone."

"Glad to be of help."

"You weren't, but thanks anyway for listening. Just keep all this between us, okay?"

"Trust me, I will tell no one." Decker gave Kippen a mock salute. "I will put my security clearance to good use for once. Oh, and Merry Christmas."

"Merry Christmas to you, too," Kippen smiled, as the ship swayed to port under a swell. "Whoa, I'd better sit."

"Good thinking," Decker agreed, as he walked down the ladder, leaving Kippen perched cross-legged on the edge of the deck.

After a brief stop on the mess deck, Decker entered the supply department berthing, stripped to a T-shirt and skivvies, and climbed in his rack. He closed the thin blue drape, turned on the overhead light, and retrieved a notebook stashed under his mattress.

Hack Wilson peeked inside the curtain and flashed a smile, his curly blonde hair wet from a shower. "I saw your light on. Are you awake?"

Decker didn't look up. "No. Go to bed."

"I can't sleep. What are you doing? Writing in your diary again?"

A slow exhale. "For the hundredth time, this isn't a diary. It's my Book of Dates. A record of what happens in my world."

"Sounds like a diary to me. What are you writing about anyway?"

"Imee."

"What about you?"

"Not 'I' and 'me.' I'm writing about Imee." Decker closed his journal. "I suddenly feel like Bud Abbott."

"Who?"

"Never mind," Decker said. "I was writing about Imee Marcos. And Bongbong. Ferdinand and Imelda's kids."

"What kind of name is Bongbong?"

"It's a nickname. He's Ferdinand, Jr."

"I'd stick with Ferdinand."

"You've got a lot to learn about your new homeland. Most Filipino's have nicknames. I know a NoyNoy, a Popoy, and a Joker. But my personal favorites are names that are bell sounds. I know a Bong, Pong, and a Dingdong. "

"I know one of those," Hack smiled.

"I'll pretend I didn't hear that."

"I'd still stick with Ferdinand," Hack countered. "Why were you writing about the Marcos family anyway?"

"It's my anniversary," said Decker. "I reported on board the *Harvey* one year ago today."

"My condolences."

"Thank you, my friend."

"So tell me, what do the Marcoses have to do with your

anniversary?"

"Nothing. I was just thinking about the upcoming elections. I suspect there's going to be trouble. The anti-Marcos forces are planning his downfall."

"They must think Luzon isn't big enough for the both of you."

Decker tucked the notebook under his mattress and closed his curtain. "Go to bed."

* * *

Kippen couldn't sit still. He got up, walked down the port ladder, and cautiously made his way aft to the fantail, while holding onto the top cable of three thin metal lines that formed a safety railing around the perimeter of the ship. The two boiler techs, smoking and talking quietly waiting to go on watch, huddled near the five-inch gun mount. Kippen knew smoking was not allowed topside at night, but he also knew most of the crew ignored the rule, expertly holding the burning end of a cigarette towards their palms in a semi-closed fist. A simple "hey guys" was all he said as he walked to the starboard side and up the ladder.

Kippen made two trips around the flight deck, deep in thought. Tired of walking in circles, he sauntered forward along the starboard side where the superstructure on his left narrowed the passageway to only a few feet. He paused amidships a few frames aft of the quarterdeck and leaned against the Mark 32 anti-submarine torpedo tubes, staring at the blue-green glow of bioluminescent plankton, churned up by the ship's propeller and sent swimming along in its wake. Lost in the solitude of the night, he thought he heard footsteps behind him.

Boots on the nonskid-coated deck.

He turned, but it was too dark. *Probably nothing,* he said to himself. *The ship makes odd noises at night.* He looked back towards the ocean and rested his elbows on the chest high pyramid of three torpedo tubes, his mind drifting again to the missing parts in the ship's inventory.

* * *

Unable to sleep, Decker opened a Herman Wouk novel that he'd been slogging through off and on while underway, hoping it'd work its magic once again. Twelve pages into his nightly reading, Decker heard the familiar din of Petty Officer Pinto next to him in the aisle, the unfortunate circumstance of having sailors sleeping above, below, and in the case of Pinto, across from him. Decker concentrated on the book with great effort, desperately hoping to avoid a conversation.

Pinto inserted a key into his locker, raised the lid, and rested it on a small support post. He methodically began undressing, neatly placing each item of clothing into his laundry bag. He reached over and pulled open Decker's curtain. "You're always reading. You should exercise your body as well."

Decker noisily turned a page.

Pinto hung a small mirror next to his locker, removed his T-shirt, and began flexing his biceps. "Take a look at these guns. They're huge."

Decker turned another page. "I'm not looking. I'll take your word for it."

Apparently satisfied with what he saw in the mirror,

Pinto spread a towel on the deck, stripped off his pants, and lay prone on the deck in his underwear.

"Jesus, dude," Decker said. "Now I know why I hate to go to sea."

Pinto ignored the comment and began doing rapid push-ups, counting aloud. Decker heard Pinto reach two hundred with a shrill grunt. "I hope you're finished."

"Just gettin' started."

"I was afraid of that."

Pinto stood and began rummaging through his rack. "Time for cardio. Join me?"

"No, and please get dressed."

Pinto laughed, threw on his T-shirt and sweat pants, and headed out of the berthing, a towel slung over his shoulder.

"Why me?" Decker sighed, closing his curtain and rolling over to face away from the aisle. Twenty-four pages later, Decker drifted off to sleep as the USS *Caine* steamed into the eye of a typhoon. Out cold by 2345.

* * *

Again the noise behind him. Kippen spun around. A shadow moved behind the captain's gig. "Who's there?"

Silence.

Kippen squinted. "Decker? Is that you? You're not going to scare me this time. Hey, I thought of something else."

A figure appeared out of the darkness. The man approached within an arm's length as clouds drifted away from the moon, casting a dim light on his face.

Kippen took a step back, reaching for the lifeline.

"Oh," he said. "It's you."

* * *

In the middle of a quickly forgotten dream, the man-overboard alarm startled Decker awake.

CHAPTER TWO
0005, MONDAY, DECEMBER 24

The alarm required a simple task: get out of bed, get dressed as quickly as possible, and report to your duty station for a head count. The berthing suddenly teamed with sailors frantically getting dressed. Decker rolled out of his rack, slipped into his coveralls and boots, and headed out the door.

Hack Wilson wasn't so lucky. He groped in the darkness for his footwear. "Damn it, has anyone seen my boondockers?" he yelled amidst the chaos.

The only reply came from an anonymous voice across the berthing. "If they were up your ass, you'd know it."

"Thanks, jerk," Hack said to no one in particular. One last sweep of his hand behind his rack located the missing footwear. He didn't bother to tie them, his lone thought was to head out the door. Only fat Ollie remained, heavily panting over the exertion of energy it was taking to get dressed so quickly. Hack ran to the port side ladder, sliding down with his hands on the rails as the ship came to a halt, rocking from side to side with the waves. He covered the last few feet in record time and threw open the door to Supply Support. "I made it," he exhaled.

"Hack, you're late," Decker said. "What the hell took you so long? You really must stop that self-abuse all night long. And to think you've only been away from dear Leeandra for one day."

Chief Fray stood in front of his desk and silenced his men with a scowl. Medium height with his thick, light blonde hair trimmed short in a buzz cut, Chief's life was being at sea. He stretched his back and surveyed the room. He spoke with an accent that gave away his Lawton, Oklahoma upbringing. "Enough out of you, Decker. Glad you could find time to join us Wilson. Where the hell are Kippen and Limpert?"

Pinto, Decker, and Hack exchanged glances. Decker was the last to see Kippen, but that had been topside, well over an hour ago. No one had seen Limpert all day.

Chief sat at his desk looking upset. He grabbed the handset of the growler, the shipboard sound-powered phone. "I'd better call the bridge."

"Hold on, Chief," Decker interrupted. "I'll double-check the berthing."

Chief shook his head. "No time for that."

"Maybe he's in his rack with headphones on and didn't hear the alarm."

"He still would've noticed the stampede of people leaving," Chief countered.

"One quick check," Decker urged.

Chief tapped his fingers nervously on his desk. "Make it fast. I can't hold out much longer before I have to notify the officer-of-the deck."

Decker raced out of Supply Support. Less than a minute later, he was back in the office, noticeably out of breath. "No sign of Kippen, Chief."

"Alright, let me call Suppo real quick. Maybe he knows where they are."

The sailors sat quietly as Chief cranked the handle of the growler. "Commander, we're missing Kippen and Limpert. Have you seen 'em? Uh, huh. No, sir. I don't know, sir. Wait, there's someone at the door."

Everyone in Supply Support focused on the door. The knob slowly turned and the diminutive Ensign Winthrop Limpert stepped into the office wearing rumpled khakis and a ball cap that looked like it was made for a much larger man's head. He carried a flashlight in his left hand, which he tapped with his right. "Sorry I'm late, fellas. I was, um, I had a hard time getting here."

Chief relayed the news to Commander Doerr that Limpert was found, and then hung up the phone. "You made it just in time, sir. I was about to report you missing."

"I'm right here, Chief," said Limpert.

"I can see that, sir," said Chief, sounding exasperated. "Damn it, we still have someone missing. I can't sit on it any longer."

Chief called the bridge to report that Petty Officer Kippen was not at muster. He hung up the growler and glowered at the blank faces staring back at him.

Moments later, Captain Girard announced on the intercom that Kippen was missing and there was a reliable report that someone had fallen in the water. "We're going to launch the helo and turn the lights on. I want all available hands to go topside to look for Kippen. Let the bridge know if you see anything. And I mean anything. It's dark as hell out there and a little rough so stay several feet away from the lifelines. We don't need another sailor overboard."

Decker and Hack waited for the helicopter to launch and then walked topside to the flight deck. The ship crawled through the water retracing its path. The two sailors sat a few feet from the edge of the ship, carefully scrutinizing the water for a sign of their shipmate.

"I can't believe Kippen's overboard," Hack said.

Decker kept his eyes focused on the ocean. "Me either, but he's a good swimmer. A little wiry guy like that can tread water for a long time."

"I hope you're right," Hack said. "I wouldn't be able to survive in those waves. I barely passed the swim test in boot camp. They'd find me floating face down."

"Not right away," Decker said. "A body that drowns will sink. It takes several days for it to float."

"That's a pleasant thought," said Hack. "Hey, what's that smell?"

Big Mo walked towards the two sailors and sat between them, staring at the water the entire time. "Damn, not much of a moon tonight with the clouds. This sucks, man. They sure it's Kippen?"

"He wasn't at muster, and he's either in the water or hiding somewhere," said Decker. "By the way, you stink."

"Tell me something I don't know," Mo sighed. "You try working in the engine room all day and night and see how you smell."

"Have you thought of a shower now and then?" asked Decker.

Mo shrugged. "Thought about it, but I was too tired after watch to clean up. Just took off my coveralls and crawled in my rack. It's the navy way." Mo spotted Commander Doerr as he approached within a few feet in the dim light. "Here comes your boss."

The supply officer sat next to them before they had a chance to stand. "What's the word, fellas?"

"It's too dark, sir," Mo said. "It's going to be tough to find Kippen, if he's out there."

"I agree," said the commander. "Are we sure it's him?"

"He's the only one missing," said Decker.

The commander and the three sailors sat on the flight deck without saying another word, silently scanning the ocean the best they could. The ship crawled along the same path of open ocean that had just been crossed. The helicopter circled the water in an ever-widening pattern. An hour later three Sikorsky SH-3 search-and-rescue helos from Cubi Point Naval Air Station joined the hunt. Four hours later, the group dropped out, one at a time. Suppo went first, telling the guys he was headed to the bridge. Mo left for watch a half hour later. Hack curled up on the deck shortly thereafter, nodding off in less than two minutes. Decker hung in for a little while longer, but his valiant effort to maintain a lookout for Kippen soon gave way to a lack of sleep. Exhaustion finally overtook him as he leaned back and rested his head on the deck.

CHAPTER THREE
0800, THURSDAY, DECEMBER 26

The search continued into its third day. No sign of Kippen. An agent from the Naval Security and Investigative Command arrived on board the *Harvey* late Wednesday evening. Unwilling to pull into port, Captain Girard had requested that the investigator fly to the ship. He wasn't about to give up the search and, just as important, one lost day at sea meant the crew would fall behind in its training schedule, a day that the captain was unwilling to forego because of an accident.

Interviews began early Thursday morning. Decker waited his turn, sitting on the mess decks with the others and writing in his Book of Dates. No one talked much. When they did have a conversation, it was in hushed tones. When did you last see Kippen? When did you last talk with him? How could he have fallen overboard? How rough was the sea that night?

Decker drifted in and out of the conversations, thinking about Monday night. He noticed Hack fidgeting with his watch. "Nervous?"

Hack dropped his hands to his sides. "A little."

"No need to worry. You should get over your fear of authority figures."

"There's a death. And an investigation. I didn't sign up for this stuff."

"Not a death yet," Decker corrected him. "They could still find Kippen, if he's been able to stay afloat."

"Then why do they want to talk with me?"

"You work with Kippen. It's a routine procedure they have to follow. Just answer the questions. It's as simple as that."

"What questions?" Hack mumbled.

"Whatever they ask," said Decker, sitting back in his chair. "I'm sure it'll be a breeze."

"You're about to find out," Hack said, pointing to the ladder leading down from the wardroom.

Decker turned and saw Commander Doerr slowly coming down the ladder from his interview with the investigators. Suppo walked over to Decker and put a hand on his shoulder. "You're next."

Decker nodded in the affirmative, walked across the mess decks, and ambled up the ladder to the wardroom. He knocked and stepped into the room. A man in his early 30s, wearing a blue sport coat and tan slacks, stood near a sofa. No tie. His short brown hair, Marine style, shaved at the sides, made him look younger than his true age. Decker noticed his service record on a table beside the investigator's chair.

"Petty Officer Decker, thank you for coming up here," the man said. "I'm Agent Bogen. Call me Scott."

"Nice to meet you," Decker smiled, extending his hand.

"Okay then," Bogen said. "I won't take much of your time. This is a routine investigation we perform when there's a missing person. A few questions and you'll be on your way. How about something to drink? Water? Coffee?"

Decker surveyed the wardroom, noticing with envy the formal dining table and plush furniture. First-class accommodations compared to junior enlisted quarters. "Coffee if there's some made. I don't want to pass up an opportunity to use officer china."

"You're my kinda guy," Bogen laughed. "I like the way you think. Sit down and I'll get you some. Might have some myself, now that you mention it."

Decker sat on a leather sofa and watched as Bogen found cups and saucers.

"Let's get some background out of the way," Bogen said as he poured coffee. "When did you report on board?"

"A year ago this past Monday, sir."

"No need for the 'sir'," Bogen said. "How do you like it?"

"If you don't mind the endless days at sea and the long workdays in port, I guess I like it okay," Decker said. "Overnight duty every four days makes up for the bad times," he added, sarcastically.

"I mean your coffee," Bogen said.

"Sorry, I thought you meant the ship. Cream and a little sugar. The real stuff, if it's there. I've never been a fan of artificial sweeteners."

"I'm with you," Bogen said. He filled two mugs and walked over to Decker. "Here you go."

"Thank you, sir, I mean Mr. Bogen."

"Don't call me that, either. Mr. Bogen's my father. Call me Scott." He sat down and took a sip of his coffee. "Okay, back to the ship. You go to sea, and the work life isn't the greatest, but how are things on board the

Harvey? Everybody get along?"

"For the most part," Decker nodded. "We all live as amicably as can be expected with five hundred guys crammed into the small living quarters of a *Belknap*-class cruiser."

"Where were you stationed before reporting on board the *Harvey*?"

"This is my first duty station. I spent two months in boot camp in Orlando, and two months in supply school in Meridian, Mississippi."

"When did you arrive in the Philippines?"

"A year ago this past Monday. I went straight from Clark Air Base to the ship."

Bogen browsed his notes. "Okay, let's see. You've been on board a year. How well do you know everybody in your department?"

"I know them all well. But, except for Hack Wilson, I don't hang out with any of them.

"Why do you call him Hack?"

"His choice. I don't think he likes Lewis as his first name. He's named after a baseball player, a former Cub great, if there's such a thing."

Bogen laughed and scribbled something in his notebook. "How well did you know Petty Officer Kippen?"

"Did? I hope he's still treading water and they find him."

"You're quite right," said Bogen. "Thank you for correcting me. Now, how well do you know Kippen?"

"I've known him my entire time on board the *Harvey*."

"How is he as a coworker? Does he seem to enjoy his work, and being on the ship?"

"As far as I can tell, he likes it as well as anybody. I've never heard him complain about anything other than the usual stuff."

"What usual stuff?"

"You know, going to sea a lot. Long workdays underway. The usual gripes sailors have."

Bogen sat back in his chair and crossed his legs. "Has he ever mentioned anything that was bothering him? Maybe something with work, or in his personal life?"

Decker paused. "No, not that I can remember."

Agent Bogen shifted positions in his seat. "You hesitated. Don't hide anything."

Decker focused on a welded seam in the bulkhead to his left. He had promised Kippen that he wouldn't tell anyone about their late night conversation. But with Kippen missing, Decker knew the deal was off. "Monday night. He came looking for me topside."

"What time was that?"

"Around 2230."

"How long did you talk with him?"

Decker shrugged. "I don't know, maybe 15 or 20 minutes. Then I went inside."

"What did you talk about?"

"He was worried about some missing parts. And his girlfriend had broken up with him Sunday. He was tossing her letters overboard."

Bogen rested his hands behind his head and stretched his legs. "What was his mood like?"

"Somewhat dejected. Must've been because of Claire."

"The girlfriend?"

Decker nodded. "She's transferring to CONUS and ended it."

"Do you know her last name?"

"Shelley or Shelby. Something like that. I never had the chance to meet her. She's in the air force stationed at Clark."

Bogen took a slip of paper wrapped in a Mylar sleeve out of his notebook and handed it to Decker. "Someone found this topside along the starboard passageway forward of the fantail. We don't have the second page with the writer's name on it."

Decker read the first line of the letter. "It's probably from Claire. He was throwing her letters overboard. The wind must've blown it back on the ship. I told him it happened."

Bogen took the letter from Decker and set it on a nightstand. "You mentioned missing parts. What did he say about them?"

"He just said some parts are missing and that he was worried he'd get blamed for them. I told him he's just being a perfectionist. I reminded him it's happened before."

"What has? Missing parts?"

"No, things that he thinks are life and death that turn out to be nothing."

"I see," said Bogen. "Did Kippen mention anything else? People who disliked him or were out to get him?"

Decker shook his head. "No, and I can't imagine him even getting into an argument with someone."

Bogen put his notebook in his lap and sat back in his chair. "Where was he when you left him?"

"On the flight deck."

"Where were you when he went overboard?"

"In my rack. Sleeping."

"Can anybody verify that?"

Decker thought for a moment, suddenly becoming nervous.

"Just one or two names," Bogen urged.

"Hack saw me."

"And he can confirm that you were asleep when the alarm sounded?"

"I was in my rack," Decker repeated.

Bogen stared at Decker. "It appears that you were the last person to have a conversation with Kippen. It's important that someone can attest to your whereabouts."

Decker started to reply when the forward wardroom door flew open. He saw who it was, and hastily shot to his feet.

CHAPTER FOUR
0800, THURSDAY, DECEMBER 26

Captain Girard lumbered into the stateroom in crisply pressed khakis, making a beeline to the coffee pot. "Sit down, sit down. Don't let me interrupt. Just looking for Cheng and the coffee."

Bogen looked at Decker, confused.

"The Chief Engineer," Decker whispered to the investigator. "He hasn't been in here the past half hour, sir," he replied to the captain.

Captain Girard glanced up from pouring coffee. "Okay well, he must be hiding from me." He turned to Bogen. "Have you talked with whomever you needed to?"

"Yes, sir, I've been able to interview most of the people on my list. Some of the others have been on watch or asleep. I'll talk to them later tonight, or tomorrow morning."

"Just do what you have to do," said the captain. "I'm saddened about the whole thing. An injury on board my ship is bad enough. To have someone fall overboard just makes me sick to my stomach."

"I understand, sir. It's a tragedy," Bogen said, sympathetically.

The captain nodded and sipped from his mug. "What's your assessment of it?"

Bogen caught Decker's eye. "That'll be all." The investigator closed his notebook and extended a hand. "Petty Officer Decker, thank you for your time. If you think of anything else that Kippen may have said to you, here is my card. Call me anytime. I'm at the embassy in Manila, so I can be here quickly if need be. When you get to the mess decks, please tell Wilson I'm ready for him."

Decker took the card and put it in his shirt pocket. "I will, sir. But that's all I know."

He walked out of the wardroom, closing the door behind him. He paused at the top of the ladder and realized that a bead of sweat had formed on his forehead. He took a deep breath, collected himself, and started to walk down the ladder. Then it hit him. A low, but audible, conversation coming through the thin metal door. He knelt to tie his shoes, his head as close to the door as he could get it without looking too obvious.

"At this stage, I haven't reached a conclusion," Bogen said. "But it looks like either an accident or suicide."

"Suicide?" the captain grunted.

"Kippen's girlfriend broke up with him the day before you got underway. Of course I'll need to talk to a few more people, but that's the way it's looking."

The captain grunted. "Yeah? Well, my money's on it being an accident. I've warned these damn sailors about walking around the ship at night. Especially on a night when the seas were a little rough."

"How rough were the seas, sir?" Bogen asked.

"Oh, nothing too terrible. Had some swells big enough to rock the ship a little."

"That doesn't sound too bad, sir," Bogen said. "Especially for a ship this size."

"You ever been to sea?"

"No, sir."

"Yeah? Well, let me tell you about the waves. It doesn't take much to rock a ship, even a ship of this size. Get a little water on deck and a sailor can lose his footing pretty easily."

"I'm sure that can happen, sir."

"You're damn right it can happen. I was just telling the supply officer that it happens to me, maybe half a dozen times every cruise. The problem isn't the waves, as much as the rolling of the sea. It can be smooth for a long stretch of ocean, then the ship hits a rolling wave, and wham, we get knocked to one side. It can take a person by surprise. Hell, we have enough broken furniture to prove that point."

"I don't doubt that, sir," Bogen said. "Most everyone I've talked to has said the same thing. And they've all been very helpful."

"What did they have to say?" asked the captain. "As far as I know, Kippen didn't have any enemies. He was 4.0 all the way in his evaluations. Never had a problem with him. And that's saying something, being stationed in a place like Subic Bay with all sorts of distractions for young men."

"From what I can gather, Kippen was well liked," Bogen said. "Everyone had nice things to say about him. I couldn't find a motive for anything malicious."

"Another reason it makes me believe it was an accident," said the captain. "Did you talk with the boiler techs who were on the fantail?"

"I did, sir. Their story is straightforward. Heard something in the water. Thought they saw a body float by. Went to the ship's store to call the bridge about the man overboard."

"We're lucky they saw him. It annoys me that they were out there smoking at night, but I'm glad they saw him," said the captain.

"It was very fortunate," Bogen said. "We also spoke to Chief Fray. Apparently, he was also on the fantail prior to Kippen falling overboard, but went inside before it happened."

"That's what Suppo told me," the captain said.

"What can you tell us about the chief?" asked Bogen.

"Solid perfomer. The top chief on board. I'm lucky to have several top-notch chiefs with me," the captain added. "Hell, they run the ship. They get things done. And Chief Fray is as good as it gets."

"That confirms what I've learned," Bogen said. "Oh, and there is one more thing, sir. It's probably nothing, but something about missing inventory items came up in my interviews with Kippen's shipmates."

"What about it?"

"Petty Officer Decker told me just now that Kippen said he was looking for missing parts."

"I'm sure it's nothing," said the captain. "We have thousands of parts on board this ship. Hell, there are more storerooms than I know about, and I'm the captain. I'll check on it and let you know if I find out anything."

"I'd appreciate that, sir," Bogen said. "As for now, I've done all I can do. I'll interview the others and be out of your hair when the ship returns to port."

"That'd be much appreciated," the captain said. "We'll

need to do a lot of work when we get back to Subic. I want you to do your job, but I also have a ship to run. We're leaving on a six-month deployment to the Persian Gulf in a few months and I'm going to need all hands working when we return to base."

"I'll be out of your way, sir. I can promise you that," Bogen said. "I'll touch base with you before I leave the ship."

Decker heard a door open and close from within the wardroom. Then silence. He sprang to his feet and slid down the ladder handrails, his feet never touching the steps. He hustled over to Hack, who was sitting alone at a table on the starboard side drinking a coke. "You're up."

Hack stood and nervously adjusted his uniform. "How'd it go? I'm sure you sailed through it."

Decker looked at the ladder leading to the wardroom. "Not exactly."

CHAPTER FIVE
1430, FRIDAY, DECEMBER 27

As the ship drew closer to the pier, a handful of sailors stood at attention topside fore and aft, waiting patiently to throw mooring lines ashore and step off the ship after five days at sea. A couple hundred yards from land, the ship turned to port and sat motionless, with its starboard side facing the pier. Pushed by a tugboat the last few feet to its resting place, the *Harvey* inched its way closer, until finally, sailors heaved mooring lines onto the pier where stevedores scooped them up, tossing them over bollards. With precision and almost without notice, the U.S. flag dropped from high amidships the instant a sailor raised an ensign on the fantail's flagpole. The *Harvey* was home, minus one of its crewmembers.

A fleet of forklifts ferried pallets of supplies toward the ship, and a large blue crane on rails moved into position, lowering the gangway. A throng of Filipino welders, machinists, and pipefitters gathered at the foot of the brow, waiting to board the ship to begin the around-the-clock work necessary to keep a navy vessel at sea.

After two hours of loading supplies, Decker and Hack finished the workday, precisely at 1700. They changed into civilian clothes. Decker into his usual polo shirt and khaki shorts, Hack into T-shirt and jeans. They walked to the quarterdeck, where Decker spent a few minutes in quiet conversation with the petty officer-of-the-watch. He finally turned to Hack. "What are you waiting on?"

"You," said Hack, waiting patiently.

"Let's go then."

They walked down the gangway and spotted Commander Doerr and his wife waiting to go up the brow. Piper Doerr stood nearly five foot ten with her yellow sundress providing a stark contrast against her tanned skin and shoulder-length auburn hair. The supply officer stood to her left, noticeably a couple inches shorter than his wife. A dedicated gym rat, the commander has maintained a trim figure and athletic build from a childhood spent roaming the mountains of northern Vermont. A khaki garrison cap covered his retreating hairline. A Naval Academy class ring on his left hand, perched above a wedding band, glistened in the sunlight. The two sailors stepped onto the pier and saluted the supply officer. The commander returned their salutes. "Decker, you know my wife, Piper."

"Nice to see you again, ma'am," said Decker.

"Piper, this is Lewis Wilson. He's been on board about a month. You go by Hack, though, right?"

It surprised Hack that the supply officer knew that about him already. "Yes, sir. But Lewis is fine, too."

Mrs. Doerr flashed a smile. She turned to Decker, took his hand, and held the handshake a bit too long. "It's nice to see you again."

Decker looked at Commander Doerr, who luckily was scrutinizing something on the ship. Piper turned to Hack. "And nice to meet you."

The commander turned his head towards the sailors and put his arm around his wife's waist, signaling it was time to go. "You guys stay out of trouble tonight. We don't need another accident to hit the department."

"We always try to," said Decker.

The commander laughed, and Decker and Hack watched the supply officer and his wife walk up the gangway to the quarterdeck. Piper's yellow sundress showing off her long, tanned legs.

Decker grabbed Hack by the shirtsleeve, nudging him to start moving. "Don't look at that. It's the boss's wife."

The walk to the main gate at the north end of the base cut through the heart of Subic Bay Naval Station. A slice of Americana in the Far East. Palm-tree-lined streets with softball fields, a Baskin Robbins, bookstore, and taxi stand. Moderate traffic with people walking— mostly sailors—heading to town on liberty. And Filipino workers heading home after the work week.

Twenty minutes later, the sailors stopped at the entrance to the main gate complex, a two-lane street and a sidewalk that passed over a small river on the Philippine side. A security checkpoint stood on the base side in the middle of the road, with Marine guards inspecting every vehicle that entered or exited. A similar checkpoint blocked the sidewalk, causing a bottleneck of foot traffic. The sailors decided to wait for the line to thin.

"Where are we going?" asked Hack.

"To California Jam," said Decker. "As soon as we make it through the crowd."

"I've never been there."

"You're missing out. Cal Jam's the best club on Magsaysay Drive. And I know the owner, Pong Dango, so I get free beer sometimes."

"I knew there had to be a reason."

"I go for the music," Decker said. "But the free beer helps."

"How do you know the owner?"

"He was my landlord when I rented a place in Olongapo for a few months. Good old man. Nightclub owner, man about town, and an avid collector of WWII memorabilia. I paid my rent on time, and he took care of me. He even lets me in the bar when it's closed."

"So, you do know a Pong," Hack mused.

"You doubted me?"

"A little. I still think it's a funny nickname."

"And here comes another example."

Hack saw a man in khakis pass. "Senior Chief Wall?"

"Senior Chief Dingding," whispered Decker. "It's the Tagalog word for 'wall'."

"That's his nickname?"

"In a way. That's what the Filipino sailors have started calling him. They find it amusing that some American names sound like everyday words. Wright, Carr, Hart, House, Byrd."

"Woods, Day, Field, Dahl," Hack added.

"Exactly," Decker agreed.

"What's he think of the nickname?"

"He doesn't," Decker said. "No one says it to his face. Everyone does it the proper way and only calls him Dingding behind his back." He nodded towards the dwindling crowd making their way off base. "Let's go."

The sailors passed through the checkpoint with a grunt from the Marine and exited the main gate onto the Shit River Bridge. The "river" was, in fact, a drainage canal that skirted the southern edge of town, separating the naval base from Olongapo. Sailors gave the canal its epithet decades ago from the water's raw-sewage smell. The name stuck. Decker and Hack were halfway across the bridge when Decker spotted a crowd of sailors throwing coins in the water. "Damn."

"What's wrong?"

Decker pointed towards the canal. "They're throwing coins in the river. It's disgusting. Making those kids dive in that filth to fish them out."

Hack watched a gaggle of grade-school-aged boys swimming in the muddy brown water. "Let's keep going."

The sailors continued their walk along Magsaysay Avenue, the main strip, with the smell of the bars, of food cooking in the streets, of fumes from the hordes of trikes and jeepneys mixing with the hot, humid air that drifted in from the sea. A sprinkling of restaurants, barbershops, pawn dealers, and massage parlors nestled among the multitude of nightclubs that lined the street. Vivid neon signs lit the sidewalk, drawing attention away from scruffy, indiscreet exteriors that belied the sumptuousness of the clubs' interiors. Music blared from each open door, creating a symphony of rock, hip-hop, and country as one walked down the street.

Up to this point, Decker had not told anyone, except the navy investigator, about his conversation with Kippen the night he went overboard. Decker looked at Hack as they walked along the bustle of Magsaysay and figured it was time.

He *had* to tell someone.

Hack listened to the story without saying a word. When they approached the entrance to Cal Jam, he turned to Decker and put a hand on his shoulder. "Let's tell Mo and Vega."

The sailors climbed the three-step staircase. A rush of cool air hit their faces as a young Filipino opened the door, escorting them into the interior. Half full, but it was early. The two-story club featured a stage along the west wall, with floor-to-ceiling speakers towering along either side of the platform. A dance floor next to the stage was nearly empty as groups of two, three, and four sailors sat at round tables and flirted with bar girls, company-owned prostitutes who floated between tables endlessly searching for their one true love for the evening. A bevy of waitresses scurried across the scene, distinguished from the bar girls by their modest wardrobe of black shirts and sensible skirts.

Big Mo sat at a corner table nursing a San Miguel. Six-foot-five inches and north of 250 pounds, he'd been coming to Cal Jam for the past three years. He liked the music, the atmosphere, and the bar girls. Depending on his mood, that order of preference often changed. Despite the heat and humidity of the evening, he sported a faded red-and-white, checkered long-sleeve shirt over a black T-shirt . His brown cargo pants groaned at the seams. An old, discolored Atlanta Braves ball cap, turned backwards, sat atop his crew-cut black hair. Black, size 17 navy boondockers completed the ensemble.

Vega Magpantay sat opposite Mo, her back to the entrance. Her long black hair tied in a French-braid ponytail. A rooky police officer in Olongapo, she was one of only two women on the force. Tonight, she had on her favorite off-duty attire: a light-green cotton tank top, denim shorts, and white tennis shoes. Her silver diamond-shaped earrings sparkled when the lights from the dance floor hit them just right.

Raised in the U.S. with her American mother, Vega had moved to the Philippines at age twelve to live with her father. She spoke fluent English, Tagalog, and Ilocano, the predominant language of northern Luzon, her dad's home province. She had met Decker one night when she came to a nightclub in town with a group of police officers to make an arrest. Lovers briefly, they now were just friends, with their romance confined to occasional nights when loneliness and a desire for intimacy overpowered her wish to keep things platonic.

Mo saw them first and leaned in close to Vega. "Here come the tools. Hack and Decker." They both giggled loudly.

"Greetings everyone," Decker said. "What, may I ask, is so funny?"

Mo winked at Vega. "Nothing. You're late."

"Sorry about that. Got held up with work. The supply business never stops, unlike the machinery on board the ship."

"Then let's trade jobs," Mo said.

"Not a chance," said Decker. "I value my nice, clean workspace too much."

Decker ordered a beer for himself and Hack and kissed Vega on the cheek. "You look lovely as ever. Merry belated Christmas."

"Thanks," Vega said, "And sorry about Kippen. Mo told me what happened."

Decker sighed and put his elbows on the table. "I need a beer. Or three. It's been a long week."

"Tell me about it," Mo said. "It still bums me out. It's

been four days and still no sign of him. He was an okay guy for a supply type. The idiot should've been more careful. It's a damn shame."

Mo noticed Decker and Hack exchange glances. "I saw that look. What'd I say?"

CHAPTER SIX
1745, FRIDAY, DECEMBER 27

Decker gave an abbreviated version of what he had told Agent Bogen and what he had overheard after his interview. "The navy investigator ruled it an accident or suicide," he added. "I stopped and chatted with Pitchford on the quarterdeck before we left the ship. He saw the message traffic about it. With no other apparent motive, the official theory is that he either lost his footing and fell overboard or jumped on his own because of Claire. The navy's going to keep searching for several more days, but, unless they find a body, the case is closed."

"I can't believe it's suicide," Mo said. "Hell, no woman's worth that." He caught Vega's eyes and turned red. "You know what I mean."

"I do," Vega said, reassuringly. "But do you guys know anything else about the missing parts?"

"I'm surprised you're interested in navy talk," said Decker. "You never seem to want to hear about our heroic efforts at sea and keeping the world safe for democracy."

"I usually don't," Vega said, taking a swig of beer. "I have to put up with sailors every day on the job." She straightened in her chair, her face turning serious. "It's just something I'm working on. The black market's a big deal in Olongapo. People are always stealing stuff from base and selling it in town. It's mostly small stuff like soap and cigarettes. Things that aren't worth the time to investigate, for us or the navy."

"All he mentioned was some missing parts," Decker said. "We don't stock soap and stuff. Another department does that."

Vega leaned in and spoke in a hushed voice. "I'm not worried about those things. The black market's been relatively quiet for a few years. Until recently, that is. Over the past few months there's been a flurry of activity. Military parts. Expensive items. We received a report a few days ago about material from the base making its way to town. You made me think of it when you mentioned the missing inventory on the ship."

Decker perked up. "That rings a bell. Kippen mentioned they were expensive items. I'd completely forgotten about that."

"You think someone on the *Harvey* is involved?" Hack asked, one eyebrow raised.

Vega took another drink of beer and leaned back in her chair. "I don't know if it's a sailor on the *Harvey*, but someone is working from the inside. Someone on base. I'm not even supposed to know about it, though. My boss doesn't think a woman should be a cop. He treats me like I'm an idiot, or his personal secretary or something. But all his paperwork comes across my desk, so, naturally, I read it. We all know who's the real idiot. And he hardly ever let's me out of the office unless I'm with him."

"That sucks," Mo said.

"Sucks big time," Vega agreed. "But at least I get to read everything that crosses his desk." Her eyes twinkled and a broad smile spread across her face. "If I can solve a case like this, it'd prove a woman can be a damned good cop."

"Why not talk to the navy police?" Mo said.

"I can't talk to anyone," Vega replied. "I can't even talk to Filipino cops in neighboring towns. 'That's not your job, young lady' is all I ever hear." She looked at Hack. "Your navy girlfriend, what's-her-name, Cassandra?"

"It's Leeandra," Hack corrected her.

"Okay, Leeandra. She works at the supply depot, right?"

Hack leaned forward and set his beer down hard. "What do you mean? I'm sure she's not involved with black market stuff. She's not the type."

"I'm not saying she's involved," Vega laughed. "But maybe she can help." She put a hand on Decker's leg. "Maybe you guys can look around the ship, too. It's about navy material, and that's your job. It'd only be natural to do some extra checking on things."

Decker leaned back and put his hands behind his head. "What do you think, guys?"

"Count me out," said Mo. "You'll come up with wild schemes, and Hack and me'll be the ones who do the dirty work."

Decker shot Mo a look of mock surprise. "When have I ever talked you into doing something you didn't want to do?"

"About every other weekend for the past year."

"I believe that's an exaggeration," Decker smiled. "I am deeply offended."

Mo nudged Hack with his elbow. "You don't need me, you got the new guy to do your 'detective' work now."

Hack put his hands up as if he'd been accused of something. "I don't like the sound of this," he said.

"Look, Decker, just go to the navy police," Mo said. "If the black market has anything to do with Kippen taking a dive, they need to be the ones to investigate."

"We're talking murder," Decker said, his voice tight.

"Hold on, guys," Vega interrupted. "I didn't say there was a murder. Besides, the navy investigator found no motive, so I doubt there's any connection between the missing parts and Kippen's fall. But I do know something's going on with the black market. Just look around the ship a little. That's all. I'm just interested in your inventory problem because if there's something fishy going on, I'll need hard evidence to go to my boss."

Decker sipped his beer, and tipped the bottle toward Vega. "Let me think."

"Maybe we should wait a week or so and see how things go in the supply department," Hack said.

"A week?" Vega protested. "Someone could cover their tracks by then."

"But maybe Kippen's body will be found and it'll be clear it was an accident."

"Even if they find him, it won't prove he wasn't pushed," Decker said.

Mo looked at Hack and pointed at Decker with this thumb. "I don't like the sound of this. All I know is that if Columbo here gets involved in whatever is going on, it ain't going to end well for anybody. Especially you and me."

"This could go on all night, guys," Vega said, changing the subject. "Let's get out of here. It's getting crowded, and the band's about ready to start."

Decker, Hack, and Mo agreed and the three sailors and police officer walked out of Cal Jam and stood on the crowded sidewalk.

"I'm headed to T's Tavern," Mo said. He looked at Hack. "Wanna tag along?"

"No, I'm going to Leeandra's." Hack glanced toward the corner. "Gotta find a ride." He turned to Decker and Vega. "What about you two?"

Vega slipped her arms around Decker's waist and looked up at him. "We have dinner plans."

"I bet you do," Mo said, with a smirk as he turned on his heel to head toward his favorite dive.

Decker laughed. "Unfortunately for me, it's not like that," he called out, but Mo waved his hand in dismissal and just kept on walking. Decker turned back to Hack. "Before we say *magandang gabi*, let me introduce you to the best trike guy in the islands, and he's right here at your service."

At the corner of Gordon and Magsaysay, a Filipino wearing a red Chicago Bulls T-shirt and faded jeans leaned against the seat of his tricycle, a red Honda four-stroke 125cc motorcycle with a metal-framed, plastic-covered sidecar. One of the most popular, cheap, and prolific modes of public transportation in the islands, trikes swarmed the streets by the hundreds. An old navy baseball cap sat on the man's thick crown of brown hair and he lit up with a wide smile when he saw the group walking toward him.

"Hack, I'd like to introduce you to my number one *pare*, Rusty Ramiro."

Rusty shook hands with Hack. "Nice to meet you, Mr. Hack. Decker is a good man. He helped my family. A friend of his, is a friend of mine." He turned to Decker. "Emil can see everything now. We feel so fortunate."

Decker smiled and put his arm around Rusty's shoulders. "We'll talk about that later. Hack, if you ever need a trike, Rusty's your guy. I've known him almost as long as I've been stationed here."

"I need to get to 501 Jones Street," said Hack.

Rusty cocked his head towards his trike and as Hack folded himself into the sidecar, he kick-started the engine and put the bike in gear, sending a cloud of exhaust fumes billowing from the tail pipe. Decker watched the trike disappear down the street among the dozens of other motorcycles. Vega tugged at his arm, and looked up at him. He gave her a squeeze and the best smile he could muster, trying to put Kippen and the subject of black market shenanigans out of his mind.

CHAPTER SEVEN
2054, FRIDAY, DECEMBER 27

Hack gripped his seat with one hand and clamped the other over his mouth to avoid breathing the noxious brew of dust, humidity, and exhaust fumes as Rusty zoomed through the side streets of Olongapo weaving in and out of traffic clogged with trikes tailgating each other. They finally came to a stop near the corner of Jones and 12th streets, where Hack saw Lee standing inside the courtyard of her apartment complex talking to her landlord, an elderly Filipina in a flowered nightgown. Hack climbed out with a grunt of thanks and flipped Rusty twenty-five sentimos.

"I'm happy to drive you anywhere, Mr. Hack."

"I'm just glad I arrived alive," Hack mumbled as Rusty roared off.

Hack and Leeandra Mansfield had first met at the bookstore on base when he stopped in because of the air conditioning. The bookstore was halfway between the ship and Main Gate, a perfect place for a pit stop on the way to town. Lee was there to buy a magazine, and they crossed paths at the checkout counter. They'd had lunch a few times, then dinner and drinks and dancing one night at the Sampaguita Club on base. Hack could've done without the dancing, embarrassed mostly at his clumsiness, but the evening couldn't have gone better. They'd been dating ever since.

Hack unlocked the courtyard gate and walked towards the two women. Lee had on baggy green gym shorts, a white T-shirt , flip-flops, and a bag slung over her left shoulder. The thick brown hair he loved to run his hands through fell just below her neck, and he imagined tracing his fingers down toward her collarbone and beyond. Unwilling to wait, Hack walked up and put his arm around Lee's waist. She cut short her conversation with the old woman, and turned to greet him with a kiss.

"Welcome home, sailor. Christmas wasn't the same without you." She took a step back to get a good look at him. Hey, what's wrong? You look sea sick?"

"I'm fine. I think the exhaust fumes must've gotten to me." He slid the bag off her shoulder. "Did you just get home from work?"

"Sort of," she said. "I worked late and then went to the gym." She patted her flat stomach. "I have to work hard to keep it this way."

"Mmmm," Hack said and put his hand over hers.

Lee giggled and then made a pouty face. "Hey, I saw you walking with Decker on base. You were across the gym parking lot from me. I tried to yell."

"Were you spying on us?"

"Of course I was." She rested her hands on his chest. "I always want to know what you're up to. Especially when you're with Decker."

"He's not a bad guy."

"He's a jackass." She smacked him lightly.

He bent and kissed her below her right ear. "Maybe

so, but underneath the jackass exterior, I think he means well."

Lee ran her fingertips down Hack's chest. "Well, just be careful. He just seems like trouble." She looked up, her mouth set in a straight line, her expression serious. "I heard about Kippen."

"Yeah…"

"Everyone was talking about it at the supply depot. What a freak accident. I met him a few times when he'd come over to check on parts. He used to call us a lot, too, about high-priority stuff. He seemed like a nice guy."

"He *was* nice," Hack said. "Everyone liked him."

"He must have been clumsy to fall off the ship like that."

"I don't know about clumsy. It might have been suicide or—"

"Suicide?" Lee interrupted.

"His girlfriend broke up with him last weekend. He was apparently upset."

"You said 'or'… or what?"

"Or he had help going overboard. Kippen mentioned missing parts to Decker, and Vega thinks it might be part of a black market operation."

"She thinks someone pushed him off the ship because of that?"

Hack shrugged. "I have no idea. I think it's just talk."

Lee frowned and leaned into him, gazing up into his face with inviting blue eyes. "Oh well, let's forget about that. I hope you can stay tonight."

Hack didn't reply but unloosened her arms, picked up her bag, and walked with her up the stairs to her doorway. As soon as she put the key in the door the power went out. A regular occurrence in Olongapo once the clubs cranked up for the evening and drained what little electricity there was coming through the lines. Tonight, it would be no air conditioning, and no television.

Lee unlocked the door and tried the lights out of habit. No luck. "Angie should be home," she whispered to Hack. "Angie, honey, *nandito ka ba*?"

"*Oo, nandito ako sa kuwarto,*" came a soft voice through the darkness.

Angie came out of her bedroom holding a candle, and wearing jeans and a deep blue T-shirt with the word "Navy" printed in white across the front.

Lee took a sack out of her bag and handed it to the maid. "Here, I brought you something." Angie lit another candle on an end table and walked into the kitchen,

"I try to help her out with meals," Lee whispered to Hack in the darkness. "She buys her food at the local market, but I know she enjoys American food, so sometimes I bring her food from the supply depot cafeteria."

Lee took the candle from the table and led Hack to the bedroom. "Let's let her eat. She's shy."

Lee set the candle on the dresser while Hack fell back on the bed. She lay on the bed and cuddled up next to him. "What do you want to do? We could go out, but the bars are always crowded. We could stay here, if you don't mind the heat."

"Let's stay in," Hack replied. "It feels good to be away from the navy for a night. I have duty tomorrow, though, so I need to wake up early."

"Good," Lee sighed. "I didn't feel like going out anyway." She leaned over to give Hack a kiss, running her hands through his blond hair. "Mmmm. You're *maganda*."

"What's that mean?

"Beautiful. Pretty." She gave him another kiss. "You look very *maganda* lying here in my bed. My *maganda Mahárlika*"

"Thanks, I think. And what's Mahár...? I can't pronounce it."

"*Mahárlika*. It means noble warrior. I heard it from a guy at work." Lee tickled him along his midsection with her left hand. "And I have some news."

Laughing and squirming, Hack grabbed her hand. "It's never a good thing when someone starts a sentence like that."

"It's a good thing this time, but there is some bad news."

"I knew it. What's the bad news?"

"I called my detailer again last night."

Hack sat up with a serious look on his face. "What'd he say?"

"Remember when I told you a couple weeks ago I'll probably have to transfer? Well, he said I have to change duty stations, and there's nothing available in Subic. They offered me something at the Pearl Harbor supply depot."

"Did you take it?"

"Not yet. I told him I'd think about it. He also had something in Long Beach and Yokasuka, but I don't feel like moving to Japan, and Long Beach doesn't sound as nice as Hawaii. What do you think?"

"I think you ought to go where you want to. I could try to transfer to Pearl Harbor when my time's up on the *Harvey*."

"That'd be nice. They have plenty of ships home-ported

there. I feel bad we just met, and now I'm going to be leaving."

"So, what's the good news?"

Lee sat up and pushed Hack onto his back on the bed. "Get undressed because I have a surprise for you."

Hack smiled. "I like these kind of surprises."

She jumped to her feet. "I'll be back. Close your eyes until I tell you to open them."

Hack did as he was told, undressing and slipping under the covers with his eyes closed. He could hear Lee open a drawer, close it, and then leave the room. Five minutes later, he heard the door open a crack.

"Still have your eyes closed?"

"Yes."

"Good. Now open them."

Hack opened his eyes and focused on Lee standing in the doorway in the dim candlelight. She had on a red silk babydoll and black fishnet, thigh-high stockings. He watched her walk slowly to the bed, her ample breasts swaying in the loose-fitting top. She slowly pirouetted, revealing that she wasn't wearing underwear. She put her hands on her hips when he was silent. "You're supposed to say I look *maganda*."

Hack turned on his side, reached out, and ran his right hand along her hip. "You look amazing," he whispered.

Lee climbed back on the bed straddling his midsection. "I'll take that." She leaned down and nibbled on his earlobe, her voice a husky whisper, "Now, where were we?"

CHAPTER EIGHT
1056, SATURDAY, DECEMBER 28

Chief Fray threw the door open to Supply Support, causing Decker and Hack to nearly jump out of their chairs.

"Decker, what the hell are you doing here when you don't have duty?" Chief bellowed. "A young guy like you ought to be out having fun on a Saturday."

"I just woke up," said Decker. "You're the one at work on a day off."

Chief hitched up his pants. "They called off the search for Kippen. Just got word of it. Why don't you guys find somewhere else to grab-ass." He scowled at Hack. "Wilson, aren't there parts in Alpha to stow? And Decker, you've got about thirty seconds to get out of here before I put you to work."

"I guess so," Hack said, looking at Decker and pointing with his eyes towards the door.

Decker stood and clapped his hands together. "You don't have to tell me twice."

Chief strode to his desk and dropped heavily in his chair. "Just stay away from Supply Support. I'm on leave all next week. I'm heading out for Baguio City later today, and I've got some important work to do before I can go. I sure as hell don't want to be disturbed."

Chief bent over and started to unlock the small safe tucked under his desk.

"We'll miss you terribly," Decker said as he stood in the doorway.

Chief didn't look up, concentrating on the lock's combination. "You better miss me," he grunted.

The two sailors walked out of the office and stood in the passageway. "This sucks," Hack said.

Decker nodded. "It's not like the news is unexpected, but I still held out hope."

"Me too," Hack agreed, turning to head aft towards Alpha storeroom. "Guess I need to get to work."

Decker showered, dressed, and left the ship at noon. He left the shipyard strolling down Dewey Avenue towards the Main Gate. The walk was his favorite part of the base, picturesque, just as he'd always imagined a tropical island. A native Missourian, he had never even seen the ocean before joining the navy, but now, after a year at Subic, he preferred the towering palms swaying in the ocean breeze to the dense canopies of the old oaks in his yard at home. Despite the heat and the shipboard life, he was hooked on the laidback lifestyle that comes with living near the equator. Alone in his thoughts, he hadn't noticed the maroon Thunderbird drive past him, turn around, then pull up beside him.

"Hey there! Excuse me, but you're on the *Harvey*, right?" asked the woman behind the wheel.

"Yes, I am," said Decker, startled momentarily by the car alongside him. The driver appeared vaguely familiar, but a hat and sunglasses hid her face.

"I thought I recognized you, Elliott. I can give you a

ride if you'd like," she said.

Decker did a double take. A beautiful woman. Blonde. Pretty smile. Nice voice. Mrs. Doerr. The boss' wife. *Damn.* He looked at the main gate complex two blocks in front of him. "Thank you, but I'm not going far. Just to the main gate."

Piper Doerr lifted her sunglasses and leaned over to the passenger window. "I'll save you a few steps. Get in. I actually want to ask you a favor."

Decker started to once again decline the invitation, but his eyes locked onto Mrs. Doerr's loose fitting top that exposed more than a hint of cleavage. "Now that you mention it, the gate *is* a long walk from here. I think I will take that ride."

Decker picked up a slip of paper from the passenger seat, climbed in, and, despite his best efforts not to stare, found his gaze trailing the distance from her bright white shoes to the hem of her tennis skirt under which her sleek tan legs disappeared. Any other woman, and he would've been pleased with the situation. *Play it cool*, he told himself. *Don't look at her. Just small talk.*

"Are you in a hurry?" she asked.

Decker shrugged. "Not really, ma'am. Just going to meet some guys for a beer." He lied, but that was the first thing that came to mind.

"Well then, Elliott Decker, let's go for a ride." She shifted the car into gear and sped along the side streets towards navy housing. At a stoplight she turned to Decker. "First of all, call me Piper. Save the ma'am crap for the navy. And if you have a few minutes, I could use a hand with something. Bob is gone for the day, and I need to carry some stuff to the garage. I really want to take care of it today. Would you mind helping me? I'll pay you."

Decker breathed in deeply and slowly exhaled. "Sure, but no need to pay me."

"Then let me make you lunch. I'd feel bad if I didn't do something."

"Okay, lunch is fine. But I don't even need that, if it's a problem."

"No problem at all," she said as they cruised towards officer housing.

Decker spent the next few minutes glancing around the sedan's interior. The faded grey fabric in the seat itched against his back where the sweat from walking had soaked through his T-shirt. Dust coated the plastic dashboard, and the armrest had a sticky film on it that made Decker slightly uncomfortable. He glanced at the words and numbers typed on the piece of paper:

Boston -1100
Dallas +2300
Detroit +1800
LA -1200

On the back, Decker read "L2-50%" scribbled in pencil. "You need this?" he asked, holding up the note.

Piper glanced at the paper. "What is it?"

"Looks like cities with plus or minus military times."

Piper grabbed the note out of his hands, looked at it, wadded it, and tossed it in Decker's lap. "Sorry I haven't cleaned up in a while. Bob's always working and writing notes. I meant to vacuum this morning, but didn't get around to it."

Decker reclined the seat and absentmindedly pocketed the note. "It's cleaner than my car back home." He lied again.

"I'm living in luxury," Piper smiled, noticing Decker scrutinizing the car's interior. "You know the old saying, 'my other car is a Mercedes?' Well, we had a new Mercedes but had to sell it a few months ago." She shrugged her shoulders. "Too many bills to pay."

"I understand that," Decker lamented.

Piper tapped the steering wheel and glanced at him. "It's old, but it gets me around. As long it runs, I can live with it. It's my reward for living in a place like this," she laughed as she downshifted and came to a stop at an intersection. "Sorry about my rant. I get this way sometimes, and I usually don't have anyone to talk to. Most of my friends are hardcore navy wives. You know the type. 'Gung ho navy', just like their husbands. They don't mind moving around every two years, dragging their snot-nosed kids from port to port. Don't mind living in godforsaken places like this, I grew up in Malibu, and now look at me! My only reprieve is an occasional trip around Asia or to the States." She glanced at Decker and smiled. "Guess what's going to happen January 13?"

Decker thought for a moment, puzzled. "I don't know, what's going to happen?"

"Bob's finally taking some time off for a weeklong trip to Hong Kong. I'm soo-o looking forward to it. I'm counting the days like a little kid waiting for summer break. He's always on that damn ship or running off to Manila. It's like he's married to the navy instead of to me."

Decker sat quietly during the twenty minute drive to

Binictican housing as Piper spilled her feelings about the military, married life, and a dozen other things that irritated her at the moment. Tucked away on the northwest corner of the naval station, the housing provided seclusion and quiet for its inhabitants. An elementary school and high school formed the centerpiece of the community. The Doerr's house was a three bedroom ranch with a carport. Nothing fancy, but adequate, roomy actually, with a spacious, manicured lawn. The boxes she wanted moved to the garage took four trips, and they were cumbersome, and much heavier than Decker had hoped.

Piper stood in the living room when Decker walked in from the garage. "See, I told you it would only take a few minutes."

"It was no problem. I was glad to help," said Decker, panting and wiping sweat from his forehead.

"How about lunch now?" asked Piper.

"Raincheck?" Decker said, stretching his back. "Thank you for the offer, but I'm not that hungry yet. I just woke up an hour ago, and it always takes me a while to get my appetite."

"You sure? I feel bad that I can't give you anything for your trouble." She peered over Decker's shoulder to the kitchen. "Andrea? Why don't you go down to the Millers. I think the house looks fine now." The maid politely thanked her and walked through the back door without saying another word.

Piper turned to Decker. "Andrea is friends with the Miller's maid. They like to get together when they can, and I don't mind. She's a nice girl and a hard worker, but her English isn't great, so there's not much conversation between us. I hate having someone here every hour, every day; but I also hate doing housework. So, I've learned to live with it. Andrea's been with us a year now. It only costs us thirty dollars a month, and I tell Bob it's another perk of living in a place like this. Do you know how bored I get? God, there are days when I could just scream. Not to mention the heat of this place."

Decker didn't know how to respond. The thought of having a young maid around all day didn't seem like a problem to him. He changed the subject. "How long have you been married?"

"Seven years," said Piper. "Bob was stationed in Nevada. I was living with my sister in Reno at the time and met him there. We got married a year later."

"He's a nice boss," Decker said.

Piper smiled. "He's a nice man. Hey, let me get us some drinks. What do you want? Beer? Iced tea? We probably have something stronger, too."

"Tea if you have it made."

"I made it yesterday," Piper said as she walked to the kitchen.

Decker stood in the quiet of the living room peering out the window, wondering what he was doing there. *What if Commander Doerr comes home? How am I going to explain this?* Panic suddenly hit him.

"Sugar?" Piper yelled.

Decker jumped. "No, I like it plain."

"Me, too," Piper said, entering the living room with two glasses of tea. "Don't worry, silly. Bob won't be home for several more hours. He called from the ship an hour ago."

"How did you know what I was thinking?" asked Decker.

"Just a lucky guess. And, by the way you were fidgeting." Piper handed him the glass. "Here's to the *Harvey*." They clinked glasses.

Decker relaxed. "Where was this taken?" he asked, pointing to a picture on the wall.

"Nevada," Piper said. "Fallon Naval Air Station. It was a couple weeks after we first met. Bob showed me around base, and I wanted a picture next to a plane."

"I don't know much about aircraft," said Decker. "But that's a sweet lookin' Tomcat. I'm talking about the F-15," he quickly added.

Piper laughed. "I get it from my dad. He was a pilot. Still is, but not in the military. It's one of his hobbies. That's where I got my name."

"I like the name Piper," Decker said. "It's unique and much better than Beechcraft."

"I thought you didn't know much about planes?"

"I know a little," Decker said. "Were you living in Nevada?"

Piper shook her head. "No, my sister and I were spending the summer at our parents' vacation home at Lake Tahoe. We'd go to Reno all the time. I met Bob at the Sands." She touched his arm. "That seems like a lifetime ago, but it's only been eight years."

"I was a freshman in high school eight years ago."

"You're making me feel old."

"I didn't mean it like that."

"I know," Piper sighed. "I turned thirty-one two weeks ago. I spent most of my 20s being a navy wife. But, hey, age is only a number, right?"

Decker nodded. "My mom says that fifty is the new forty. I told her I'd take her word for it. I haven't told her this, but she's always been old to me."

"I hear it's the opposite with parents," Piper said. "I'm sure you're still a little boy to her."

Decker, a faraway look on his face, stared at the picture of the happy couple posing next to the aircraft.

"A peso for your thoughts," Piper said.

Decker smiled. "At least that makes them worth more than a penny." They both laughed and turned to face each other.

"Thank you for your help today," she said.

Decker set his glass on the coffee table and extended his hands until they rested gently on her waist. "I was happy to help." He drew her a few inches closer.

She looked up at him and started to say something. A glance downward. Awkward hesitation. "Don't," she whispered, slowly removing his hands. "You'd better go."

Decker closed his eyes. Thoughts of Vega, and then of Commander Doerr walking through the door vanquished any natural instinct he had to argue. "Alright," he exhaled.

"Finish your tea and I'll take you to the gate."

"Thanks, I'm done."

Piper pulled into a parking lot behind a row of taxis. She put the car in park and pushed up her sunglasses. "Thanks again for the help. I get depressed living out there at times. You were good company."

"So were you," Decker said. "Sorry for the ... you know."

She smiled and put the car in gear. "Hey, don't worry about it."

"Goodbye," was all Decker could think of to say as he climbed out of the car. Piper waved. Decker started to raise his hand, but she was already speeding away.

He walked across the Shit River Bridge, numb to the familiar sights, sounds, and smells of Olongapo. He decided to stop at Cal Jam to have lunch and get his mind off Commander Doerr's wife. As he sat in the club, his mind drifted to Kippen and the black market. He pulled out his Book of Dates, added his run-in with Piper, and inserted the note he had found in the car. A waitress took his order, pancit noodles, lumpia, and a beer. He waved at Pong behind the bar and settled into his chair, contemplating what his next move should be.

CHAPTER NINE
0720, SATURDAY, JANUARY 4

The three sailors had few opportunities to tak about Kippen the following week. Decker had duty Friday, so Hack spent the night with Lee, having dinner at the Sampaguita Club and going to a movie at the base theater. Despite only a few hours sleep, he awakened early Saturday morning and lay in bed listening to Lee's rhythmic breathing as she slept. He thought about the previous week and the two things that he had done that he hoped he'd never have to do again. On Monday, he had helped Commander Doerr inventory Kippen's personal effects before shipping them to his parents in some small town in Indiana. Everything the man owned—clothes, souvenirs from port visits, letters from home, socks, boots, and books—was sent packing to his relatives.

On Wednesday, he had attended a memorial service for Kippen at the base chapel. Captain Girard said a few nice words, and Commander Doerr spoke eloquently of Kippen's life, a story gleaned from Kippen's personal effects; details of a man that few sailors had known well. The last speaker, the *Harvey's* chaplain, droned on for way too long and came dangerously close to putting the crew to sleep. Midway through the monologue, Hack heard a sailor in front of him whisper to a friend, "Kippen's the lucky one. He doesn't have to sit through this." Hack frowned at the comment, but twenty minutes later, with no end to the oration in sight, he was in complete agreement with his shipmate.

By Thursday life began to get back to normal in the supply department. The commander mentioned the ship had received orders for a new guy, Petty Officer Swischer, who would transfer from a ship in San Diego next month. Navy life goes on.

Hack squinted at the clock on Lee's dresser. 0720. He gazed at Lee's nude body sleeping next to him, the sheets covering only her lower legs. On her left side facing away from him, her well-proportioned hips and butt were tempting. Hack put his hand on her thigh and thought about waking her but knew he didn't have time. Decker would be off the ship by 0800 and they had promised to meet for coffee, a decision Hack now sorely regretted. He pulled the sheets up to Lee's shoulders, quietly rolled out of bed, grabbed his clothes, and peeked out the bedroom door. Angie was nowhere to be seen so he scampered naked the few feet to the bathroom, holding his clothes in front of him just in case. A quick shower and he was out the door, in a trike, and on his way to Magsaysay.

Hack arrived at Cal Jam and looked at the clock behind the bar. 0750. Pleased with himself that he was a few minutes early, he walked around to the back entrance. He found the place dark and a little creepy this time of day. Pong Dango greeted him as soon as he opened the door.

"Good morning, Mr. Hack," Pong said. "Your friend is already here."

"He is?" Hack said, surprised at the news.

"Not he," Pong said, pointing to a table near the window facing the street. "She."

Hack spotted a woman at a table near a window. She sat facing the street with her hand wrapped around a large coffee mug. The smoke and beer and music from the previous night had faded. A few people milled around, bar girls mostly, and an old man was in the far corner sweeping the floor, removing any sign that hundreds of people were packed into the place just a few hours ago. A big man for a Filipino, Hack watched Pong shoo the girls away from the bar and then walk over and talk with the old man cleaning the floor. Hack stepped past them and sat down across from Vega.

"I didn't expect to see you here. Mind if I join you?"

"Of course not." Vega patted the chair next to her. "Sit here. Elliott said he was going to be here so I thought I'd stop by and see him. Sorry if I'm barging in."

"No, not at all," said Hack, noticing for the first time how young she looked to be a police officer. "I didn't mean it like that. I'm just surprised to see you."

Vega surveyed the empty bar. "Where is he, anyway?"

Hack shrugged. "It's still early. He won't be here for another half hour at least. It'll give us a chance to talk."

Vega scooted her chair closer to the table. "Okay, want do you want to talk about?"

"Let me ask you something about Decker."

"I'm afraid of what you're going to ask."

"No, it's nothing like that," said Hack. "What's the deal with Rusty?"

"What do you mean?"

"Remember when Decker introduced me to Rusty a

few days ago? He told Decker that 'Emil can see everything.' I asked Decker about it at work, but he changed the subject. It made me curious."

Vega leaned back. "Ah, that. You're right. He doesn't like to discuss it for some reason."

"Are we talking about the same Decker? I didn't think there was anything he didn't like to talk about?"

"I'll tell you," Vega said, turning serious, "But you've got to keep it to yourself."

"I won't tell a soul," said Hack.

"Okay, here's a brief version. They met when we were going out. Rusty would give Elliott a ride to and from work when he'd stay overnight with me."

"He's told me that much."

"I hope not in too much detail!"

Hack laughed. "Not about spending the night, but about Rusty giving him trike rides all the time."

Vega grinned. "Good. Anyway, Rusty had an accident with his trike about eight months ago. Ran into the back of a jeepney stopped in front of him. He had Emil riding with him and the kid hit his right eye on a piece of metal in the sidecar. Punctured it pretty badly. Rusty took him to the hospital, but he couldn't afford medical treatment. They were going to just sew it up and the kid was going to have to live with only one eye the rest of his life."

Hack grimaced. "Damn, that's awful."

"I'm sure it was and I felt sorry for the little guy. Elliott felt the same way and offered to pay for Emil to have surgery in Manila. It was a lot of money, but still a lot cheaper than it would've cost in the States. Even an enlisted guy could afford it if he wanted to, and Elliott wanted to."

"Why doesn't he talk about?" asked Hack. "That sounds like the kind of thing Decker would brag about."

"You've got to hear the rest of the story. The kid ended up needing two more surgeries. Elliott had to take out a loan, and he never told Rusty he was forced to do that. I pitched in a little money, but I don't make much. Elliott ended up paying ninety-five percent of the cost of the surgery, and he still owes the bank quite a bit. It's why he's no longer renting an apartment in town, and it's probably why he changes the subject whenever it's mentioned."

"I still don't see what the big deal is," said Hack. "I'd tell people if I did something nice like that."

"Well, number one he doesn't want Rusty to feel bad, but there's more to it than that. Has he told you about his cousin?"

"Rusty's cousin?"

"No, Elliott's cousin. I think he was two years younger. He was killed one day when they were kids out riding their bikes. He must've been around Emil's age. They were riding along a busy street and, of course, Elliot's showing off, riding with no hands and pulling wheelies and stuff like that. Then his cousin swerved into traffic by accident and got hit by a car. Elliott saw it happen."

"Damn," Hack mumbled.

"He doesn't talk about it often, but sometimes when we'd be alone in the middle of the night, I'd wake up and see him staring at the ceiling. Sometimes he'd want to talk about it."

"He probably thought of his cousin when Emil had the accident," said Hack.

Vega nodded. "Probably so. Elliott thinks he should've

been able to prevent the accident. I told him it wasn't his fault, but he's still carrying around a lot of guilt. I think Emil gave him a chance to do something to help and, you may not see it behind his bravado, but that's why Elliott's always trying to fix any wrongs. He's still reliving the bike ride."

"Damn," Hack said again.

Vega reached across the table and put her hand on Hack's arm. "Please don't tell him I told you, okay?"

Hack smiled. "I won't."

"Promise?"

"I promise. You can trust me."

Vega squeezed his arm. "I know I can. That's what I like about you."

Hack blushed. "Why aren't you and Decker still going out? I know he likes you. He talks about you a lot when we're at sea."

"I like him, too," Vega said. "We've become close friends, and I like hanging out with him, but, I don't know, I think I'm ready for a more serious relationship. Maybe someday I can see Elliott like that, but not now. He's a sweetheart, but he's got too much of a wandering eye."

Hack laughed. "It's hard not to be like that around here."

"He just needs to find the right kind of girl. I've been trying to think of someone I could set him up with, but I haven't found the perfect girl for him yet." She let her hand drift down Hack's arm until she took hold of his hand.

Goosebumps made the hair on his arms and the back of his neck stand at attention.

"Your girlfriend's lucky." She squeezed his hand and he found himself squeezing back.

At the back of the bar, Decker appeared carrying a plastic bag. Pong poured him a cup of coffee, and Decker waved to a gaggle of girls while he waited.

Vega let go of Hack's hand and abruptly stood up. "I need to find the ladies' room. Be right back."

Hack nodded wordlessly and watched Vega walk across the empty nightclub and disappear through a set of double doors.

Decker sauntered up, threw the bag under the table and plopped down across from Hack. "What's going on? You look like you just lost your best friend."

CHAPTER TEN
0800, SATURDAY, JANUARY 4

"I think I'm still half asleep," Hack said. "Vega's here. Had to go to the head."

"I was hoping that wasn't your lipstick on the coffee cup," Decker said. "Were you talking about me?"

"There are more interesting things in Olongapo than you to talk about." Hack looked his watch, wanting to change the subject. "How'd you get here so early?"

"Trick of the trade, shipmate," Decker said. "At precisely 0730 I told the officer-of-the-deck I had to take some trash off the ship. Which was not a lie. I did have to take some out. But as soon as I got to the dumpster, I made a bee-line to the machine shop next to it."

"The machine shop?"

"The machine shop. The view from the quarterdeck to the pier side entrance to the shop is blocked by the dumpster. I walked behind the dumpster, threw the trash in, and slipped into the shop. A few seconds later I exited the shop on the other side of the building."

"How did you know how to do that?" Hack asked.

"It was easy," Decker said. "Unlike most of my shipmates, present company included, I never like to waste my time. I noticed the shop's door one night when I was on quarterdeck watch a few weeks ago. I watched shipyard workers coming and going from behind the dumpster so I assumed there had to be an entrance on that end of the building."

"What about your uniform? Weren't you wearing it when you left the ship?

"I had two bags of trash. One bag was the real trash, the other bag had my civilian clothes in it. That's why I have this trash bag underneath the table. I changed in the bathroom at the Spanish Gate cafeteria. I'll stash my uniform at Vega's."

"All that for a half hour?" Hack asked.

"A half hour to the rest of the world, but precious weekend time to me," Decker said.

"I don't like taking those kinds of risks," Hack said. "At least not yet."

Decker took out his Book of Dates and began writing. "You'll learn. Just takes time."

"I suppose," Hack said, watching Decker scribble into his notebook.

Decker had made it all week without telling Hack about his run-in with the commander's wife. Though he wanted to keep it a secret, the story was too good not to share, and now he was dying to give Hack the scoop. He stopped his writing, took a sip of coffee, and spilled the whole story.

"She's the boss's wife!" Hack said. "What about the 'don't look at that' stuff?"

Decker pulled an envelope from his back pocket and handed it to Hack. "She sent me this two days ago."

Hack read the note, shook his head, and flipped it across the table. "It's a thank you card."

"With her phone number."

"Even more of a reason to steer clear. So what's their house like?"

"Typical navy housing," Decker said, sliding the card into his back pocket. "And she was driving an old Thunderbird. Quite a mess."

"What's she like?"

"Nice woman. Intelligent as well as attractive. Grew up in Malibu and you know what they say about Malibu girls, don't you?"

"No, what?"

"I don't know either, but I'm sure they say something about them," said Decker, looking through the dim light at the back entrance. "Enough of Piper, here's Mo and Vega."

"Look who I ran into," Mo said as he pulled up a chair at the table and spread a *Stars and Stripes* newspaper in front of him. Vega, back from the bathroom, kissed Decker on the cheek and sat next to him.

"How was your week? Was anyone talking about Kippen?"

"Everybody was talking about him," Decker said. "And it gave me an opportunity to assess the situation."

"Crap. I was hoping you'd forget about it," Mo sighed, studying his paper. "Now let me check the scores before you go all Magnun P.I. on us."

"Not a chance I'd forget," Decker said, looking around the bar. "In fact, I've given the situation a great deal of thought and I'm back to where I left off last weekend. Which is nowhere."

Mo didn't take his eyes off the newspaper. "My vote is for an accident."

"Maybe," Decker said. "But there are a few things that don't add up."

"I agree," Mo said, excited. "Like this. The Hawks have won three in a row."

"I'm not talking football," Decker said.

"Basketball."

"Whatever," Decker said, exasperated. "Let's focus on Kippen."

"What doesn't add up?" Mo grunted. "If it was foul play, there's no motive. Everyone liked him."

"The inventory," said Vega.

"That's hard to believe," said Mo. "Would someone really kill over missing nuts and bolts?"

"Not just nuts and bolts," Vega protested. "We're talking big ticket items that are impossible to find in the civilian world. People pay big money for this stuff."

"So you've said before, but I think you're jumping to conclusions. You don't even have any suspects."

"The guys topside that night are suspects," Hack said. "And the people in the supply department who have the ability to order repair parts."

Decker raised his eyebrows. "I overheard Agent Bogen tell the captain that Chief Fray and two boiler techs were topside the night Kippen went overboard."

"Forget the boiler techs." Mo folded his paper. "They don't have access to the supply system."

"That leaves Chief," Decker said.

"Yes, but Pinto, Commander Doerr, and Ensign Limpert also have access to the system. They can order parts," Hack added. "Where were they that night?"

"We know Chief was topside the night Kippen went overboard. But we don't have anything on the other two."

"I can't see Chief Fray doing something like that," Mo interjected.

"Maybe not, but," Decker turned to Hack, "remember last Saturday when you had duty? He came down to Supply Support in a huff. He kicked me out and told you to stay clear of the place. Said he was working on something important before he left on vacation."

Hack sat back in his chair. "He gave me some work to do in Alpha Storeroom. I guess he thought it'd keep me busy long enough. I didn't go down to the office the rest of the day."

"Sounds farfetched to me," Mo said. "Chief's a decent guy, and if you think something fishy is going on, you guys should talk with him first."

"Not if he's a suspect," Decker said. "Besides, if I stick my nose in this business, I want to take an indirect approach."

"What do you have in mind?" asked Hack.

"We can take a look around the office ourselves. Chief has a safe under his desk that I've always been curious about it. No one else has the combination. Not even the supply officer. I sit directly behind Chief and I've been watching him open it over the past few months. Helps pass the time at sea."

"Do you have the combination?" asked Mo.

"I think so," said Decker. "I'm not positive about the last number, but I think I have it. He opens it too fast. I can't exactly determine where he stops the dial."

"You should open it when you have duty," Hack said.

"Not a chance," Decker said. "Too many people could walk in, including Chief or Suppo."

"Do it late at night," said Mo.

Decker shook his head. "There needs to be a lookout." His eyes widened as if he just had the most brilliant idea in the world. "Hack, you could do it."

"Why me?" asked Hack. "I'd be worried about getting caught, too."

"Uh oh, here it comes, Hack," Mo said with a laugh. "This is where he wrangles you into doing his dirty work."

"I don't mean on your duty night," Decker said, ignoring Mo. "Stop by the ship when I have duty. Tuesday night I'll be on the quarterdeck watch from 2000 to midnight. That'll be a perfect time. I'll be able to alert you if anyone comes on board."

"How are you going to do that?" Hack asked, his voice laced with skepticism.

"Easy enough. I'll call Supply Support if Chief or Commander Doerr come aboard. It'll take either one at least three or four minutes to get to the office. And that's if they walk straight there. Chances are they'll stop off at the wardroom or chiefs' mess first. That'll give you plenty of time to close the safe and get out of there."

"Where am I going to go? It'll look suspicious if I'm sitting in the office when I don't have duty. And if I leave Supply Support to head to the berthing, I might run into them."

"There's a storeroom directly below the office. It's a hatch so you'll have to unbolt it before you open the safe. If need be, just jump down there and close it behind you. If someone walks in, it's highly unlikely they'll notice that it's unbolted."

"I don't like the sound of 'highly unlikely,'" said Hack.

"Go aft," Mo said. "The emergency diesel generator is

back there. Go straight aft from Supply Support, stay on the port side and you'll run into it. I've been on the ship three years, and I've yet to see a supply type back there."

"Perhaps," Decker said. "If you have enough time you can go aft. But it's a clear shot along the passageway from Supply Support to the diesel room. Someone could easily spot you. If it were me, I'd use the storeroom. That way you never have to leave the office."

Hack thought it over for a few seconds, looking dubious. "Why don't *you* come to the ship when *I* have duty?"

"Won't work," Decker said.

"Why not? It only works if I'm the one breaking into the safe?"

"I'd be more than happy to do it, but you're still new on board. It's not just Chief Fray and the commander we have to worry about. I know everyone on board and can warn you if I suspect any trouble."

"Don't listen to him," Mo said.

Vega had been silent, listening to how the conversation unfolded. She reached across the table and put her hand on Hack's arm. "It'll only take a few minutes. Maybe we'll learn something about a connection to the black market operation. I don't know if there's a murderer on board the ship, but what if there is? You'd be doing Kippen a favor."

Hack sat back and rubbed his eyes, obviously deep in thought. A few moments later, he dropped his hands. "Okay, I'll do it," he said, avoiding Vega's stare. "But you've got to be sure you keep an eye out for me."

Decker raised his beer bottle. "Believe me, you'll have nothing to worry about. I'll be on the lookout. It'll give me a reason to stay awake while I'm on watch." He turned to Vega. "Do you have something to write with? I've lost my pencil."

Mo laughed and finished the last of his beer. "You guys are nuts. This is crazy."

"It's not crazy at all," replied Decker, taking a pen from Vega she had dug out of her purse. He glanced behind him to see if anyone was standing nearby. Satisfied that they had privacy, he pulled his chair close to the table and wrote a series of numbers on a napkin. He handed it to Hack and cleared his throat. "Okay, here's the plan."

CHAPTER ELEVEN
2015, TUESDAY, JANUARY 7

The plan was simple. Hack would walk aboard ship on Decker's duty night while he had the quarterdeck watch from 2000 to midnight, the perfect spot to be a lookout and the perfect time of night to snoop around while most people were off the ship. If all went well, it'd be a routine evening. No one in the duty section would suspect otherwise.

Hack spent the early hours of the evening pensive, walking around base for two hours. He met Lee at the Sampaguita Club for a beer. She could immediately tell something was up.

"You're acting weird." she said. "You're not breaking up with me, are you?"

Hack sat his beer down and put his chin in his hands. "No, of course not. It's nothing like that. I have to go back to the ship tonight."

"For work?"

Hack shook his head. "Not exactly. Decker and I are planning a break-in."

"A break-in of what?"

"Promise not to tell anyone?"

"Of course, silly goose. Who am I going to tell anyway?"

Hack whispered quietly about what Vega had said about the black market operation, its possible connection, in Decker's mind, to Kippen's death, and the plan to break-in to Chief's safe.

Lee listened with obvious skepticism. "I knew Decker'd get you involved in something like this. And his girlfriend sounds just like him."

"Decker's not getting me involved. I agreed to help. And Vega's got nothing to do with it. It's our idea."

"It's Decker's idea," Lee corrected him. "So what do you expect to find?"

"We're not sure, but it's strange."

"What is?"

"No one but Chief has the combination to the safe."

Lee laughed. "What's wrong with that? That's the whole idea of having a safe, sweetie. It keeps people like you and Decker out of it." She sat back in her chair. "How are you going to open it if you don't have the combination?"

"Decker figured it out. He's been watching Chief the past few months."

Lee reached across the table and held both of his hands. "You shouldn't get involved like this. Do you have any idea what could happen to you if you get caught?"

Hack squeezed her hand, running his thumb in tiny circles on her soft skin. "I try not to think about it. Decker has quarterdeck watch so it'll be safe. I'll have a lookout. If he has the right combination, I can be in and out of the safe in five minutes."

Lee let go of his hands and sat back in her chair. "I still think you shouldn't do it."

"I have to. I promised," Hack said, looking at his

watch. 2030. "In fact, I need to be going. I'll stop by tomorrow night."

Lee finished her beer and pulled out five dollars from her jeans. "I'll buy," she said. "I'll save the rest of my money to bail you out of the brig, if that's even possible in the navy."

"That won't be necessary," said Hack. "I hope." He pushed his chair back and stood, taking a deep breath as if to steel himself for the night's adventure.

Lee stood, too, and wrapped her arms around his shoulders. "Just kidding. Please be careful, okay? Promise me that?"

Hack kissed her forehead. "I promise." His eyes drifted around the club. Everywhere people were having fun, partying, laughing and carefree. How was it that Decker had talked him into this scheme of his? He'd much rather be heading back to Lee's place to spend the evening with her. "What are you doing tonight?"

"I have a few errands to run," Lee said. She looked up at Hack with a worried expression. "I better get home."

Hack said good-bye and left the club at 2040. He walked up the gangway fifteen minutes later. *Perfect timing*, he thought, *except* ... Decker had been on watch for an hour. Hack saluted the officer-of-the-deck, Lieutenant Duncan, and motioned discretely to Decker that he wanted to talk.

Decker led him to the far end of the quarterdeck. "What's up?" he asked, taking a peek at the officer-of-the deck. "We're looking suspicious."

"I can't get in," Hack whispered.

"Sure you can. You can be in and out in five minutes."

"It's not that. I forgot my keys at Lee's apartment."

Decker dug a keychain out of his pocket. Three keys and a yellow Tweety Bird fob around a silver metal loop.

"You actually walk around with this in public?"

"It's my good luck charm. And don't leave the ship with it. My rack key's on there."

Hack nodded and walked across the quarterdeck and down the portside ladder. Standing on the mess decks, Hack scanned the room to see who was on board. A few guys were sitting around playing cards, others were watching television. No one to be worried about.

He walked aft along the starboard passageway, past the supply berthing and down the port ladder. He continued aft along the passageway to Supply Support, pausing as he inserted the key. Above him, the noise of a shipyard worker using a needlegun scaler on the main deck reverberated throughout the stern of the ship.

Hack looked up and down the passageway. No one in sight. As stealthily as possibly, he unlocked the door, turned on the lights, and nearly jumped out of his shoes.

"Wilson. What are, um, it's nice to see you," stammered Ensign Limpert. "I didn't think, well, I didn't know you had duty."

"I don't. I just came down to do a little work, sir" said Hack. "Were you in here in the dark?"

Ensign Limpert nodded his head. "The dark, well, I don't like lights on when I'm on the computer. Mine isn't, um, well it crashed. I thought, um, I figured I'd come down here to do some work."

"I see," said Hack. "I'll come back."

"No, I'm almost, well, I'm finished," said Limpert. "Let me get out, um, I'll shut down the computer and I'll be out of your way."

Hack watched as Ensign Limpert turned off the computer, grabbed his hat, and shuffled towards the exit.

"Sorry to bother you," Limpert mumbled as he opened the door to leave.

"No problem," said Hack, but Limpert was already heading forward in the passageway.

Hack grabbed the growler next to Chief's desk and called the quarterdeck. Decker answered immediately.

"Quarterdeck, Petty Officer Decker."

"Limpert's on board."

"Who is this?" asked Decker, smiling.

"You know who it is, damn it. Limpert's on board. You didn't tell me that."

"How do you know?"

"Because he was in Supply Support!"

"You're kidding?"

"I wish. He was sitting down here with the lights off."

Decker was silent for a few seconds. "In the dark?"

"Yep, in the dark. He was sitting at Chief's desk on the computer."

"Why Supply Support and, more troubling, why were the lights out?"

"He said his computer wasn't working in his office and that he prefers it dark when he's on the computer."

Decker thought for a moment. "That's odd. Where is he now?"

"I don't know. He walked out a minute ago."

Decker looked aft along the starboard side. "Oh, here he comes. Looks like he's going to leave the ship." Decker paused while Ensign Limpert walked down the brow. "Must've been working on payroll. He probably knew I was on watch and thought he'd have the office to himself. I had no idea he was still on the ship."

"You sure no one else is on board?" asked Hack.

"As far as I know."

"That's not very comforting," said Hack.

"I'm sure of it," Decker said, not sounding completely convincing. "It's safe to proceed. Hey, you know what else?"

"What?" asked Hack, exasperated.

"Limpert's hat looks like it's three times too big for his head."

"I know," Hack chuckled. "And I'm sure it's the smallest size they make."

"I bet his wife—"

Hack hung up the growler before Decker could finish his sentence. He knew better than to trust his shipmate completely, so he grabbed the wrench next to the hatch that led to a storeroom below the office and loosened the six bolts. *Better safe than sorry*, he said to himself.

Satisfied that he had an escape route, Hack turned his attention to the safe. He set the keys on the desk, got on his knees, and slowly turned the dial. 36 right. 12 left. 24 right. No joy. Decker had warned him he wasn't sure about the last number. Hack turned the dial once again, this time trying a different ending number. 36 right. 12 left. 26 right. He tentatively pulled down on the handle. It opened effortlessly. He was in.

Hack took a quick look at the safe filled with file folders. *Damn*, he thought. *I'll need an hour to go through all this stuff.* But five minutes later he determined that most of the folders contained causality reports that ships submit when they need critical repair parts to maintain their warfighting capabilities. Most were classified documents with various ship locations and ship movements peppered throughout each report.

Hack was almost ready to give up when he came across a folder at the back of the safe. Labeled "Inventory," he thumbed through it, noticing the file had been updated during the past week with a recently-run report.

Hack quickly scanned the documents. He didn't know what he was looking for, but he tried to digest all of the names, dates, and figures that he could. Lost in concentration, the 1MC nearly scared him to death. *Harvey, departing.* The captain was going home for the night.

Hack exhaled and sat on the deck to stretch his legs. He quickly composed himself and began reading through the documents again when the growler began humming. *Not now, Decker*, Hack thought. He raced to the phone and was barely able to get out "Supply Support" before Decker interrupted.

"Get out of there. Now!"

"What's going on? Is someone here?"

"Hell yes! The commander and Chief Fray are both on board. Commander Doerr walked up the brow as soon as the Old Man rounded the corner to leave. I had to pass the word that the captain was leaving. But never mind that. Get the hell of there! Suppo said he's here to meet with Chief."

"Holy shit! Chief's on board?"

"Apparently he is, shipmate. Let me say that—"

"I knew this would happen," Hack growled, hanging up on Decker before he could finish his sentence. For the briefest of moments, the worker with the deck scaler above the office stopped allowing Hack to hear the sound of voices in the passageway. He grabbed the files, threw them in the safe, and closed the door as quietly and quickly as possible. He lunged across the office, dove into the hatch, slipped down the ladder, and closed the hatch to the storeroom just as the office door opened. In complete darkness, Hack dared not move. A step either direction could knock over something and give him away. It was then that he remembered: *Decker's keys.*

The conversation above him was barely audible. Chief was doing most of the talking. Something about inventory. *Perfect*, Hack thought. *They must be discussing the missing items.* The conversation lasted only five minutes when he heard Suppo say he was leaving. Hack, motionless, felt his heartbeat begin to return to normal. But his luck ran out when Chief Fray started for the door.

"Damn idiots," Chief said. "They left the hatch open. I'll catch up with you, sir." Hack heard Chief Fray grunt as he knelt to grab the wrench. Hack cautiously felt his way along a row of bins, wanting desperately to move away from the opening in case Chief took a look down the hatch. But Chief was in no mood to mess around. He tightened the bolts, mumbled something Hack couldn't understand, and left the office, slamming the door behind him.

For the next thirty minutes Hack waited in the dark wondering how long it would take Decker to come look for him. He sat on the deck and tried to think positive thoughts to rid himself of his anxiety. To his great relief, ten minutes later he heard the door to Supply Support open and a familiar voice calling out. "Hey, Hack, you in here?"

"Thank you, God," Hack said to no one in particular. "I'm down here!"

Decker unbolted the hatch and Hack climbed out, relieved his temporary confinement was over. "Why aren't you on watch?"

"I got worried and told Lieutenant Duncan I had to go to the head. Chief and the commander left the ship about twenty minutes ago, and I didn't see or hear from you."

"I barely made it to the storeroom in time. I started to—"

"No time for your life story," Decker said. "I need to get back to the quarterdeck. Did you see what's in the safe?"

"Several folders. Mostly routine supply stuff that's classified. Casualty reports that have been filed over the past couple of years. There was one folder that might be of interest. Chief labeled it 'Inventory.'"

"Did you look inside?"

"I'd just opened it when you called. I barely made it to the storeroom in time."

Decker took off his hat and scratched his head. "You see what was in it?"

"Requisition lists, mostly. And a slip of paper with the name 'Allen Sumner' written across the top and several more names written below it."

Decker's eyes widened. "Allen Sumner?"

"You know him?" Hack asked.

"No, it's not anybody on the ship."

"There's one more thing." Hack glanced at the desk.

"What's that?"

"Your keys. I forgot to grab them when I hid in the storeroom."

Decker turned and saw Tweety Bird sitting plain as

day on a white desk calendar.

"I doubt if Chief noticed it," Hack said. "And if he did, he probably assumed you left it there sometime earlier today."

"Then how did the door get locked?"

Hack looked around the room as if the answer might be hiding in a dark corner. "I don't know...."

Decker thought for moment. No time to worry about it now. "You sure that was the name?"

"What name?"

"Allen Sumner."

"Positive. At least I think I'm sure."

Decker put his hat back on and checked his watch. "We've got to find out for sure, but I need to get back to the quarterdeck. I'll call when I get there. Open it up again and make copies of the papers."

"Pay attention this time," Hack said. "I don't want another close call."

"I'll do my best," Decker said, leaving Supply Support and jogging up the ladder to the main deck.

Two minutes later, Decker called from the quarterdeck to say it was clear. Hack locked the door to the office and once again opened the safe. He quickly grabbed the folder and made copies of the documents. Hack returned the original documents to the safe, locked it, and made sure everything on Chief's desk was returned to normal. He grabbed Decker's keys, closed the door to Supply Support, and headed to the quarterdeck. He was relieved to see the officer-of-the-deck in conversation with a fellow officer returning from liberty. Hack walked over to Decker and they stepped next to the life line, looking at the water below. "I've got the copies."

"Where?"

"In my back pocket."

Decker didn't lift his head. "Keep them there. And let's not talk about it anymore on the ship. Not even tomorrow. Let's meet at Cal Jam after work."

Hack nodded and began walking towards the brow. He turned to Decker and handed over the keys. "What if Chief saw them? They were laying right there...."

Decker followed him to the edge of the quarterdeck. "If he noticed the keys, he may be on to you. But what's worse, he's going to think *I'm involved*."

Hack heard him but didn't reply. He was already heading down the gangway, feeling lucky he was able to leave the ship.

CHAPTER TWELVE
1830, WEDNESDAY, JANUARY 8

"I brought the copies," Hack said, anxious for Decker to have a look at them.

Decker brushed aside the news. "Hang on a minute," he said. "I have to finish this."

Decker and Hack sat in Cal Jam at their favorite table near the window, Hack staring at people walking down the sidewalk and Decker writing in his Book of Dates. Ten minutes later, Hack took a drink of beer and decided to interrupt. "You about done writing?" He looked around the bar. "Where's Vega tonight? I expected her to be here."

Decker finished a sentence and closed his notebook. "She's working until 1900. I'm supposed to meet Mo here, but he's obviously stood me up. Where's Lee tonight?"

"Working late, too. I'm going to stop by there a little later."

"Working late?" Decker said, surprised. "I thought she had a nine-to-five job?"

"So did I."

"Well then, what can be so pressing at the supply depot to make her work late?"

"I guess they have their busy times, too. She said they

have stuff piling up for all the ships deployed throughout the Pacific. It seems to happen frequently. Makes me wonder if shore duty is that much better than sea duty."

"It is. Trust me on that one. Sea duty, in case you haven't noticed it yet, can really be a miserable undertaking. All that time at sea, then your reward for returning to port is duty every four days. Not much time to do anything meaningful. Wait 'til you've been on board a year, and you'll be ready for shore duty, too."

"I'm glad we're not at sea this week," Hack said. "I'm worried Chief knows we were snooping around. He didn't mention it today, though, so maybe we got lucky."

"Maybe," said Decker, raising his beer bottle. "And that, my friend, is a perfect segue. Let's have a look."

"About time," Hack said, pulling the papers from his back pocket and setting them on the table. There were four requisition lists and one page of handwritten notes.

Hack drank his beer as he watched Decker flip through the papers. "What do you make of them?"

Decker picked up one list, examined it closely, and pointed to the columns. "It's a list of repair parts that were ordered. Each item is listed by stock number. Here's the quantity ordered and over here is the date at the top when the order was placed. The requisitions were submitted December 24, December 26, and December 31."

"Doesn't do us much good," Hack said, sinking into his chair.

"I'm afraid you're right. Where's the copy of the note with Allen Sumner's name written on it?"

"It's in there along with several more names."

Decker flipped through the requisitions and found the document. Across the top of the note Chief had written "Allen Sumner," along with several other names listed below it.

"I don't recognize any of these names," Decker said. "There must be over twenty on the list. Some are first and last names. There's James Owens, John Thomason, and Wallace Lind. Then some words like 'brush,' 'strong,' and what appears to be 'stormes'. Typical Chief Fray, though. He misspelled it with an 'e' before the last 's.' And there's a Hank and Zellars." Decker rubbed his forehead. "They don't mean anything to me. They're not sailors on the *Harvey*."

"They don't mean anything to me, either. They could be anybody. Maybe they're guys Chief knew at his previous commands."

"Or they could be names of people who are helping him," Decker said. "If Chief's running a black market operation, he wouldn't be able to do it alone. Maybe they're not even here at Subic. Maybe they're spread out all over the navy, each one working their own angle at their local supply command."

"Maybe," Hack agreed. "But we have no way of tracking them down."

Decker suddenly stopped reading. A broad smile formed across his face. "I was wrong. I do recognize one name."

Hack leaned in to see what Decker was looking at. "Which one?"

Decker held the paper so Hack could see and pointed to a name. "Mansfield. I thought you said you didn't recognize any names?"

Hack took a sip of beer and sat back in his chair. "I saw that, too. It's a common name."

Decker raised his eyebrows. "Really? How many Mansfields do you know besides Leeandra and Jayne?"

"Plenty," Hack said. "And who's Jayne?"

"Never mind about her," Decker chuckled. "Although she obviously could have been related to Lee." He tapped the paper with his finger. "It's interesting her name appears on here."

Hack took another drink of beer, annoyed. "I know plenty of Mansfields. I just can't remember first names. It doesn't matter, though. We've probably got it all wrong. If they're people helping Chief, he'd be dumb to write the names down like this."

Decker held up his index finger on his right hand. "Not really. Maybe he needs to remember the names. It's not like he had the paper lying around on his desk. He kept it in his safe. And he's the only one with the combination."

"And there are initials written at the bottom," Hack said.

"A. A.," Decker said, reading the name. "And something that looks like 'j-bee' written next to the name."

"Do they mean anything to you?"

Decker stared at the ceiling for a moment. "Nothing. Could be someone on the ship with those initials, but no one comes to mind. Could be that he attends AA meetings, but I don't think he drinks that much. And I have no idea what 'j-bee' is supposed to mean. Maybe it's a nickname for someone."

Hack slumped in his chair. "We're back to where we started. Which is nowhere."

"We have all of this," Decker said, holding up the papers.

"But if we can't make sense out of them, then it doesn't do us any good."

"It's a start and, I should add, more than we had a couple days ago."

Hack picked up the paper with the handwritten notes. "Who are these people? Where are they are stationed? We don't even know who Allen Sumner is."

"Mo might know. He's been on board the *Harvey* for three years." Decker scanned the room. "I was hoping he'd be here by now."

"Maybe he found a better offer," Hack smiled.

"Wouldn't surprise me," Decker agreed. "But I've got another idea. When are you going to Lee's?"

"In a few minutes. She should be off work soon."

"Ask her ... wait, don't turn around," Decker said. "Pretend we're talking."

Hack glanced behind him. "We *are* talking."

"I mean a serious conversation."

"Okay, what do you want to talk about?"

"Never mind," Decker sighed, peering over Hack's shoulder. "Pinto, what are you doing here? I thought beer was bad for your caloric intake?"

Pinto hovered over the table, obviously wanting to join his shipmates. "One beer a month is good for the system and it's my birthday today so I wanted to celebrate. Mind if I join you?"

"We're just leaving," Decker said pointedly. "And we're not going to another bar," he added. "We'll have a beer with you next month. It'll be a belated birthday beer."

"Very funny," Pinto said. "Which way you headed?"

"To the trike stand," said Hack.

"I guess I'll head back to base if you guys are leaving," Pinto replied. "I'll walk with you."

"Suit yourself," said Decker, "The Amo Band's getting ready to play. You should stay and listen. I highly recommend it."

Pinto put his hands in his pockets and took a quick look around the club. "Not tonight," he said abruptly.

Decker looked at Hack, pointing with his eyes towards the door. The three sailors walked out of the club and down the sidewalk towards base. They said their goodbyes in the midst of a gaggle of trikes at the corner of Magsaysay and Gordon. Decker and Hack watched as Pinto made his way upstream against the flow of foot traffic leaving base.

"That was weird," Hack said.

"Tell me about it. I've never seen him in Cal Jam before."

Hack looked towards the Shit River Bridge trying to see Pinto. He turned to Decker. "You were getting ready to ask me something before we were interrupted."

"I forgot what it was," Decker said.

"You started to say 'ask her' and then Pinto showed up."

"Oh, yeah," Decker said. "When you see Lee, ask her if she can print out *Harvey* requisitions from the past couple months. We only have a few lists and it'd help to see what's been ordered over an extended period of time."

Hack hesitated. "I'm not sure she'll do it. She's a by-the-book girl and isn't thrilled I'm involved in this in the first place."

"You *told* her?"

"Not everything," Hack lied.

"Just have her get a few printouts," Decker paused while a group of young sailors walked by, clapping each other on the shoulders and bragging about booze and women, obviously first-timers on the strip. "We're stuck in neutral, but maybe we can learn something if we have more data. It'll give us a more complete picture."

"I'll ask," said Hack. "But don't expect her to help."

"You can charm her," Decker said, checking his watch. "I've got to get to Vega's."

"What are you doing with Vega?" Hack asked, signaling the nearest trike driver and wondering why he cared what Decker and Vega were doing together.

Decker ignored the question. "Just make sure you get Lee to help."

"Maybe you should talk to her. You're the one who seems to be able to get people to do things they don't want to do." Hack climbed in the side car and gave the driver Lee's address.

"Don't forget to ask her!" Decker called out as the trike roared away in a cloud of dust. Another trike suddenly pulled close to him, narrowly missing his feet with the front tire.

"Hey, you almost hit me."

"Not a chance, *pare*," said Rusty. "I'm an expert driver. Climb in. It's been a slow night."

Decker moved a step towards Rusty's side car, but a small Filipino grabbed him by the arm, jerking him backwards, almost off his feet.

"Need a ride?" the man said. "I get you there fast."

"*Hindi*," Decker said firmly, prying the man's fingers from his arm. "And get out of my way." The man mumbled something in Tagalog and walked towards a group of drivers milling on the corner.

Decker rubbed his arm where the man had had a hold of him. "You know that jerk?" he asked Rusty.

"I've never seen him before, but I can tell he's *walang pakinabang.*"

"What's that mean?" asked Decker.

"Good for nothing," Rusty said. "Now grab your nuts and hang on."

CHAPTER THIRTEEN
1905, WEDNESDAY, JANUARY 8

Rush hour Olongapo style. Trikes and jeepneys jockeyed for position, horns blaring, zigzagging through the maze of streets. Lost in jumbled thoughts about Vega and Allen Sumner and Chief Fray, Decker hadn't noticed the yellow and red trike that pulled within a few feet of the motorcycle. Rusty waved with his left hand for the guy to pass, but the driver stayed in position. Rusty yelled something in Tagalog and then turned to Decker. "Must be *loko, pare.*"

Decker glanced behind him, but couldn't see anyone in the side car and the bike's decorative top obscured the driver's face. But Decker did notice a gun appear in the driver's hand as the trike pulled alongside. Rusty saw it too and swerved just as a shot was fired. He put on his brakes to let the trike pass, but the driver, as skilled as Rusty, slowed and pulled in front to block Rusty's path. Thinking quickly, Rusty slammed on the brakes, executed a perfect 180, and sped back towards base.

Decker turned and saw the trike resume the chase. "Head to Magsaysay," he shouted to Rusty. But it was too late. The trike, a bigger and faster bike, gained on them until the driver pulled alongside, aimed his weapon, and fired two more shots.

"Watch out, *pare*," yelled Rusty, as the bike crashed headfirst into a roadside, open air *sari sari* store. Decker flew out the sidecar and tumbled over the store's counter, crashing into a large sack of rice. Rusty held on to the bike as long as he could as it slid to a stop on its side. As Decker recovered his senses, he did a quick check of his hands and feet.

"Everything still works," he mumbled, and pulled himself to his knees to peer over the counter. Two young Filipinas rushed to his side, asking if he was alright.

The girls helped Decker to his feet in the middle of merchandise strewn across the floor. He shook himself off and saw the trike, its front tire still spinning as Rusty pulled himself from under the wreck. With a crowd of onlookers gathering, Decker rushed to Rusty's side and saw blood running down his left leg. A young woman appeared at his side with a towel, and Decker wrapped Rusty's leg as best he could.

"You hurt anywhere else?"

"Don't think so," Rusty whispered. "Sorry I couldn't get you to Vega's."

Decker held Rusty's head off the hard concrete of the street. "That's the least of our worries. We've got to get you to the hospital."

Decker took out his wallet and opened it. Forty-eight dollars and a hundred twenty-five pesos. He gave Rusty most of the cash and helped him into another trike for the ride to the hospital. With no phone nearby, Decker tore a page from his notebook, scribbled a note, and wrote an address across the top of the page. He gave forty pesos to a kid standing nearby and sent him to deliver the message to Rusty's wife. Decker picked up the spilled trike and paid another kid eighty pesos to walk it to Rusty's house.

Decker walked to the *sari sari* store and examined the damage, wondering how much it was going to cost him. A police siren behind him gave him pause. He turned and saw a brown Toyota 4Runner pull up several yards from the scene. A middle-aged man exited the vehicle's driver side. He had on jeans, a light blue polo shirt, and a police baseball cap. A young Filipina emerged from the passenger side. White blouse, khaki pants, and a similar police ball cap. Two more cops rode to the scene on bicycles and started clearing the area of bystanders. The man and woman walked towards Decker.

Decker smiled. "You're a sight for sore eyes."

Vega grimaced at Decker's familiarity. She gestured with her left hand to the man standing next to her. "This is Inspector Navarro. What happened?"

Decker explained the trike chase and gunshots and how Rusty crashed his bike. He described the Filipino who grabbed his arm at the trike stand, but was unsure if it was the same man. He assured Vega and Inspector Navarro that Rusty was on his way to the hospital, injured but otherwise doing well.

The inspector raised his eyebrows. "Is that what really happened?"

"Of course that's what really happened," said Decker. "Ask the fifty people who witnessed it. We could've been killed."

Inspector Navarro crossed his arms. "No need to get angry with me, young man. I just find it strange that someone would want to follow you and shoot at you.

Does not make sense to me." He turned to Vega. "It appears this man knows you. What's his name?"

"Decker. Elliott Decker, sir. He's a friend of mine."

The Inspector smiled. "I see. Navy, not Marines, I presume from your haircut."

"Yes, navy. I'm stationed on the *Harvey.*"

The inspector reached for a notebook in his back pocket. "Interesting. Where were you earlier this evening?"

"Cal Jam for a little while. That was the only place I've been."

"Cal Jam, huh? Nice place. Don't go there myself. Too many sailors, but they have pretty girls." He leered at Vega. "But pretty girls are everywhere."

Vega ignored the comment and focused on Decker. "Did you get a look at him? The trike driver?"

"No, I couldn't see his face. Just that it was a man. Maybe Rusty can tell you more, but the guy was wearing a cap and he had a cover on his trike that blocked the view of his face.

Vega nodded. "What about his trike? Can you describe it?"

Decker shook his head. "Only that it was red and yellow. But half the trikes in town are red and yellow."

Inspector Navarro looked both ways along the street. "Where were you headed, Mr. Decker. Do you live around here?"

Vega urged him with her eyes to fib. Decker then remembered Lee lived somewhere in the area. "I was going to visit a friend," he said. "His girlfriend lives nearby."

"And does this supposed friend and his girlfriend have names?"

Decker hesitated but Vega nodded for him to cooperate. "Hack and Lee."

Inspector Navarro eyes narrowed. "I thought you said one was a girlfriend?"

"It is. Her name's Leeandra Mansfield. She goes by Lee. My friend is Hack Wilson. But I don't see why it matters who they are."

The inspector scowled. "It's not for you to ask questions, Mr. Decker." He adjusted himself in front of everyone, forcing Vega to look away and roll her eyes. He cleared his throat. "It is very interesting. I believe I know the girl who you speak of. A pretty American girl. Perhaps I should take her down to the station for questioning someday."

Decker didn't like what the inspector was intimating about Lee, but he had no desire for a confrontation with the police chief. He knew the inspector was fishing for something, and he wasn't in the mood to play along. He had no idea why someone would want to shoot at him. Maybe Chief Fray was behind it or perhaps the guy was after Rusty and he just happened to be in the wrong place at the wrong time.

To Decker's great relief, Inspector Navarro scribbled a few lines in his notebook and ended the interview. "Be careful, young man. I hate to see sailors get involved in local grudge matches. We'll talk to this Rusty at the hospital and get his statement."

"I'm not involved in anything," Decker said.

The inspector raised an eyebrow. "Good, then keep it that way. I have to go now and I hope our paths never cross again."

"Me, too" said Decker, but the inspector was already

walking towards his truck, talking with two male police officers.

Vega moved close to Decker, keeping a careful watch on the inspector. "Are you okay? I couldn't believe my eyes when we pulled up and I saw it was you."

"I'm fine," Decker said. "I'm glad you showed up." He pointed discretely at Navarro who was standing with a foot on the front bumper of his vehicle issuing orders to his men. "That guy's a jackass. How do you put up with it?"

"It's not easy," Vega said. "But I have to if I want to have any shot at advancement."

Decker wiped the sweat from his forehead. "It's hot out in the street like this. You're about to get off work, right?"

"Not too much longer," she said. "Depends on how long it takes to get the paperwork wrapped up for this."

"I was actually heading to your place. Can I meet you there later?"

Vega shuffled her feet. "Not tonight, okay? But let's get together soon. We have to talk." She turned and jogged back to Navarro's truck before Decker could answer.

Decker watched her move away, annoyed at himself that he was admiring her butt in the tight khakis. "We have to talk. That's never a good thing," Decker said out loud.

A voice from behind startled him. "You need to get your head looked at. You're starting to talk to yourself."

Decker whirled around. "What are you doing here?"

Hack grinned. "I was in front of Lee's apartment and heard the commotion. By the time I saw that it was you, the police showed up, and I didn't want to get involved."

"Smart thinking," Decker said. "I had the pleasure of meeting Vega's boss, the Supreme Jackass himself, Inspector Navarro."

"I don't feel so bad about staying away. What happened anyway? Where's Rusty?"

Decker told Hack about the chase and shooting, Rusty's injuries, and his conversation with Inspector Navarro and Vega.

Hack shook his head in disbelief. "Well, Lee's not home. She must be still at work. Let's go back to Cal Jam."

"Good idea," said Decker. "Maybe Mo's there by now. But let's take the backstreets. That guy could still be out there." Decker looked again at the wrecked *sari sari* store. "How much money do you have on you? I gave all I had to Rusty to pay his doctor's bill."

Hack opened his wallet and counted the bills. "Twenty-eight dollars and a few pesos."

Decker reached in and took the money from Hack. "I'll pay you back. This'll help get the store put back together." He handed the money to one of the young women cleaning up the mess.

She smiled and bowed her head. "*Salamat po,* sir."

"*Walang anuman,*" said Decker. "I'll come by tomorrow and see if that's enough to cover the damages." He turned to Hack. "I need a beer."

Hack cocked his head. "I didn't know you could speak Tagalog?"

"I don't. I only know the basics to survive around here. Thank you. You're welcome. How much? Things like that."

Hack put his wallet back in his pocket and started

walking with Decker towards Magsaysay. "Whichever language you use, I hope you know how to buy beer without any money."

Decker put his arm around his friend's shoulder. "That, my boy, is my specialty."

CHAPTER FOURTEEN
1945, WEDNESDAY, JANUARY 8

Mo looked up as Decker and Hack approached the table. He threw up his hands in mock disgust. "Great. You finally show up just when I thought I was arranging to have some fun on my own tonight."

"We've got news," said Decker. His face grew serious and he put his elbows on the table. He spent the next ten minutes telling Mo about his adventures earlier in the evening.

When Decker finished, Mo sat back in his chair. "This *is* big news. You know what this means?"

"No, what?" asked Hack.

Mo nodded toward the bar. "I should be on my way home with that lovely lady instead of sitting here with you two jerkoffs."

Decker spied a girl across the bar sitting with another sailor. "I'm sure you'll have another opportunity with her. We need to do some serious brainstorming about who would want to shoot me."

The beers arrived and Decker and Hack exchanged glances. "Mo, how 'bout buying this round," said Decker.

"Where the hell's your money?"

"I gave what I had on me to Rusty, and Hack gave his

money to the owners of the *sari sari* store."

"Great," Mo grunted and handed the waitress sixty pesos. "Add one more to the list of people after you. And this is the second thing tonight that is cutting into my liberty money."

"What was the first?" asked Hack.

"I was late leaving the ship and had to do an exchange with a street vendor. Gave me fifteen pesos to the dollar."

"You got ripped off, my friend," laughed Decker.

"Tell me about it," Mo agreed. "I told him the official rate was twenty and a half to the dollar, but he pretended not to understand. Seeing that he was my only option at the time, I gave in."

Decker tipped his bottle towards Mo. "You are a true friend and shipmate. Now, let's talk this through. I don't mean to seem selfish, but someone appears to be out to get me and I suddenly find that very troubling. First Kippen and now this."

Hack took a swig of beer. "Chief Fray's the obvious choice, especially if he knows we were snooping around his safe."

"You should've listened to Vega," said Mo. "She told you something like this would happen."

Decker ignored the comment. "What do we know about Chief?"

"He's your chief," Mo said.

"I mean besides that. What does he do off the ship? Who are his friends?"

"He's married," Hack said. "I saw his wife, or I assumed it was his wife, with him one day on the ship. She was there to pick him up for lunch."

"I've met her, too," Decker said. "Several times in fact.

A Filipina."

"Nice looking woman," Mo added.

Hack smiled at Mo's comment. "She's okay, but not as nice as Mrs. Doerr. And maybe that's who chased you. Maybe the commander found out you were at his house."

"Woah, back up," Mo said, choking on his beer. "What's going on with you and the commander's wife?"

"*Nothing* is going on." Decker shot Hack an angry glance. "Hack's just running his mouth. Now, let's get back to Chief Fray. We've established that he is, in fact, a chief and that he's more than likely married. We're going to have to do better than this."

"I don't even know what ships he's been on," Hack said. "Has he ever talked about that with you guys?"

Mo stared at his beer bottle. "I've heard him talk about the *Midway* before. I think that was his first ship."

"And I know he was on the *Holt*," Decker said. "That's the ship he made chief on. A fast frigate. I believe that was his duty station before the *Harvey*."

"I think he's been on the *Stoddard*, too," Mo said. "He always talks about this numbskull supply officer he used to work for. I'm pretty sure it was the *Stoddard*."

Decker took out his notebook and pencil and wrote down the ship names. "I've heard those stories, too." He examined the list. "Let's see. That gives us the *Midway*, *Stoddard*, and *Holt*. Any more duty stations?"

"I can't think of anywhere else," said Mo. "But I don't work with him every day."

Decker twirled his pencil in his right hand. "I think I've heard him mention being in San Diego. Or maybe Long Beach. He talks about Southern California sometimes. I can't remember the duty station, but it was on shore. Let's add it to our list. We're probably missing something, but this is a good start."

"How does this help us?" asked Hack. "He was on those ships a long time ago and we'd never be able to get a crew list. Plus, we're stuck in Subic and have no way of tracking down those ships wherever they are home ported."

Decker leaned back in his chair. "Okay then, let's think more locally. We know he's married. Do we know anything about his wife? What the home situation is like?"

"I think they have a kid," Mo said. "A boy. Something like four or five years old. I've seen him with Chief a few times at parties."

"I've seen the kid, too," said Decker. "But let's focus on navy personnel. Who are his friends on the ship? Do we know of any friends he has at other places on base?"

"All I know is he hangs out with other chiefs," Mo said. "I've seen him with Chief Barker and Senior Chief Genet on liberty."

"And I saw him with Chief Blanchard in Hong Kong once," Decker said.

Mo took a big swig of beer and belched. "He seems to keep to himself on board. 'Course he hangs out in the Goat Locker a lot. But we can't go in there."

"Where?" asked Hack.

"The Goat Locker. The chiefs' mess," Decker said. "It's what everybody calls it. Including the chiefs."

"That's a dumb name."

"I agree," Decker said. "But that's what they call it. Even more sad than the name is the fact that they like calling it the Goat Locker."

The three sailors sat in silence as the Amo Band began playing. The loud music blared from the floor-to-ceiling speakers making any attempt at a conversation impossible. Five songs later, the band took a ten-minute break and Decker resumed. "The bottom line is we don't know much about Chief Fray. We know the basics. Where he was stationed in the past. He's married with a kid. He hangs out with a couple fellow chiefs while on liberty. That's about the extent of it."

"Why don't you follow him for a couple days?" Mo said. "If you want to play detective, that's the way they do it in the movies."

Decker's eyes brightened. "Mo, I think you may be on to something. That's a brilliant idea."

"How are we going to do that?" Hack asked. "We don't have a car. He knows all three of us so he'd surely see us if we try to follow him."

Decker looked at Hack. "Not if you're careful."

"If *I'm* careful?" Hack asked.

"You're the perfect person to do it," Decker said. "You're new on board. New enough he won't easily recognize you in civilian clothes. All you need is a hat of some kind. You'll blend right in."

Hack pointed to Mo. "What about him?"

"Not a chance," Decker said. "He'd stick out like a sore thumb. No offense, Mo."

"None taken," Mo shrugged. "I'm glad you feel that way."

Hack turned to Decker. "Okay, what about you? You know the base and town better than I do. You'd be able to track him much more easily than me."

Decker considered the wisdom of Hack's comment. "I

hate it when you're right, but it makes sense. Okay, let's both do it. I don't want to do it alone, though."

"You were ready to send me out there alone!" Hack said.

"That was before I realized how little you know the surroundings."

"Then why don't *you* do it alone?" Hack argued.

"I would, but I'd stick out, too. Chief knows me too well. Besides, I don't look like the kind of guy that would be trailing someone."

Hack frowned. "That doesn't make any sense."

Decker set down his beer and folded his arms. "It makes perfect sense. You have that innocent look about you. You can blend into the background. No one will suspect you're following someone. I'll be there as your wingman to guide you."

"I've seen how well you handle that role," Hack said, finishing the last of his San Miguel. "But if we do it, let's give ourselves a week. If Chief's involved with some-thing, he'll make a move at some point during the week."

Decker raised his beer bottle. "Okay, we're in for a week. Hack, you have duty tomorrow, right?

"I think so."

"Then we'll start Operation Chief Watch on Friday."

"What do you want me to do? I'd be more than happy to follow the commander's wife," Mo said with a leer.

"At this point, nothing," said Decker. "You'll be the muscle when we need it.

Mo polished off the remainder of his beer and set the bottle down with a grunt. "Great."

CHAPTER FIFTEEN
1735, FRIDAY, JANUARY 10

Decker and Hack waited near the machine shop behind the dumpster, out of sight from the *Harvey's* quarterdeck. Decker looked his watch. "Chief's a man of habits. He always leaves the ship at the same time."

Ten minutes later, at exactly 1745, the two sailors watched Chief Fray depart the ship. He had on his work khakis, not bothering to change into civilian clothes. He walked down the pier forward of the *Harvey*, turned right on the shipyard access road, and passed through the security gate exiting the ship repair facility. He continued walking north one block to the Spanish Gate where he made a pit stop for ice cream. Decker and Hack entered the adjacent cafeteria, ordered cokes and fries, and sat in a corner booth. Decker had his back to the Baskin Robbins, but Hack could see Chief through the window that separated the two eateries.

Decker picked at his fries. "What's he doing now?"

"Sitting there slurping his ice cream."

"What did he order?"

"Looks like a hot fudge sundae."

"The fat bastard," Decker smirked. "But don't look at him. Keep your eyes on me. What's he doing now?"

"How can I tell you what's he doing if I'm looking at you?"

"Use your peripheral vision."

"Why don't you just turn around and take a quick look?"

Decker shook his head. "It'd be too obvious. What's he doing now?"

"Are you going to ask me that every ten seconds?"

"Yes."

Hack glanced over Decker's shoulder. "He's flirting with the ice cream girls."

"Are they cute?"

Hack took another peek. "One of them's okay. Too young for Chief, though. The other one's kinda big."

"Which one is he talking to?"

"The big one."

Decker put his head in his hands. "We could be here all night. What's he doing now?"

"Ordering more ice cream."

"He's finished with his sundae already?"

"No, but he's ordering another one."

"Maybe it's his dinner," said Decker.

Hack stole another glance. "I don't think so. It looks like he's leaving. He's getting some napkins. He's heading out the door."

"Let's follow him," Decker said. "Which way did he go?"

"The west exit. He's headed for the street."

Decker and Hack walked into the ice cream store and watched through the window to the sidewalk. They saw Mrs. Fray parked on the curb in a maroon Cadillac Brougham next to the Spanish Gate. Little Fray sat strapped in the backseat. Chief Fray got in on the passenger side, kissed his wife, and handed the extra sundae to his kid. Mrs. Fray put the car in gear, looked over her left shoulder, and sped away.

"I bet they're going home," Hack said.

Decker watched the station wagon drive out of sight. "You're probably right. No luck tonight. We'll follow him again next week." He turned to his left as the girls greeted a customer. "Let's get a treat. The big one's yours."

And so it went the following Monday. Decker and Hack followed Chief Fray to Baskin Robbins whereupon he ordered a hot fudge sundae, flirted with the ice cream girls for a few minutes, ordered an extra sundae, and then departed at exactly 1805 out the front door. Waiting for Chief would be Mrs. Fray parked on the street in front of the Spanish Gate. Little Fray in the back seat. Monday night Hack had duty. Tuesday night it was Chief Fray's turn. Decker had duty Wednesday night. Thursday night, the two sailors returned to the stakeout.

CHAPTER SIXTEEN
1735, THURSDAY, JANUARY 16

Decker and Hack hadn't bothered to follow Chief Fray from the ship. They knew where he'd end up. Chief entered the Baskin Robbins at his usual time, ordered his customary hot fudge sundae, and departed the premises at exactly 1805. But tonight Mrs. Fray was nowhere to be seen. He exited the ice cream store and walked down Dewey Avenue heading west. Decker and Hack, caught off guard, followed Chief when he was a block away.

They found themselves exposed walking down the same sidewalk on the same side of the street. Decker took a quick look around the area. "If he turns around, we're busted. He's probably heading to the chiefs' club. If so, I suspect he'll turn right on Aguinaldo and follow that to the club. Let's take Bonifacio and follow him a block south of his position."

The two sailors turned right on Bonifacio and walked a half block until they were in front of the base mess hall. A long line of sailors had formed along the sidewalk extending several yards west.

"Let's stand in the chow line," said Decker. "We'll blend in with everyone and watch for him to walk down Aguinaldo."

Decker and Hack waited in line at the mess hall for ten minutes. Plenty of time for Chief to pass by them a block west walking north on Aguinaldo. When another five minutes passed, Hack knew that even the slow-walking Chief should have made his way north by then. "Great plan. Now we've lost him. Want to eat since we're here?"

Decker quickly read the menu posted on the door. "No thanks. I've had enough navy cuisine for one day. And how can you think about food at a time like this?"

"It's easy. We lost him," Hack said. "We can try again next week."

Decker folded his arms and contemplated their situation. "I don't understand it. If he continued straight on Dewey, there's nothing but officer barracks and administrative offices in that direction. If he turned left on Aguinaldo, he'd be heading to the pier. I doubt if he was heading there. He can look at the water anytime he wants to. I was sure he'd turn right. Let's backtrack and see if we can find him."

The two sailors got out of line and backtracked down Bonificio to Dewey Avenue. Three sailors were walking east heading for the Spanish Gate. Two sailors were heading west. None of them was Chief Fray.

"Let's walk towards Aguinaldo," Decker said. "Maybe we'll run into him."

"What if we do?" asked Hack.

"Not to worry," Decker said. "It would be normal for us to walk around base. We'll just say we're heading to the enlisted club or something."

Decker and Hack continued walking along Dewey until they reached the intersection of Aguinaldo. The base library and movie theater were to their right. Decker scanned both directions. "No sign of him. That's odd."

"Maybe he's watching a movie."

"Why would he watch a movie?"

"His wife could be busy. Killing time."

Decker grimaced at what was showing. *Ernest Goes to Camp.* "I doubt he's in there. It's one thing to run a black market scheme, but quite another to watch a movie like that."

They stood at the corner of Dewey and Aguinaldo, contemplating their next move. Decker pulled at his T-shirt , which was stuck to his body with sweat. "It's too hot to be standing out here. Let's head to the Sampaquita Club."

They turned right on Aguinaldo and were almost out of sight from the library and theater when Hack saw something out of the corner of his eye. Chief Fray sitting in the library, his back to the window. Hack grabbed Decker by the arm and discretely pointed with his thumb. "Look over there."

"He's been in the library the whole time," Decker said. "I suspected that."

"You're full of shit," said Hack. "You had no idea he was in there. So what do we do?"

Decker surveyed their surroundings, finding a perfect hideout. "Let's go across the street and wait for him to leave."

"To the miniature golf place?"

"Sure, we can play a few holes. Loser buys the first round at Cal Jam. We'll be in perfect position to watch the library."

"Okay. You're on."

Decker and Hack were on the eighth hole negotiating

the windmill when Chief Fray emerged from the library.

"There he is," said Hack.

"I see him. He's just standing there looking at something."

"Maybe he's waiting on his ride."

"Can you see what he's holding?"

Hack squinted towards the chief. "I don't think it's a book. Looks like a piece of paper."

"Let's keep playing and see what he does," Decker said.

From the eighth green, they watched Chief walk down the sidewalk heading back to the Spanish Gate. When he reached the gate, Mrs. Fray sat waiting in a Caddy.

"Well, we know where he was going," Decker said. "Now we need to find out what he was doing in there."

"How are we going to do that?" asked Hack. "It'll be impossible to find out what he was reading."

"Maybe he left some books lying around," Decker said. "And if you don't see anything that looks obvious, you can ask the librarian. Maybe Chief asked her for help."

"I'm not going in there alone," Hack said. "You do it. Or we both go in."

"Someone has to stand guard outside. What if Chief comes back?"

"Okay then, I'll stand guard. You go in."

"It has to be you," said Decker. "If I go in, they won't believe me when I ask for help. You look like you need help."

"That doesn't make any sense."

Decker put a hand on Hack's shoulder. "It makes perfect sense. Just go in, take a look around, and see what you can find. If Chief didn't leave any books or magazines on the tables, just ask the librarian. It's as simple as that."

"I can't believe you talk me into these things."

"Five minutes. That's all. I'll wait out here by the theater ticket window like I'm going to watch a movie." Decker frowned again at the "now showing" poster. "I hope no one sees me, but it's a risk to my reputation that I'm willing to take."

"You're a brave man," Hack said as he walked to the library entrance.

"Wait," yelled Decker. "One more thing."

Hacker paused and turned around. "What?"

"I was up two strokes. You owe me a beer."

Hack shook his head and opened the door. "Why am I the one doing this?" he mumbled, drawing looks from a woman exiting the library.

CHAPTER SEVENTEEN
1820, THURSDAY, JANUARY 16

Hack walked into the library and paused at a magazine rack to survey the landscape. At a far table a mother and middle-school-aged son were studying an encyclopedia. Near the reference desk, a sailor, asleep on a couch, had been reading *Sports Illustrated*, which was spilled open in his lap. A cheery-looking librarian sat behind a desk in the middle of the room. Mid-forties with a slim build, her spiked yellowish hair, bright red lipstick, and thick makeup reminded Hack of the Joker from the Batman television series he used to watch as a kid. She peered over the book she was reading and smiled at him.

He walked towards the back of the room where the mother and son were sitting. Two large tables filled the space. The son had books spread out on the table in front on him. Astronomy books, Hack noticed. Probably a class project. The other table was empty. Hack walked to the west end of the library, a research room that was separated from the main part of the library. Hack browsed the shelves. All military stuff with most of them focused on the navy. He saw two carts filled with books, but no books on any of the tables. He walked over to the carts. One was filled with magazines and journals. A note on the cart read "New Material." The other cart had several Jane's military books on it. Hack counted. Eight books in all. Five of the books were on fleets of the world. Three were specifically about the U.S. navy. *Doesn't tell me much,* Hack said to himself. *Books about the navy in a navy library.*

Hack walked over to the librarian, who still had her nose in a book.

"Excuse me, ma'am," Hack said.

The librarian set aside her book and smiled. "Yes? May I help you?"

"I'm doing some research with a friend. I believe he was just in here. I was wondering if you could tell me what he was reading?"

The librarian lost her smile. "That is information I cannot share. Even if I knew who you were talking about, which I don't, I still wouldn't be able to give you that information."

"He was just in here a few minutes ago."

"We have many people come in here. I don't keep track of everyone."

Hack raised his right hand a couple inches above his head. "A tall guy. Crew cut. Big gut. Surely you noticed him."

"Several people fit that description. Besides, it's our policy not to share reader information with anyone. Even if you were an admiral, I wouldn't tell you. I'd rather lose my job than do that."

Hack rubbed his mouth with his hand. "But he's my friend. We're working on a project together. He said he was going to leave some material for me."

"What's your name?"

"Why is that important?"

"If he left something for you, I'll check our hold shelf. If you give me your name, I'll check to see if we have material for you."

Hack did a quick inventory of items on the desk. There were two dictionaries and a thesaurus between book ends shaped like ships anchors. Next to one bookend was a letter opener. *The bookend would work well*, he thought. *A blow to the head with that and then move to the letter opener.*

"If you give me your name, I'll see if we have a hold for you. I can't look if I don't have a name," the librarian said, smiling.

"It's not that important. I'll come back later," Hack said, turning to walk out of the library.

"You should talk with your friend..." said the librarian as Hack closed the door behind him. He didn't bother to hear her finish the sentence. He'd had enough of the library.

He walked next door to the theater. Decker was nowhere in sight. He started to believe Decker had left him, but then heard a voice across the street.

"What are you doing over there?" Hack yelled.

"Waiting for you," Decker said, crossing the street to meet Hack. "I thought I saw someone I knew coming up the street. I crossed over so they'd think I was headed to play miniature golf. But that's not important. What did you find?"

"Very little."

"Any books left out?"

Hack nodded. "I found a few on a cart. Could've been books Chief was reading."

"What were they?"

"Navy books."

"What do you mean navy books?"

"Books about the navy. Most were about world navies. A few were about the U.S. Navy."

"You sure he was reading those?" asked Decker. "I doubt that he was reading navy books."

"Why not?"

"Because he's in the navy."

"Maybe he likes his job so much he reads about it in his spare time."

"Did you ask the librarian?"

"Yes. She looks like the Joker."

"Who?" asked Decker.

"The Joker. From the Batman TV series. She had makeup on like that."

Decker laughed. "She looked like Cesar Romero?"

"Who?"

"Never mind. What did she say when you asked her about what Chief was reading?"

"Get lost."

"She said that?"

"In so many words. She said it was classified information. She never discloses what people have read. Must be some sort of library code of honor."

"Or the U.S. Constitution," Decker added. "Did you tell her it's important?"

"I told her I was working on a project with the guy who was just in here."

"Did she buy it?"

"No. And I felt like hitting her in the head with a bookend. Or stabbing her with a letter opener."

"Did you?"

"Of course not, but it was nice to think about for a few seconds."

"I'm glad you kept your cool," Decker said. "I've always had a soft spot for librarians. Besides the fact that they organize the world's knowledge, they can be quite hot. Have I ever told you about our elementary school librarian, Mrs. Abbott? She made going to school—"

"Whatever," Hack interrupted. "So now what?"

"I'm headed to Vega's to see if she's home. It's driving me crazy that I haven't seen her since that day she told me we needed to talk."

"Did she say what it was about?"

"No. We're already 'just friends' so it's not to break up with me. I hope I can catch up with her tonight. And I have duty tomorrow. Let's regroup Sunday at Cal Jam."

"What time?"

"Better make it the afternoon. I have the mid watch Saturday night."

"I'll be there," Hack said, looking down the street where Chief had walked. "He was researching something."

Decker nodded in agreement. "We have to find out what led him to the library."

"Maybe he was getting a book for his kid."

"I didn't see him leave with any books."

"Me either," Hack agreed. "All I saw was a piece of paper. Something had to be written on it. He was reading it before he walked away."

"Then we need to know what's written on that piece of paper."

"How are we going to do that?"

Decker wiped the sweat from his forehead and put his hands in his pockets. "I don't know yet, but I'm beginning to believe it's important that we find out."

"All *I* know is it better not involve *me* trying to get in and search Chief's pants."

An intense tropical rainstorm blew through Luzon midday Saturday, and the remnants, heavy skies and a light drizzle, lingered through the late afternoon as Decker and Hack sat in Cal Jam drinking San Miguels and plotting their next course of action. After a flurry of conversation, Decker turned to gaze out the window and Hack watched the customers come and go from the bar. After a few moments, the silence was more than Hack could take. "What are you thinking about?"

"Vega. I haven't seen her since the shooting. She said she wanted to talk. I think she's avoiding me."

"Maybe she's been busy. I'm sure her job keeps her going at all hours of the day and night. She'll touch base soon."

Decker sipped his beer. "Maybe. I know I'll run into her eventually. This place is too small not to." He lifted the bottle from the table and paused before taking another drink. "Did you ever ask Lee if she could print *Harvey* requisitions?"

"I mentioned it," said Hack.

"What'd she say?"

"Nothing. She just laughed."

"I'll take that as a no," said Decker. "We have no choice but to go back in."

"Back in where?" Hack's face clouded.

Decker shifted in his chair to face Hack. "We need copies of recent requisition lists."

"I thought we were trying to find out what was written on the note Chief had when he left the library?"

"We are, but that's going to be difficult to ascertain."

"Maybe he put it in the safe? *You* can check it this time."

"I already did."

"When?"

"Last night after I got off watch. It was 0400 so I had a pretty good idea no one would surprise me."

"That's what we should've done the first time."

"But it was more fun the way we did it."

"Fun for *you*! You weren't the one hiding in the storeroom. Do you have any idea how close I came to getting caught?"

"I have a pretty good idea," Decker smiled. "Hey, it was a team effort. I was lookout. A very important—I would say critical—element of any break-in."

"And, if I remember correctly, you weren't a very good lookout. You didn't know Limpert and Chief were on board and you let the commander walk right by you without any warning."

"My hands were tied. I had to acknowledge the captain. Navy protocol comes first."

"You were still a terrible lookout," said Hack, sitting back in his chair. "So the note wasn't in the safe?"

"I found the same stuff as before. Nothing's been added."

"Then how are we going to get recent requisition lists?

"It's Saturday, right?"

"Yeah, so…?"

"Your next duty day is Tuesday. When do you have watch?"

"Noon to 1600."

"That's perfect," said Decker. "You have the evening free."

"Why is that important?"

"Limpert always works late, right?"

"I don't know if he's working, but he stays late most days. I see him about every duty night. But what's Limpert got to do with it?"

"He's our way in."

"Way in where?"

"To the computer system," said Decker. "We don't have access to the requisition part of the system. But Limpert has access to everything."

"I thought you told us the other night that he doesn't know how to order parts?"

"He doesn't. Or I don't think he knows how. But that's not important. What's important is his access to the system. He's the Assistant Supply Officer. Even if he doesn't know how to order parts, he has the access to do it. I'm sure of it."

Hack thought it over for a moment. "What do you expect me to do? Just walk up to him and ask to use his computer? He's a strange little man, but I don't think he's *that* strange."

"You're not going to ask him. You're going to get on his computer while he's away from his office."

"Jeez, Decker, and just how do you think I'm going

to do that? Besides, I think we ought to wait until your duty day."

"We have to do it soon. There's been one death already and one near miss. And, to be frank, I worry that what happened to Kippen could happen to me next. Or you. But I'm especially worried about me."

"Thanks for the concern," Hack said, with a scowl.

"I'm the one who's already been shot at," Decker protested.

"Yeah, well, you're the one who got me mixed up in all this. And you know what? We're so focused on Chief, don't forget your involvement with Mrs. Doerr. Have you ever thought that she could be the reason someone was shooting at you?"

Decker shook his head. "I seriously doubt that. If the commander knew I was at his house, he'd be more apt to make my life miserable on the ship, not hire a trike driver to chase me around and shoot at me."

"I still think you ought to take your own advice and steer clear of her. A beautiful woman says 'hi' and off you go."

Decker hated when Hack was right, but also hated admitting it. Time to change the subject.

"How'd we get on the topic of Piper Doerr?"

"Listen to you calling her by her first name. You're playing with fire, Decker."

Decker ignored the warning. "We need to focus on the missing parts and the black market operation. The navy's obviously not pursuing it, Vega's no longer talking to me, but someone is out to get me and there's the fact that Kippen might've died because he knew too much."

Hack flagged down a waitress and ordered another

round of San Miguels. "I still don't understand how I'm going to get on Limpert's computer."

"I'll be there to distract him."

"Why don't *you* get on the computer and I'll be the one to distract him?"

"I have to be the one to distract him. You wouldn't be very good at it."

"Why not? I can be as good at distracting as you. Besides, I don't know the computer system too well."

"It can't be too difficult. You learned about it in A-school."

"That was a few months ago. I barely remember half the stuff they taught me. Let's wait until your duty day."

Decker shook his head. "We'd have to wait until Wednesday and I don't want to lose two days. I could be killed as soon as I walk out of here tonight."

"What's so important about these lists? The other requisition lists didn't give us anything other than what's been ordered and when."

"We only have four lists. If we get a few more recent ones, we may be able to find a pattern."

"Okay, still … I don't know how I'm going to get on his computer. He's probably got some sort of password protection or something. And even if I can get on, I'm not sure I'll be able to find what we need." He looked at Decker. "You should be the one on the computer. You know what you're looking for."

Decker sat back in his chair and took a swig of beer. "Alright, if you insist. I'll be the computer man. You can distract him."

Hack shot Decker a surprised glance. "Wait, that was too easy."

"No, it's set. You agreed."

"But how am I going to distract him?"

"It'll be easy to do," said Decker. "I have the perfect plan."

"That's what you said last time."

"I've got every detail worked out. Trust me."

Hack took a drink and wiped his mouth. "I wish you hadn't said that."

CHAPTER NINETEEN
2000, TUESDAY, JANUARY 21

Decker watched as the big hand on the clock in Supply Support struck twelve. The little hand rested on the eight. "Time to go," he said, softly. "If we wait any longer, he might leave the ship."

"You sure this is going to work?"

"Have I ever led you astray?"

"Several times," said Hack.

"It's a simple operation this time."

"I've heard that before."

"Let's run through it again," Decker said. "We know Ensign Limpert's sitting in the Disbursing Office. I'll go visit him and ask for help."

"What do you need help with?"

"A computer question. If he's not already logged into the system, he'll have to log on to help me."

"I'm with you so far."

"In five minutes, you call the quarterdeck pretending to be Suppo. Use your best Commander Doerr voice."

"How do I do that?"

"Be confident. Act like you're in charge. That's all it takes to be an officer."

Hack sat down in Chief's chair, swiveling back and

forth, his mouth set in a worried frown. "I don't know if I can pull it off."

"Of course you can. Ask them to pass the word for Limpert to report to the wardroom. Be quick and to the point. When Limpert leaves his office, I'll print the documents. It'll take two or three minutes at most. We'll meet at Cal Jam after work tomorrow to look at them."

"How will I know he's on the computer? I might have them pass the word before he's logged on."

Decker rubbed his forehead. "That's a good point. Tell you what. After I leave Supply Support, wait exactly five minutes and then walk by his office. I'll give you a signal when he's logged in."

"What signal? I don't want him to see me standing in the passageway."

"He won't see you. Stay forward of the office door. I'll leave it cracked open a little and say something loud enough so that you can hear."

"What are you going to say?"

"If it's a go, I'll say 'I'm thirsty'."

"I'm thirsty? That's the best you've got?"

"It's a natural thing to say."

Hack stood and paced the office deck. "I'm not sure about this. Isn't it unauthorized use of the 1MC? That's a security alert if someone finds out we're screwing around."

"No one will know it's you and, besides, I doubt that Limpert will realize he's been had."

"Why are you so sure about that?"

Decker shrugged. "It's his personality. He'll think about it for a few minutes and then get lost in something else, probably a computer game."

Hack continued pacing. "I don't want to risk impersonating an officer."

Decker walked over to Hack and put a hand on his arm to stop his pacing. "You won't be impersonating anyone. Don't even tell them you're Suppo. Just tell them you need Limpert to go to the wardroom. They'll assume you're the commander." He took Hack by the shoulders and looked deep into his eyes. "Do it for Kippen."

Hack removed his ball cap and ran his fingers through his hair. "Okay, I'll do it."

Decker clapped his hands. "It'll go smoothly, my friend. No need to worry. Give me five minutes to get settled and then walk by the Disbursing Office. I'll give you the code word. All you have to do is walk back to Supply Support, make the call to the quarterdeck, and you're home free. I'll do the rest. As soon as Limpert walks out, I'll close the door behind him, print the documents, and it'll be mission accomplished."

⊁ ⊁ ⋈

Hack nodded and mumbled "I'm thirsty" as Decker left the office. Exactly five minutes later, Hack walked out of Supply Support and headed forward along the starboard passageway. He rounded the mess decks and smiled, thinking to himself that he was, in fact, thirsty.

Hack turned aft and walked slowly towards the Disbursing Office along the port passageway, pausing to listen to the conversation. Nothing. He tiptoed aft a few more paces, pausing next to the barber shop, a few paces from Limpert's office. This time he heard it. Decker's unmistakable voice saying that he was thirsty.

Hack quickly passed through the mess decks again and jogged aft down the starboard side. Once in Supply Support, he grabbed the growler's handset, turned the dial to the quarterdeck, and cranked the handle, knowing he would lose his nerve if he hesitated for even a second.

"Pass the word, Ensign Limpert lay to the wardroom," Hack snarled in his best Commander Doerr voice.

The petty officer-of-the-watch didn't skip a beat. "Yes, sir," he said.

Hack hung up the growler and exhaled as a wave of relief rushed over him. He listened intently for the word to be passed over the intercom ten seconds later: *Ensign Limpert, lay to the wardroom.*

Hack exhaled and raced out of Supply Support. He made it to the mess decks just in time to see Limpert head up the ladder to the wardroom. Hack walked over to the vending machines and decided on a coke. *Take your time,* he said to himself. He dropped his coins in the machine, pushed the button, and picked up the soft drink can from the tray. Satisfied that no one was milling around the mess decks had noticed him, he made his way aft along the port passageway.

Slowing by the Disbursing Office, he put his ear to the door and closed his eyes. The relief he had felt seconds earlier instantly vanished. Fear spread through his body. He had hoped to hear the clicking of a printer in action, but, instead, it was the sound of Decker pounding on something. Decker cursing. Hack opened the door a few inches and peered inside. "What's going on?"

Decker stood over the printer on a desk along the starboard bulkhead, panic in his eyes. "The printer's jammed!"

Hack glanced forward along the passageway to the bottom of the ladder that led to the wardroom. "We don't have much time. I'm sure Limpert'll be back very soon."

"Thanks for stating the obvious. If you see him, you've got to stall him."

"How the hell am I going to do that?"

"Think of something."

"Like what?"

"I don't know, just do something!"

Hack turned again towards the ladder and saw khaki pant legs and the unmistakable small feet of Limpert trudging down the ladder. Hack closed the door to the Disbursing Office and thought for a second about heading aft, leaving Decker to his own devices. Instead, he headed forward to confront Limpert. They met a few feet from the office door.

"Wilson, I was called, well, I'm not sure. I thought someone wanted to see me, but I guess, you know, um, never mind."

Hack bent over holding his stomach. "I don't feel so well, sir."

Limpert put his arm around Hack's waist to steady him. "Are you going to, you know, throw, I mean, vomit?"

Hack shook his head. "I don't think so. Not yet. Must be something I ate." He handed the ensign his soft drink can.

"You need, well, you should, um, go see the corpsman," Limpert said.

"I don't think it's that bad," Hack mumbled.

"You should, I think, you know, you should go see someone," Limpert urged. "Let's go in my, um, I'll call to see who's the duty corpsman today. I think it's, well,

I'm not sure."

"No need for that, sir," Hack said. "I think it's passed." He leaned against the bulkhead opposite the Disbursing Office and wiped his forehead. "I'm not sure what happened. I just need to stand here for a couple minutes. I'm afraid if I move, it'll hit me again."

Limpert waited until Hack collected himself and then guided him towards the office door. The Assistant Supply Officer slowly turned the knob.

"Wait," Hack said.

But it was too late. Limpert opened the door and looked at Decker. "We need, um, can you, well, I need help."

Decker sat in a folding chair at Limpert's computer terminal, the keyboard in his lap and his feet propped on the desk. "Hack, my boy, what's gotten into you?"

"He, um, well, I think he's, you know, sick," Limpert said.

"I'm feeling better now, sir," Hack said.

"He doesn't sound well to me, sir," said Decker.

Limpert sat Hack in a chair next to Decker. "That's what I, well, we need to get him to sick bay." He turned to Decker. "Call to see, um, have them page the duty corpsman."

"Aye, aye, sir," Decker smiled.

"Really, I'm feeling much better," Hack argued. "I think it was the coke I just drank. It didn't sit well or something, but I'm better now."

"Best not to take any chances," Decker said.

Hack shot Decker a look that could kill. "I said I feel okay."

"Could be something, um, well, it could be contagious,"

Limpert said. "You need to see the corpsman. That's a, you know, well, that's an order."

CHAPTER TWENTY

Intuition? A hunch? Hack didn't know what to call it, but the feeling of being watched had nagged at him for a block. As he passed through the shipyard onto Dewey Avenue, he glanced behind him towards the Spanish Gate.

A swift scan.

Three sailors exiting the cafeteria, crossing the sidewalk. A woman approaching, head down. Two men behind the woman. One with distinctive blond hair. The other middle aged, short hair, wire-rim glasses. Brief eye contact with the blonde-haired man. The kind where you catch someone staring and they look away quickly.

Hack suddenly felt alone. He had avoided Decker most of the day, still angry about his time in sick bay. *Three blocks to the main gate.* Hack picked up his pace and crossed the street at an angle. A peek over his left shoulder. No sign of the two men. He breathed a sigh of relief. *Must be nerves. Decker's fault for getting me mixed up in this investigation.*

One more block to the gate. Hack made it in record time.

An unfortunate Filipino searching for his ID card

held up the line. Hack took the opportunity to survey the crowd behind him. Dozens of Filipinos heading home. Several sailors on liberty. One American stood out in the crowd. His blond hair noticeable. To his right stood a middle-aged man.

Hack anxiously fished his ID from his wallet and the marine waived him through the checkpoint. He hustled across the Shit River Bridge, arriving in front of Cal Jam at 1725. One more look down the street towards base. No sign of the two men. Hack shrugged, walked through the door, and flopped in a booth near the window.

Decker pushed a beer across the table without lifting his eyes from his Book of Dates.

Hack stared at the bottle in front of him. "How did you know I'd be here? I thought about not coming."

"I'm actually surprised to see you. You didn't talk to me all day."

"Can you blame me? I spent most of the evening sick in bed."

"I thought you were faking it."

"I was until the corpsman gave me some medicine. Then I got sick." He shuddered. "Vomited half the night."

"It was perfect cover," Decker laughed. "Limpert forgot all about being paged. I think he was genuinely worried about you."

"I'm glad someone was," said Hack, taking a sip of beer. "Hey, it's still ice cold."

"Of course it is."

"I thought you said you weren't expecting me to show up?"

"I wasn't," Decker said, gesturing out the window with his right hand. "I saw you walking up the sidewalk."

"Next time I'll be more evasive."

"Then you won't have a cold beer waiting for you."

"Good point," Hack sighed. He waited for Decker to finish writing another sentence. "I saw two guys following me."

Decker set his pencil down and reached for his beer. "It was your imagination. No one was following you."

"It sure seemed like it. I saw them walking behind me when I left the shipyard. I saw them again when I was leaving the base. Did you see anybody behind me on Magsaysay?"

Decker shook his head. "Nope. It was just you and half the Filipinos in Olongapo."

Hack leaned back in his chair. "I'm sure I was being followed."

"Probably a couple sailors," Decker said. "A lot of people get off work this time of day."

"I don't think they were sailors. Too civilian looking."

"What do you mean by that?"

"They looked out of place. Even in civilian clothes, you can spot a sailor a mile away. One was young enough to be in the military, but his hair was too long."

"You noticed his hair? That's a bit troubling."

"It was blonde like it had been bleached. Reminded me of a surfer."

"And how many surfers do you know?"

"None," Hack admitted. "But I've seen them in movies. The other guy was older, but I didn't get a good look at him."

"Could've been an old master chief," Decker said. "Hell, some of these lifers have been in over thirty years."

Hack peered out the window, scanning both directions

along Magsaysay Drive. Several people ambled along the sidewalk in both directions, but none were the two men he had seen walking behind him earlier. "Maybe you're right. It gave me a funny feeling, though."

Decker waved his hand. "Forget about them. We have more important issues at hand." He pulled a stack of folded papers from his back pocket. "Let's take a look at the requisition lists. I was able to print two recent ones."

They each took a printout and spent the next few minutes scrutinizing the data. Decker gave up first, tossing aside the papers he was reading. "This doesn't do us much good. It's the same as before. A record of what's been ordered."

"Maybe we're missing something," Hack argued.

"I don't see anything," said Decker. "Unless…"

"Unless what?"

"Unless you check the inventory on board ship against these printouts."

"Why am I the one to check the inventory?"

"Chief doesn't watch you like he does me," Decker said. "You're the new guy. He assumes you don't know anything yet. All you have to do is check the big ticket items. Anything over one thousand dollars."

Hack sat back and shook his head. "No way."

Decker didn't persist. He grabbed the lists from Hack. "Let's see. This was submitted on January 2. What day of the week was that?"

Hack thought for a moment. "It was a Thursday."

"I'm not even going to ask how you remember that." Decker looked at the other list. "These orders were placed yesterday, January 21."

"What do you think it means?"

"Nothing," Decker said, handing the papers to Hack. "Keep these in a safe place until you're ready to do the inventory."

"Why do you want me to hold on to them?"

"Because you have the other documents. We need to keep all of them in one place."

"Why can't you keep them? I'll give you what I have and then you'll have everything."

"That'd be too complicated."

"That doesn't make any sense."

"It makes perfect sense," said Decker. "You've got the other papers in a safe place, right?"

"I think so."

"There's your reason. I don't know any safe places to hide things."

Hack grew weary of the argument and folded the papers into his back pocket. "I still think we ought to concentrate on the names. Especially Allen Sumner."

Decker shook his head. "I'm beginning to think we need to work the problem from the other end."

"What other end?"

"Who's buying this stuff after it finds its way off base."

"Maybe the people Chief had on his list? Which brings us back to the names."

"That's a dead end for now," Decker said. "We need to find someone with an insider's knowledge of the local black market scene. We find out who's buying, we find out who's supplying."

"What about Vega? She'll know."

"I haven't talked with her in several days. In fact, I have no idea when I'm going to see her again."

Hack shrugged. "I don't know anybody else in town

besides Lee's maid. And Rusty, your trike guy. And I don't really know either one of them too well."

Decker suddenly sat up. "Hack, my boy, you're brilliant."

"What did I say?"

"Rusty. He could be our ticket into the local underworld."

"How's he doing anyway?" asked Hack.

Decker sat back and rested his hands on top of his head. "I ran into his wife a couple days ago. She said he's doing fine. About ready to start driving again."

"That's good. But how is he going to help? Vega said it's probably someone at the supply depot."

"I'm not worried about the depot at the moment. Rusty's hinted at a previous job. He hasn't talked much about it, but I think I'll pay him a visit while he's still recuperating."

"What other job?"

Decker leaned forward. "I don't know exactly, but it's time I find out a little more about it."

CHAPTER TWENTY-ONE
1745, FRIDAY, JANUARY 24

Decker crossed the quarterdeck at 1730, passed through the main gate a few minutes later, and stood at the end of the Shit River Bridge. He looked down Magsaysay Drive and smiled at the sight of the long line of neon signs that lined the street. *Not tonight*, he said to himself, resisting the pull of the bright lights. He turned right on 1st Street and walked past the beckoning bargirls standing at the entrances of the smaller clubs that sprinkled the landscape a block or two either side of the main strip. He weaved his way through the mass of kids, street vendors, and trikes and jeepneys sharing the narrow roadways. A left on 6th Street and a right one block later on Kessing put him in sight of his destination.

Decker found Rusty sitting on his front porch, his leg propped on a milk crate. The damaged trike leaned against his cinder block house, a painful reminder of the shooting and subsequent wreck. A red sports car blocked a narrow concrete driveway.

"Hello, *pare*," Rusty shouted, excited to see Decker. "Long time, no look."

"Rusty, you are truly a man of leisure" replied Decker. "Is that your Camaro?"

"*Hindi, pare.* It is friend's car. He let me borrow it this morning. Went for long drive. Weny told me get out of house."

Decker laughed. "How's the leg?"

Rusty tapped his knee with his hand. "Doing okay. Only eighteen stitches. The bullet barely got me. Want to see?"

Decker held up his hands. "No thanks, my friend. I'll take your word for it. How long until you're driving the trike again?"

"The doctor said I work next week." Rusty swatted a fly buzzing near his face. "No ships visiting so business would have been slow anyway."

Decker looked at the bike and back at Rusty. "How about dinner? I've avoided navy chow all day and I'm beginning to regret it. I'll run out and pick up something for you and Rowena and the kids. You have rice, right?"

"Of course we have rice, *pare.* Always got to have rice."

"Okay then," said Decker. "Give me five minutes and I'll be back with dinner."

Decker flagged down a trike and was at a nearby market in two minutes. He bought several pieces of freshly cut chicken, a bag of santol fruit, and a couple of kalabasa, one of his favorite vegetables. He caught a trike back to Rusty's house and walked across the street to the local *sari sari* store and bought eight San Miguels and four sticks of Marlboro cigarettes. Though he didn't smoke, he knew Rusty would appreciate it.

The kids came running out as soon as they heard Decker return. He set down the packages and scooped up one in each arm. The boy, Emil, especially liked Decker and pleaded with him to grab his arms and spin him around. Decker let go of Elenita and took hold of Emil's arms and spun him around eight times several feet off the ground. Decker set him on his feet and they all laughed as the little boy stumbled along the sidewalk dizzy and giggling. Elenita, just beginning to learn English in school, always enjoyed Decker's visits, finding it the perfect time to practice speaking with an American.

She tugged at Decker's shirt tail as he watched Emil finally regain his balance "Hello. How are you?"

Decker knelt down to her level. "Hello, I am doing fine. Thank you for asking." With that, Elenita lost her nerve and, with her younger brother hot on her heels, ran inside the house to find her mother who had scooped up the sacks of food and was preparing the dinner.

Decker pulled up a folding chair, opened two beers, and sat next to Rusty on the porch. The street was quiet except for the sound of kids playing in the distance and the periodic interruption of a trike or jeepney zooming by. As dinnertime approached, street vendors appeared, slowly walking the neighborhood selling maize and balut, reminding Decker of stadium vendors back home, yelling the name of their products.

The two friends sat quietly for a few minutes, deep in thought. Rusty finally broke the silence. "Thank you for dinner. It is nice of you."

Decker picked up a toy at his feet and set it aside. "Glad to do it. We haven't talked since the shooting and it's been forever since I've seen the kids. I think Emil has grown two inches since I last saw him."

"They are growing. We are so thankful that Emil can see with both eyes. I wish I could be home more often, but work keep me busy. No time for rest until I got shot. But something is on your mind. I can tell. I have a good, how you say it, feeling about things like that."

Decker laughed and took a drink of beer. "You're right, my friend. I'm in a bit of a quandary."

"What is her name?"

"I do have a bit of a delicate situation on that front, but that's not what I'm thinking about at the moment. Did you hear about the sailor who died on the *Harvey* a few weeks ago?"

"*Oo,*" Rusty nodded. "I saw it in the paper. Did you know him?"

"I did. In fact, Petty Officer Kippen worked in my department. He was a decent guy."

"Sorry about that, *pare*. Fell overboard, right?"

"That's the official navy version," Decker said. "An investigator flew out to the ship after it happened. He nosed around, talked to several people. Came to the conclusion that it was either an accident or a suicide over his ex-girlfriend."

Rusty eyed Decker. "You agree with that? Something in the way you say it. I think you have doubts."

"You can read my mind," Decker smiled. "I do have doubts. And part of my doubt comes from a conversation I had with Kippen the night he died. He told me about an inventory problem with the ship's repair parts."

"What kind of problem?"

"Missing parts."

Rusty studied Decker's face. "I did not know your friend, but I am sure sailors misplace things all the time."

"That was more or less my first reaction. 'So what?' I told him. 'It's probably just a computer problem'. But he didn't think so, and now I'm beginning to believe he was on to something. Hack and I snooped around the ship some and then came the shooting. Unless that trike driver was after you for some reason, it makes me think we've stumbled into something serious."

Rusty took a swig of beer, picked up a Marlboro and lit the cigarette, slowly blowing smoke out of his mouth.

"Hey, that was supposed to be a joke," Decker said, studying Rusty's face. "Now it's my turn to ask. Is there something on your mind?"

Rusty didn't look up. "Could be the black market, *pare*."

Decker cocked his head. "You think so? Vega said the same thing. She told us the local cops are investigating a growing black market operation in town."

"Do not trust the cops," Rusty scoffed. "Vega is an honest girl and means well, but she is new on the force. I bet anything that Inspector Navarro and his cronies are paid to look the other way where the black market is concerned."

Decker let that sink in while he finished his beer. "How big is the black market around here?"

Rusty shrugged his shoulders. "Not sure anymore. Used to be everywhere. American cigarettes, shampoo, and candy bars. You name it, you could buy it in town. Still can if you know where to look."

"How does that stuff make its way off base? The Marine guards search everybody and everything that leaves the base. They search me half the time and, I must say, I'm an honest looking guy."

Rusty smiled. "It is not easy to move parts off base, but it can be done. I can prove it. Visit Filipino stores in town and you will see navy stuff. I cannot afford it, but I know where I could get it if I wanted to."

Decker reached for two more bottles of beer and opened one for Rusty. "I had no idea. I guess I've never paid attention to stuff like that."

"Why you care? You can buy those things anytime. For Filipinos, they are luxury items."

"Well, I don't know if that explains the missing items," Decker reasoned. "Cigarettes and soap are quite different from circuit cards and ball valves. I doubt if there's a market for those kinds of things in town."

"Not in this town, *pare*. Other places. I know a man who tell you stories. His name is Mr. Fortuno. He used to be big in the black market. He retired a year ago after Marcos' power started to fade. I worked for Fortuno when I was younger. Nice guy, but not someone to take lightly. He was one of the Rolex 12."

"The what?"

"The Rolex 12. A special advisory group under Marcos in the early '70s. The president gave them a Rolex watch. They gave their support to Marcos's martial law policies and took control of everything. The military. National police. Businesses. Casinos. Even political opponents. Rumor has it that they ordered the murder of Benigno Aquino. Not a pleasant group to be associated with."

"What's happened to them?"

"A few of them are still with Marcos. General Ver and Danding Cojuangco are close advisors, at least for now. I heard that Juan Enrile and Fidel Ramos will support Cory Aquino. I have no idea about the others."

"What about Mr. Fortuno?"

"He had disagreement with Ver four or five years ago.

When you do that, you are on the outside. Ver has all the power of the group. There was even a rumor the Rolex 12 had a contract out for Fortuno. Many people are surprised he survived this long."

"Sounds like a charming fellow," said Decker.

Rusty's face brightened. "He is. Gave me my first job. I drove a truck for him. Did not know what I was carrying, of course, but he paid me good and I needed the job. Only found out later he was in black market business. He would take things from the navy base, Clark Air Base, too, and ship them to Manila. From there I have no idea where they ended up. All I know, he was a rich man. Still is."

"You're lucky you survived that," Decker said.

"I *am* lucky. I met Weny while I was driving for Mr. Fortuno. She made me quit. Never liked him. Said she could tell he was no good the first time she met him. I did not have another job, but I did not want to lose her."

Decker ran his finger around the top of the bottle. "I understand that," he whispered.

"I felt so lucky to meet her. I said, 'God will take care of me and Weny.' So, I left Mr. Fortuno. Been driving a trike ever since. It was a blessing. I do not have much, but I have a nice family and I feel lucky about that."

Decker sat up in his chair. "You got quiet when I joked about the guy shooting at you. Do you think someone from your past is after you?"

Rusty shook his head. "I doubt it. I left on friendly terms. I do not think about those days very often, but you reminded me of it."

Decker stood and paced along the porch. "Then I was the target."

"Afraid so."

"But who was behind it?" asked Decker. "I don't know many people in town, and, come on, who would want to harm me?"

Rusty exhaled and blew a series of smoke rings. "Always remember this. Many people live in Olongapo, but it is a small town."

"What do you mean?"

"People talk. And more people listen. If you have money, you can find out about anyone."

Decker stopped his pacing and returned to his chair. "You ever stay in touch with this guy, Mr. Fortuno?"

Rusty nodded. "I saw him a few years ago. Remembered my name. Asked me to come back to work for him. He says I was always trustworthy. Probably meant that I did not talk a lot. Some guys talked too much. Would get drunk and brag to their friends. Then one day they would disappear. Some were fired. Some had accidents. Never seen again. Scared me, but I needed money and Mr. Fortuno was nice to me."

Decker leaned back and propped his legs on the free edge of Rusty's milk crate. "Doesn't the military do anything about it? Seems it would be easy to stop, even for the navy."

"They try, but there are many people going on and off base. And trucks from the supply depot have official papers."

"Maybe I can talk to this Mr. Fortuno," Decker said. "He may be able to fill in some details about what's going on."

"You cannot just go and knock on his door," Rusty said, speaking quietly. "He would never see an American who showed up at his house. He is careful. You could be somebody working undercover."

"How do I get to him then?"

Rusty turned and looked through the screen door. Satisfied that Weny was still in the kitchen, he took a drink of beer and glanced at Decker. "I can go with you. Don't tell Weny. She kill me if she knew I was going to see him."

"I don't want to get you in trouble. Just take me there or tell me where I can find him. I'll bring Hack along. I'm sure he'll be eager to go. If Fortuno throws us out or refuses to see us, so be it. At least we've tried. A shipmate died and I've been shot at. I have to find out what's going on. No one else seems to want to pursue it."

Rusty stood and gestured to Decker to follow him inside. "*Sige, pare.* I will talk to him and try to set up a meeting. Might be a few days, but I see what I can do. Now, let's go eat."

CHAPTER TWENTY-TWO
1905, SUNDAY, JANUARY 26

Hack and Lee stood on the sidewalk at the west end of the parking lot, arms wrapped around each other, when a silver car pulled into the lot. "I think that's your ride," he whispered, as two women in the front seat waved in their direction.

"Yep, there they are. And on time for once." She put her hands on his chest. "I'll see you when I get back from Manila. It'll only be a week. Don't let Decker get you into trouble while I'm gone."

"Don't worry about that. Not today anyway. He's got duty."

She patted his backside. "Then don't get into trouble on your own." She planted a long and lingering final kiss on his lips, grabbed her suitcase and climbed into the back seat. Lee waved good-bye through the back window, and Hack suddenly found himself in an unusual position. Alone.

Hack hung around base for most of Sunday afternoon, wandering out the gate close to sundown. A few minutes later he found himself standing on Magsaysay at the entrance of Cal Jam with an unwelcome companion at his side.

"Sunglasses?" a young boy pleaded, tugging at Hack's shirttail.

"No thanks," replied Hack. "It's almost dark out."

"Cheap," the boy countered.

Hack shook his head.

"One hundred pesos."

"No money," said Hack.

"Eighty pesos," the boy offered, knowing the sailor was fibbing.

Hack thought about ducking into the bar to rid himself of his new friend, but decided against it. Cal Jam was too big, too loud, and not the kind of place he wanted to visit alone. Instead, Hack walked to the next block, turned right, and found what he was looking for. The Sea Gull. Quiet, small, and just far enough off the main strip to give him the peace and quiet he was looking for.

Hack took two steps inside the bar and took off his new pair of sunglasses, his eyes quickly adjusting to the dim lighting. A dozen or so sailors, each one sporting an assortment of tattoos, lounged at cheap wooden tables. In a far corner, he spotted a few grey beards, retired sailors, who decided to retire in the islands. Hack smiled. Perfect. He didn't recognize a single soul.

Sitting alone at a table in the back of the room, Hack stared at his beer bottle, peeling the edges of the label and thinking about Lee in Manila. When he finally looked up, he surveyed the room and wondered how he had ended up in the Philippines. Just a few months ago it was boot camp in Orlando, his first trip ever out of his home state. Before that it was high school followed by a dreary succession of part-time jobs: farm hand, overnight clerk at the one and only hotel in town, and then a short order cook. He hated them all, but Halsey, Nebraska, didn't offer much.

One night in early July he had driven down to the Middle Loop River and planned his escape. The navy. A month earlier he had watched a movie at two in the morning, *The Gallant Hours*, and learned about the man, who he had assumed, was the town's namesake, Admiral "Bull" Halsey. In the moonlight, skipping stones along the bank of the river, he thought about the movie and decided to make his own adventures at sea. He drove to Kearney the next day and signed up. Only later, after receiving orders to boot camp, did Hack learn the truth from the local librarian: Halsey Yates, a 19th century railroad surveyor, not the admiral, was the town's namesake. Six months later he took a sip of beer and shrugged off his naiveté. *It's worked out fine*, he told himself. *I'm farther from home than I could ever imagine and I've met the kind of girl I didn't even know existed.* He set down his bottle and glanced around the Sea Gull, finding comfort in being anonymous and alone with his thoughts.

That's when he noticed them. They didn't fit in. Too neatly dressed. Clean and pressed T-shirts and jeans. Spotless tennis shoes. Two guys who had tried to dress down for the occasion but couldn't quite pull it off. Not the attire of someone who'd been walking around Olongapo all day. The younger of the two men stood out in Hack's mind. The blond hair. The surfer.

Alarmed, Hack got up to leave, but a voice distracted him. A young woman approached his table. "Company?" she asked.

Hack didn't want to be rude his first time in the Sea

Gull. "Uh, I guess so. Sure."

The girl sat down, smiling warmly. "What your name?"

"Hack. What's your name?"

"Lucy. Buy me drink?"

Hack ordered her a cocktail and paid the 120 pesos for what he knew was mostly soda with very little, if any, alcohol content. She had long brown hair down to her waist. Her beige top revealed nothing on underneath. Her red skirt, showing a great deal of thigh, made Hack slightly uncomfortable when she scooted her chair close to him.

Across the room, the two men, deep in conversation, seemed oblivious to Hack and anyone else in the bar. Hack peeked over Lucy's shoulder and studied them. He dubbed the surfer dude Biff. The other man, somewhat older, maybe in his early 40s, Hack thought he'd seen before. It took him a couple minutes and then it struck him. David Letterman. The same hair style, glasses, and facial expression.

"Where you stationed?" asked Lucy.

"The *Harvey*."

"My boyfriend is on USS *Midway*."

Hack looked puzzled. He knew her job description at the Sea Gull. "Boyfriend?"

She dug a picture out her pocketbook. A portrait of a small boy, around two years old, wearing a blue jumpsuit. His hair, dark brown, contrasting with his blue eyes.

"Cute kid," Hack said, honestly. "Are you going to get married?"

"I tell him I want to. I write him often. He never write me."

Hack didn't know how to respond. He had seen several Filipino-American kids running around Olongapo. Most, he knew, were the results of one night stands during port visits. The fathers, only in town for three or four days, were long gone and either unaware of their kids or, like Lucy's paramour, knew the truth and chose to ignore it.

"Maybe you'll hear from him soon," Hack said, trying to sound reassuring. He glanced once more towards the two men and this time caught Biff looking at him. Hack quickly turned towards Lucy. "I'd better go."

He downed the remainder of his beer and said good-bye to his female companion, obviously heartbroken over his swift departure. He left a twenty peso tip on the table, handed Lucy another twenty peso bill, and walked out of the bar.

Hack breathed in the humid night air. He waved away two trike drivers who were eager to give him a ride. It was only a block to Magsaysay and four more blocks to the main gate. Nice night to walk. And to think. He was sure the two men were the same guys who had followed him on base a few days earlier. Curious, and, by now, more than a little paranoid, Hack strolled half a block south and stopped at a *sari sari* store.

"Hi, sailor," said a high school-aged girl. "What you want?"

Hack scrutinized the items for sale. "Gum, please. Peppermint."

"How many sticks?"

"The whole pack."

As the girl reached for the merchandise, Hack stole a quick glance towards the Sea Gull. Biff and Dave were standing near the entrance talking to each other. *Probably stalling*, he guessed. Hack paid for the gum and continued to walk towards Magsaysay.

This time, though, he picked up his pace.

Hack made a right turn on Gordon Avenue and started to jog. A half block later the sights and sounds of the crowd on Magsaysay came into range. He hit the strip at a steady clip, veering away from the direction of the base. He slowed to a brisk walk and hailed the next jeepney coming down the street. The driver slowed the vehicle, Hack jumped in the back and found an opening next to an elderly Filipino. His heart racing, he peered out the back over the head of a young mother. Biff and Dave were nowhere in sight.

"I have to tell Decker," he said out loud, drawing looks from everyone on board. He did a quick scan of his fellow passengers: two elderly Filipinos, one young woman and her three kids, and two drunk sailors, one passed out and the other nearly so. A familiar face sat across from him.

"Wilson. I'm surprised, um, it's nice to see you," Ensign Limpert said. "Are you, well, you seem to be in a hurry."

Hack's eyes widened in shock. "I'm surprised to see you, too, sir. Do you live out here?"

Limpert shook his head. "No, I'm just, well, I come out here once in a while. I have a, um, it's a guy I know. Where are you going?"

Hack said the first thing that came to his mind. "I'm visiting my girlfriend." He looked out the jeepney and had no idea where he was. "In fact, I need to get out at the next block."

"I thought she, um, doesn't she live on Jones close to base?" Limpert said.

"She moved," Hack said, startled not only that he knew who Hack was dating, but also that he knew where she lived. Luckily, Lee had taught him how to ride a jeepney. He handed two pesos to the passenger next to him who passed it to the driver. He rapped the roof of the jeepney two times, said "*para*," and climbed out the back when the vehicle came to a stop.

"See you later," Hack said, exiting onto the street. To his surprise, Limpert climbed out of the jeepney right behind him.

"This is my, um, I need to get out here, too. Good night, Wilson."

"Good night, sir," Hack replied as he watched Limpert toddle down the sidewalk.

Hack was lost. He was several blocks from base, away from all things American. He saw a Jollibee fast food restaurant across the street and decided to get something to eat. Fifteen minutes later, he caught a trike back to a few blocks from Magsaysay. He spotted a hotel with a vacancy light and decided to spend the night. He bought two San Miguels from a *sari sari* store across the street and booked a room on the third floor. It was plainly furnished, but clean, and had a decent sized bathroom and fresh sheets on the bed. He opened a beer and pulled a chair in front of the window. For the next half hour he watched the traffic and the people moving in both directions along the street below. He finished his first beer, burped, and sat it on the window ledge. *Things are getting crazier, he thought to himself. And more dangerous.*

CHAPTER TWENTY-THREE
1955, MONDAY, JANUARY 27

Hack stood on the corner of Fendler and 3rd and looked up at the sign. The Bumper Bar. He didn't know why Decker chose this place, but he shrugged his shoulders and headed inside. A young Filipina met him at the door, taking hold of his right arm and guiding him inside the club. She wore a black sleeveless dress falling mid-thigh and her hair was tied in a knot on top of her head with a red chopstick holding it in place. The hostess greeted him with a smile. "Good evening, sir. You like table?"

Hack looked over the crowded room. "I'm waiting for a friend. He should be here by now."

"How he look?" the girl asked.

Hack saw the crowd of sailors in the bar and didn't know how to distinguish Decker. "I'll take a table if one's available," he said. "I'll look around for him."

The girl took hold of Hack's hand and led him to a table in the middle of the room. "I get you beer," she said, turning to speak to a waitress.

Hack sat sipping his beer for the next few minutes, adjusting to the crowd and noise. A DJ in the far corner interrupted his thoughts, announcing that it was time to start the karaoke. Hack turned to look, but couldn't see where the voice was coming from. He settled back into his chair and began to curse Decker for being late until, a moment later, he heard a familiar voice booming through the speakers. Decker on stage, microphone in hand, belting the Manfred Mann tune, "Do Wah Diddy." Jeez, the guy was nuts.

Hack shook his head and watched in amazement as half the bar joined in, singing the chorus with beers hoisted in the air. Decker leaned back and belted the next line, and again the barroom patrons finished the stanza.

Hack hid his face in his hands and waited for the song to finish. A loud cheer erupted when Decker walked from the stage, sailors high-fiving him as he moved through the crowd towards his friend's table. He grabbed Hack by the shoulders, still excited from the experience. "Why didn't you tell me you were here? You could've joined me."

"No way I'd ever do that. And I didn't know you were here until I heard you singing."

"I didn't want to sing, either," Decker said. "But my fans insisted.

"I'm sure they had to twist your arm," said Hack.

"Only slightly," Decker smiled. "I do it as my tribute to Roberto del Rosario."

"Who's he?"

"A Filipino who has a claim to inventing karaoke. The man responsible for bringing bad singing voices out of the showers and into public places."

"How do you know these things?"

"By reading books. You should try one sometime."

Hack rolled his eyes. "How long have you been here? I didn't see you in the berthing before I left the ship. I thought you were going to stand me up."

"Would I ever do that?"

"Yes."

"Not tonight," said Decker, looking at his watch. "I've been here for a half hour. And I'm ready for you to buy the first round."

"I'm not buying!" Hack said. "I've already had the first round while I was waiting on you."

"It's *my* first round," Decker argued. "And it goes by seniority. Rule of the seas."

"Whatever," Hack said, ordering two more San Miguels from a waitress. "So what's so urgent? All day, I could tell you were dying to talk." He looked around the bar. "And why this place?"

"The Bumper Bar is legendary," Decker said. "This is where I first met Vega. She came in with some cops to arrest a drunk who'd been beating up a girl down the street. Her colleagues didn't let her handle any of the arrest, so I got to chat with her for a couple minutes. Long story short, the bad guy got a one-way ticket to the brig, and I got a date out of it."

"It doesn't look legendary to me," said Hack, scrutinizing the surroundings.

"Looks can be deceiving," Decker replied. "And you are correct, I do have something to talk about, but didn't want to get into at work. Not sure who's listening or watching."

Hack perked up. "What is it? I've got something I'm anxious to tell you, too."

"I had a very interesting conversation with Rusty

Friday night," Decker said, ignoring Hack's comment.

"How's he doing?"

"Almost back to normal. The bullet just grazed his thigh. I guess that's why there was a lot of blood. All it took was a few stitches."

"Ah, that's where you were," Hack said. "I woke up Saturday and you weren't in your rack. I figured you were either hooked up with Vega or making a big mistake with some girl in town."

"Thank you for the confidence in my judgment," said Decker. "But, sad to say, I was doing neither. I had dinner and a few beers with Rusty and ended up on his couch for the night."

"So you wanted to tell me you slept at Rusty's?"

"Yes, I mean, no. He also told me a few things over beers. The shooting, as you can imagine, freaked me out, and I needed to know if Rusty had any thoughts about it."

"And did he?"

"Indirectly. I told him about what's been going on with the missing inventory. He'd heard about Kippen falling overboard, but hadn't heard anything other than it was an accident. I told him our thoughts."

"You sure you can trust him?" asked Hack.

"Absolutely. He's trustworthy."

"I'm sure he is. I'm just leery of the bamboo telegraph that I'm beginning to learn about. Word travels fast around here."

"I agree with being cautious," said Decker. "But Rusty's safe to confide in."

"So what did he say?"

"He thinks the shooting was directed at me rather

than someone from his past."

Hack's eyes widened in surprise. "Rusty has a past that could make someone want to shoot him?"

"Apparently mild-mannered Rusty used to be in the black market game. He was a low-level guy, just a truck driver hired by someone named Mr. Fortuno, who, I gather from Rusty, was sort of the godfather of the Olongapo black market."

"When was this?"

"Several years ago. He needed the money and Fortuno paid him well. He kept Rusty around because he was loyal and hard working."

"Sounds like Rusty from what little I know of him."

"It does, and he apparently had a good deal going as a driver. But all that changed after he met Weny. She made him quit and Rusty didn't say it, but he sounded like he was glad to get out before he got in too deep."

"Did they let him go that easily?" asked Hack.

"Yeah, seems so. Must have thought he didn't know enough to be a threat."

"Okay, so Rusty worked for this guy. You could've told me that on the ship, so I know there's more to all this. I'm afraid to ask, but I will anyway. What are you planning?"

Decker leaned into the table. "I want to go see Mr. Fortuno and find out what he knows."

"Damn," Hack mumbled. "I knew you were going to say that. You sure it's a good idea? It sounds to me like this Fortuno character's in the same category as Mrs. Doerr: stay away because no good can come of it."

"Perhaps, but Rusty told me that Mr. Fortuno's no longer in the business. He got out recently after a falling out with one of Marcos's cronies."

"I still don't think it's a good idea. Besides, what reason would he have to talk to you? He has no idea who you are or what your agenda is. Talking to American sailors about his black market business—whether he's still in it or not—is probably not high on his priority list."

"That's what Rusty said," Decker said.

"Good. I'd listen to Rusty. Sounds like he's got a good head on his shoulders. Besides, how could you get in to see him?"

"Rusty said he'll take me there."

"Damn," Hack mumbled again. "Does he still stay in contact with him?"

"Off and on. He said he ran into Mr. Fortuno a few years ago and the old man remembered him and asked to come back to work for him. Rusty said he runs into him now and then."

"Is Rusty going along?" asked Hack.

"No. He's going to take me there, but I promised him I'd keep him far away from it. If his wife found out he was doing this, it'd be bad news for everyone involved."

Hack chuckled. "So you're just going to show up on this guy's doorstep?"

"Yes, but it won't be unannounced. Rusty's going to set up the meeting. We'll just be looking for background information on the black market business so I can try to piece together what's going on."

"I still don't think you'll get anywhere," Hack said. He raised his bottle to take a drink, then stopped. "Wait, I thought you said Rusty wasn't going along?"

"He's not," Decker replied.

"Is Vega going with you?"

"Nope. I still haven't spoken to her since the shooting. I need someone who doesn't appear confrontational."

Hack sat back in his chair and waved his arms in front of him. "Oh no you don't."

"It'd only be a quick visit to see what we can learn. It'll look better if two of us go and we can—"

"It was a bad idea we got involved in this in the first place," Hack interjected. "And now it's a terrible idea. It's one thing to poke around Supply Support. That's where we work. We know that stuff. But going to see someone like Fortuno is out of our league. We don't speak the language, we don't know the culture. Besides, we've got nothin' to go on. Just some supply department documents from the *Harvey* that may or may not mean anything. You're the one involved in this, but I'm not part of it."

"Hey, you're in this whether you like or not."

"Because of you!" Hack replied.

"Point taken, but think of Kippen. And besides, Rusty assured me Mr. Fortuno is no longer in the business. He'll have no reason to fear us."

Hack laughed. "I doubt if he would fear us even if he was still in the business."

"Maybe not, but I've got to find some answers. A shipmate might have died because of this, and then I was chased and shot at. I don't know what's going on, but I can't go on like this. I'm scared every time I walk around at night on the ship. I'm scared every time I leave base and walk around town. I have to do something, but I don't know what else to do. At least if I go see Mr. Fortuno, I'll be doing something."

Hack glanced at Decker who looked more than

mildly distraught. Against his better judgment, he gave in. "Alright, I'll go if Rusty sets it up and thinks it's safe. But you do the talking. I'll just sit there. And don't give him our names." He took a swig of beer and slowly set the bottle on the table. "Just tell me when."

"Agreed," said Decker, raising his beer bottle in salute. "Now, you had something to tell me. What happened in your world that's got you so agitated?"

"I'm not agitated."

"You've been fidgeting the entire time I've been sitting here. And quite contentious. It's not like you. Let's have it."

Hack leaned in so the people at the next table couldn't hear. "Alright, Sunday night when you had duty I went out for a beer."

"And that scared you?"

"No, jackass. It's who I met while having a beer. I went to the Sea Gull. You know the place?"

Decker thought for a moment. "Rings a bell, but I can't place it. Is it on Gordon?"

"I don't know what street it's on. It's a block east of Magsaysay. But that's not important. It's just a dive with engine room types hanging around."

"Mo's kind of place."

"That's exactly what I thought."

"Anyway, I was there by myself drinking a beer."

"Any girls with you?"

"Yeah, one sat with me."

"What was her name?"

"I can't remember. Linda. No, it was Lucy."

"You sure it was Lucy?"

"Yeah, why? You know her?"

"No. Just wanted to set the scene in my mind. What'd she look like?"

"I don't know. Long dark hair. Brown complexion. Brown eyes."

"Very funny," Decker said. "I mean general superficial features the average sailor would notice."

"I didn't pay attention," Hack lied.

"Okay, continue," Decker urged. "You were sitting at a table with Lucy who may or may not have had a nice body."

"I was sitting there minding my own business and in walked two guys."

"A priest and a rabbi?" Decker smiled.

"What?"

"Never mind," said Decker. "Please continue."

"Okay, two guys walked into the bar. It took me a minute, but I recognized them from somewhere."

"Am I supposed to guess where?"

"No, you haven't seen them before. They were the two guys who followed me the other night after work."

"Who you *thought* were following you," Decker said. "As I remember, you weren't positive they were after you and I didn't see them behind you when I saw you walking down Magsaysay. My trained eye surely would've spotted them if they'd been there."

"Your trained eye?"

"Yeah. I'm very observant."

"Whatever. Anyway, they probably got lost in the crowd of people leaving base that day. But Sunday they must've followed me to the Sea Gull."

Decker sat back and crossed his legs. "Then I doubt if they were following you."

"Why do you say that?"

"It's simple. Why would they take the trouble to avoid detection and then show their faces?"

"That's what I can't figure out."

"Did you talk to them?"

"No."

Decker looked at Hack, skeptically. "Then what makes you think they were following you?"

Hack sat back in his chair. "Well, I saw them the other day. And then I saw them at the Sea Gull. And they were looking at me. It's too much of a coincidence to see Biff and Dave twice like that."

"You know their names?"

"No, it's what I call them," Hack said. "The younger guy with bleach blond hair reminds me of a surfer. I call him Biff."

"And how did you come up with 'Dave'? He remind you of your best friend from grade school or something?"

"David Letterman."

"Letterman? Hack, my boy, you need to expand your culture beyond *Beach Blanket Bingo* and late-night television."

"Their names aren't important," Hack said, his brows knitted in a pensive vee.

"Okay, what happened next? Did you approach them?"

"No way. They creeped me out. I finished my beer and got the hell out of there."

"Let me guess. You think they followed you?"

"I don't think they did. I *know* they did. I stopped at a *sari sari* store and waited and saw them leave the bar right after I did."

"You should've confronted them."

"Are you nuts? I was too scared. I ran to Magsaysay, hopped on a jeepney, and didn't get off until I was a couple miles from base. And guess who was on the jeepney with me?"

"Johnny Carson? Annette Funicello?"

Hack rolled his eyes. "No, Ensign Limpert."

Decker choked on his beer. "Limpert? Where was he going?"

"I have no idea. He got off when I did, but I stopped to eat and he walked the other direction."

"I've never seen him in town," Decker said. "I can't imagine his wife letting him run around at night like that."

"He wasn't exactly running around," Hack said. "I don't think he'd been drinking and he didn't seem lost. He knew where he was going."

"He's a strange little man," Decker mused. "How'd you get back to base?"

"I didn't," Hack replied. "At least not right away. I took a trike back to within a few blocks of Magsaysay and got a hotel room."

"Alone?"

"Yes, alone."

"I spent the night there and snuck back to the ship early this morning."

Decker reflected on Hack's story. "It sounds to me like your imagination is running wild."

"I know it was Limpert," said Hack. "I talked to him."

"I believe that," Decker said. "I mean about Biff and Dave."

"I know what I saw," replied Hack.

"What you *thought* you saw, shipmate. Are you sure they were the same guys who were following you the other day?"

"Yes." Hack paused. "Well, not exactly sure, but pretty sure. They fit the discription."

"Any number of guys walking around base fit those descriptions. Look around this bar. Clean these guys up and half of them would look like your boys."

Hack's eyes drifted around the room. "Maybe you're right."

"Of course I'm right. And why would they visit the same bar as you if they wanted to be discreet?"

"I don't know," Hack shrugged.

"And I don't know either. Just doesn't make sense. Let's forget about those two jokers and concentrate on the task at hand. We need to put together some talking points before we meet Mr. Fortuno. Someone's out to kill me and I need answers." Decker took out his Book of Dates and pencil and tore a page from the back of the notebook. "Now, what do we want to know from this guy?"

CHAPTER TWENTY-FOUR
1310, SATURDAY, FEBRUARY 8

The two sailors sat across from Rusty—Hack staring at the scenery, Decker writing in his Book of Dates—as the jeepney jostled its way towards the northeast end of town.

"Catching up on your life story?" asked Hack.

"It was a big day yesterday, my friend," Decker said, not looking up. "Election day. It could be the end of the Marcos era, but I doubt if he'll go quietly."

Rusty nodded in agreement as the vehicle slowly ascended a steep incline. Decker and Hack watched the city of Olongapo spread out from the bay towards the mountains. To the south lay the Bataan Peninsula, famous for the site of the American and Filipino armed forces' last stand against the Japanese invasion force in early 1942. Famous, too, for the infamous Bataan Death March following the U.S. surrender of the Philippines to the Japanese in May 1942.

"His wife died several years ago," Rusty said, breaking the silence. "He spent little time with her anyway. He had two small kids when I worked for him. They must be grown by now. He used to spend all of his time in his office, but he built this place in the hills several years ago. It's where the wealthy people live. It even has an underground bunker. No windows and a secret passage through the rear wall that leads to a building next door."

"Why does he need something like that?" Hack asked.

"An escape route," Rusty explained. "In case the police show up. No one is supposed to know about it, but I found out by accident when a maid let it slip."

A few blocks from Fortuno's house, Rusty tapped the roof. "*Para, para.*" The jeepney came to a stop and the three men exited out the back.

Rusty wiped the sweat from his forehead. "We wait here. My friend Baby will take you the rest of the way. He will wait for you while you visit Fortuno. He has a blue trike. Can't miss him. Please tip him enough, *pare,*" Rusty admonished, winking at Decker.

Five minutes later, Rusty began fidgeting with his watch. "He is late. Sorry about this. He is on Filipino time." He nervously shuffled his feet. "I want to stick with you guys, but if I am not home soon, Weny will be suspicious."

Decker and Hack understood completely. They said their goodbyes as Rusty caught the next jeepney headed towards base. A couple minutes later the sailors spotted Baby motoring towards them. They climbed in the trike and rode the remaining six blocks to a spot near Fortuno's house.

Baby cut the engine and edged it towards the side of the street. He turned to the sailors. "Half block more," he said. "His house is at the top of the hill. Black metal fence around it. Easy to spot." Baby pointed with his lips towards the opposite direction. "I wait in the café. Walk there and I will be waiting."

They agreed to the plan and Decker handed Baby a wad of pesos. The sailors walked up the hill the last few feet to the edge of a manicured lawn. An imposing structure built into the hillside, Fortuno's house jutted over the side of the cliff, giving an illusion from below that it was suspended in air. From street level the house was equally appealing. A short but wide driveway led to a covered parking area big enough for four cars. They both noticed the Rolls Royce, Mercedes coupe, and a large Land Cruiser 4 X 4.

The sailors walked along a stone path that led to the main entrance. Two white columns framed the entrance, and a large mahogany door that was at least twelve feet tall loomed in front of them. Decker and Hack exchanged glances.

"This is your idea," Hack said. "Go ahead and knock."

Decker hesitantly extended his hand and knocked timidly three times. They listened. No sound coming from within. Decker knocked louder and this time they heard footsteps walking through the house. Decker leaned into Hack and whispered, "It's a woman."

"How do you know that?"

"Sounds like feminine footsteps in heels."

The door opened and Decker was indeed correct. A tall, beautiful Filipina greeted them with the door slightly ajar, her left hand resting on her cocked hip. She eyed them suspiciously from head to toe. "What do you want?"

Her firm demeanor got Decker and Hack's attention, but what they focused on mostly was her beauty. Young, probably early twenties, Decker guessed, with soft but finely-toned features. He thick brown hair fell a few inches below her shoulders. She wore a loose-fitting yellow top and extremely short white cotton shorts that accentuated her olive skin. *She has to be six feet tall,* Decker thought to himself, trying to compare her with his six-foot-two frame.

"We're here to see Mr. Fortuno," Decker said softly. "I believe he's expecting us. Please tell him that Decker and Hack are here to see him. Friends of Rusty."

The woman inspected them a second time, wary of the presence of American sailors. She glanced behind her, then turned to face the sailors. "Very well. Wait here. I'll see if he's free." She closed the door and they heard the distinctive click of a lock.

"Sounds like we struck out," Hack said. "I bet she's going to leave us standing here."

"I think you could be right," Decker agreed, looking up at the sky as thunder boomed in the distance. "And it's going to rain. Let's give it five minutes and get out of here. I suddenly have a bad feeling about this place and I don't want to get caught up here in a storm."

Hack marked the time with his watch. "I hope Rusty's message got to him. Who do you think the girl is?"

"Could be his maid," Decker said.

"She didn't look like a maid. Not dressed like that."

"Could be his girlfriend."

"A girlfriend that young?"

"Happens all the time, especially with old men who have money. It's the life of the rich. Young women don't mind. They get to spend money on anything they want. The old man gets what he wants before he dies and, in the end, the young woman gets the money. That's what makes the world go round. Trickle down economics."

"I don't think that's what it's called. But whatever it is, I hope I never get like that."

"Like what? A rich old man or a young man marrying an old woman with money?"

"Neither one."

"Well, I think you're safe on both accounts."

Another minute passed and Decker and Hack were about to walk away when they again heard the foot falls of high heels walking across hardwood floors. The door opened and the woman, who this time introduced herself as Olivia, invited them inside and told them to follow her.

They passed through a long entryway that opened to a large family room with slick mahogany floors and large windows facing the city below and Subic Bay beyond. Hack glanced at Decker with a better-behave-yourself look as both of them eyed Olivia's perfectly formed derriere while she walked ahead of them. She led them across the family room to a screen door that opened to an expansive deck hanging over the hillside.

Hack was the first to take a tentative step on the wood flooring. "An engineering marvel. I just hope it holds our weight," he whispered to Decker.

Decker didn't have time to reply. His eyes met Mr. Fortuno's glare. The old man, sitting at a table under an umbrella in the far corner of the deck, took off his black-framed reading glasses and sized up the two sailors. He wore a long-sleeve white cotton shirt, untucked and unbuttoned to mid-chest, tan slacks, and dark brown Mephisto boat shoes. His white hair, thin across the top, curled along the back of his shirt collar. A stack of papers and a glass of bourbon sat in front of him. He didn't bother to stand.

Olivia announced their entrance and went over to the man, kissed his forehead, and asked him if he wanted anything. Mr. Fortuno smiled at the young woman and put an arm around her hips. "*Hindi bale na lang, anak,*" he said with a faint smile. "We'll be fine. I'll have Jimmy get our guests something to drink."

With a gold Rolex dangling from his wrist, Mr. Fortuno dropped his left arm from Olivia's hips and patted her on the butt as she walked away.

Olivia pouted. "Okay, Daddy. I'll be inside if you need anything. I'm going to call Abbey."

"Oops, not a girlfriend," Hack whispered to Decker with a bemused smile.

CHAPTER TWENTY-FIVE
1335, SATURDAY, FEBRUARY 8

Olivia spun in her heels and sashayed into the house. Mr. Fortuno cleared his throat, drawing the sailors' attention. "Welcome to my home, gentlemen. Would you like a drink? Perhaps a beer would be nice." He peered over Decker's shoulder at a servant standing a few paces behind the two sailors. "Jimmy, *dalawa* Heinekens for our guests, please."

Decker and Hack hadn't noticed Jimmy, who had obviously followed them through the house and out onto the deck. Jimmy bowed slightly. "Yes, sir."

Mr. Fortuno stretched his back in the chair and waved Decker and Hack forward. "Sit down please. Don't be shy. Any friends of Rusty are welcome here."

Decker was relieved at how friendly Mr. Fortuno appeared to be. Expecting a rude, mob boss type, Mr. Fortuno seemed a pleasant old man, pleasant in the grandfatherly sort of way.

They spent the next few minutes answering Mr. Fortuno's questions: where they were stationed, how long they had been in the navy, where they were from in the States.

Mr. Fortuno gestured towards his house. "You met

Olivia. She lived in California for several years. I wanted her to have a top notch education. She attended high school at Harvard-Westlake in Los Angeles and went to college at Stanford."

"Impressive," Decker said. "I'm not familiar with the high school, but, of course, I'm well aware of Stanford's reputation."

Mr. Fortuno grabbed his bourbon glass and put his elbows on the table. "In truth, it disappointed me. I wanted her to go to what you Americans call the east coast for college. She was stuck on staying in California, though, and I couldn't change her mind. Her younger sister is at Stanford now. Two more years until she graduates. Olivia spent the last few months in Hawaii visiting friends and then arrived back home three months ago. I'm afraid they're both infatuated with life in the U.S. I doubt if Abbey will ever move back with me. Younger siblings are like that, I suppose."

Jimmy returned with two Heinekens and frosty mugs for Decker and Hack. He refilled Mr. Fortuno's glass of bourbon and refreshed his ice.

"Are you fellows hungry?" Mr. Fortuno asked.

"No, sir," Decker said, eliciting a look of disappointment from Hack.

To Jimmy, Mr. Fortuno said, "That will be all for now. If we need anything, I'll ring."

"Yes, sir," Jimmy said and retreated to the house, nodding at the two sailors as he departed.

The three men sat on the deck not speaking for the next few minutes. Decker and Hack gazed at the city of Olongapo and Subic Bay below from a vantage point they had not experienced before. The streets were clearly defined, weaving like a maze through the houses and buildings. The naval base's few buildings and large, green open spaces were in sharp contrast to the crowded city. The tops of cranes and ships at the piers were barely noticeable. The water of Subic Bay appeared various shades of blue and turquoise, and clearer and more pristine than it looked up close. Grande Island, the small island at the mouth of the bay, was like a speck on the map spread out below them. Storm clouds gathered over the bay, creating a dark contrast with the water.

Mr. Fortuno broke the silence. "I moved here for the view about twenty years ago. We used to live northwest of the city in the country. The older I got, the more I wanted to find a place where I could relax and enjoy the scenery."

Hack held his stare on the city below. "It's beautiful up here. I had no idea Olongapo was so big."

Mr. Fortuno nodded. "Two hundred thousand people crammed into such a small area. That's why I like living in the hills. Gets me away from the crowds and noise of the city."

Mr. Fortuno glanced over at Decker and Hack who still looked mesmerized by the view. "But you two didn't come visit me for the view. You are friends of Rusty. He was a good employee for me. Someone I could trust to do the job. He told me you wanted to ask me something."

Hack looked at Decker, raising his eyebrows to urge Decker to do the talking.

Decker took a drink of beer and cleared his throat. "Did you hear about the sailor who died on the USS *Harvey* a few weeks ago?"

"Yes, I saw that in the paper several days ago. As I

understand it, the poor guy fell overboard. Must be terrible for his family. When you guys have kids, you will understand that."

"Probably so," Decker said. "But it shook us up pretty badly the way it was. I'd known him for about a year."

Mr. Fortuno sat back in his chair and took a sip of bourbon. "I've been around a long time, gentlemen. I've seen and heard many things. Something tells me you have more to say about this young man's death."

"Alright, I'll put our cards on the table," said Decker. "I don't buy that it was an accident or suicide. I knew him well enough to know he wouldn't just fall off the ship. And he wasn't suicidal."

Mr. Fortuno sat his glass on the table and folded his arms. "Interesting news, but what's this got to do with me? I have no connections with the navy anymore and certainly no connections with their investigators."

"Kippen's death hit close to home," Decker said. "We both worked with him in the same department. What concerns us is, if it was murder, who did it and why? And it's because of the 'why' that we're here."

Mr. Fortuno peered over his reading glasses, looking impatient with the conversation. "Sorry, fellows. I still don't follow you. I told you, I have no dealings with the navy and I'm beginning to not like your insinuations." For the first time Decker and Hack got a glimpse of another side of Mr. Fortuno. Nice, friendly exterior, but underneath, not far underneath, was the forceful personality of a mob moss.

Hack spoke up. "We're not saying you had anything to do with it. That's the furthest thing from our minds."

"Glad to hear that," said Mr. Fortuno. "Now get to

your point. It's going to rain soon."

Decker stood and leaned against the deck railing. "We think …I think …Kippen may have discovered something on the ship. Some missing parts, maybe thousands of dollars worth of material. I was talking with Rusty about it a few days ago and he told me of … well, he told me how sometimes navy supplies go missing and end up out in town."

"On the black market you mean," said Mr. Fortuno. "It's okay to say those words. Many people thought— probably still think—that I was involved in the black market during my career. But contrary to what people say, I ran a legitimate business. I had dealings with the navy—like everyone does who operates a business in Olongapo—but I never ran anything but a legal business."

"We weren't suggesting anything otherwise, Mr. Fortuno," Decker said. "Rusty never said you were in the black market," he added, lying to protect his friend. "But he said you might know the lay of the land. Who's operating the black market in town. We want to find Kippen's killer and we're also beginning to get worried about ourselves if the operation is continuing on the *Harvey*."

"Rusty is correct," said Mr. Fortuno. "I do know many people in town, but I'm retired now. I'm afraid I can't help you with this one, gentlemen. Now if you'll excuse me, I have another appointment."

Jimmy appeared again on the deck. Decker and Hack stood, thanked Mr. Fortuno for his time, and followed Jimmy indoors. Olivia greeted them once inside and told Jimmy she would show them out.

She moved between Decker and Hack and took each by the arm, leading them to the door. "How did the meeting go," she asked.

"Went fine, thanks," Hack said. "Your father is a nice man."

"He is," she said. "A lot of people say otherwise, but he's kind and gentle." Before opening the door, she squeezed each of their arms. "Let me give you some advice. Don't come back. He doesn't like people bothering him, especially American sailors. I'm surprised he was willing to see you today. He must think a lot of this Rusty I heard him talk about." She let go of their arms and opened the door.

Decker gave Olivia his best smile. "We would never think of bothering your father again. I hope we weren't a bother for you?"

Olivia's face softened. "You were no bother. Where are you guys stationed?"

"The USS *Harvey*," Hack replied.

Olivia lowered her head and giggled.

"Did I say something funny?" asked Hack, looking at Decker.

Olivia took hold of Hack's arm. "No, it's not you. I know someone on the *Harvey*. Ensign Malata."

"I think you've got the wrong ship," Decker said, confused. "I don't know any Ensign Malata."

"That's not his real name," Olivia said. "It's Ensign Limpert. Malata is Tagalog for 'limp'. I know it's not a nice thing to do, but it's what Emily and I call him. Not to his face, of course. It's just sort of a joke between us."

"How do you know him?" asked Decker. "And who's Emily?"

"She's been my best friend since grade school. Her dad used to work for my father years ago. We grew up together. She works at the supply depot on base now. I guess she met Malata there. I've met him a couple times when he'd be over at her house."

Hack turned to Decker. "I guess he does get off base once in a while."

"Emily says he visits now and then," Olivia said. "He actually can be funny and a big flirt, even if his wife is along."

"Are we talking about the same guy?" asked Decker.

"Short and skinny with clothes that hang off him like their two sizes too big? Malaki wife about five times his size?"

"Yep, that's him," said Decker.

"I don't think he has many navy friends," Olivia added. "Emily's nice to invite him over." She nervously glanced behind her. "Now you really must go."

Decker extended his hand. "By the way, I'm Decker. Elliott Decker."

"And I'm late for an appointment," she said, shutting the door.

Decker and Hack stood on the porch for a few minutes contemplating their recent conversation with Mr. Fortuno. Decker raised his arms above his head. "I'm in love!"

"I love you, too," said Hack.

"I wasn't talking about you, jackass."

"I was hoping you'd say that."

Decker pointed his eyes towards the Fortuno house. "Did you see that ass in those shorts?"

"I happened to notice."

"And those legs?"

"I noticed that as well."

"I'm in love."

"You said that already."

Decker shot Hack a giddy smile. "Did I?" He surveyed the threatening skies as thunder boomed overhead. "Unfortunately, besides the fact that Mr. Fortuno has at least one very attractive daughter and that she knows Ensign Limpert, we didn't learn anything."

"Maybe not," said Hack. "But at least we tried."

"I thought he'd at least give us something to go on," said Decker. "But I agree with the lovely Olivia. I'm surprised he even saw us at all."

"Do you believe him when he said he's no longer in the black market?" asked Hack.

"I have my doubts," Decker said, waving his hand at the house. "Rusty said this is his retirement home. I was expecting a small place with a white picket fence."

They stepped off the porch headed for their rendezvous with Baby at the corner café. They felt the rain as soon as they hit the street. Big drops at first, with a cool breeze and a crackle of lightning.

"Great," Decker said, looking up at the sky the precise moment the big drops turned into a downpour. "Let's run for it!"

Soaked and out of breath, Decker and Hack spotted Baby in a back booth, his back to the door. Decker put his index finger to his lips to quiet Hack while they tiptoed towards their new friend without being noticed. As they approached within a couple feet, Hack slid in the opposite bench seat and Decker jumped into the seat next to Baby, putting an arm around his shoulder.

"People of the Philippines. We have returned," Decker announced.

A wide smile formed on Baby's face. "I am so glad to see you guys. There are stories of people going in that house and not coming back out again. I was afraid for you two. I did not want to tell Rusty I lost you."

"That would've been very careless of you," Decker said. "Now, let's get something to eat." He flagged down a harried waitress and ordered three helpings of pancit, an ample serving of rice, and three cokes. "We can ride out the bad weather in here."

"Good plan," Hack said. "For once I'm glad it's raining. I'm starving."

Decker and Hack recounted their conversation with Mr. Fortuno and answered Baby's questions about the layout of the house and who they met inside. Fifteen minutes later the waitress brought their order. They ate their meal at a leisurely pace, enjoying the cuisine and the company of Baby. Thirty minutes later the waitress handed Decker the bill.

"*Salamat po*," Decker said, glancing at the ticket to ensure it was the correct amount. He quickly scanned the food and drink items listed on the receipt and started to set it aside, but something caught his eye. A note was attached to the receipt by a paperclip. Someone had scribbled two handwritten sentences across the bottom of the note. He turned to look at the door, and then at the waitress. "Who gave you this note?"

"Some man," said the waitress. "He came in and handed it to me. Gave me one hundred pesos to deliver it."

"*Salamat*," Decker said, handing the small piece of paper to Baby. "Hey, can you read this?"

"*Oo*, it says pancit and rice. Three orders. You can't read that? Where are your glasses?"

"I don't need glasses," Decker said. "I was talking about the note."

Baby studied the writing for a few seconds. "Sorry, *pare*. I cannot read it. It is probably nothing."

Decker handed the note to Hack who held it at various distances from his face. "I think it's a message, but I have no idea what it says."

"Must be from Mr. Fortuno," Decker whispered, lowering his voice to remind Hack they needed to be discreet.

Hack nodded and silently mouthed, "We'll talk later at Cal Jam."

The rain continued for another thirty minutes when a break in the weather gave them the opportunity to head back to base.

The trip downhill back to the heart of Olongapo took half the time it had taken to reach Mr. Fortuno's house. Baby dropped them at the corner of Gordon and Magsaysay and the two sailors walked into Cal Jam still pondering their trip to Mr. Fortuno's house. They sat at their usual table by the window, studying the handwritten note lying on the table in front of them.

"I still can't read it," said Hack.

"Me either," said Decker. He took out his pencil and pointed to the first sentence. "It looks like a name here, but I can't make out the other words."

"I think it's a name, too," Hack agreed. "Three words. The first letters are capitalized. But a name of what?"

"Could be a person."

"Or a town," Decker countered.

"But more likely a person."

"Or a town."

Decker turned the note towards Hack. "What about the second sentence? A word then a colon followed by two more words. And the last two words are underlined."

Hack picked up the note and held it at different angles. "Whoever wrote this has terrible handwriting."

"I assume it's Mr. Fortuno," said Decker.

"It could be from his daughter?" Hack offered.

Decker shook his head. "I doubt it."

"Why not?"

"Because beautiful women have exquisite handwriting. Always perfectly legible."

Hack looked dubious. "Is that right?"

"It's a fact of nature. I read about a research study once. They proved it scientifically."

Hack rolled his eyes. "I'm sure there's one beautiful woman out there who has sloppy handwriting."

"It's possible, but it would be an evolutionary anomaly."

"A what?"

"Never mind," Decker said. "I'm certain this is from her father. Olivia would've told us something at the door. All she did was warn you not to come back. Advice, I might add, that you should follow."

"Warned me? What about you? She was talking to both of us."

"She was clearly talking to you. She said not to come back to see her father, and she was looking at you when she said it. If I go back there, it won't be to see the old man. It'll be other business."

Hack ignored Decker's rambling. "Maybe the note's from Jimmy, Fortuno's butler guy. Did you see him at the café?"

"I didn't see anyone I recognized. But I was sitting with Baby with my back to the door. You see anyone?"

"I wasn't paying attention," Hack said. "The place was too crowded. Someone easily could've walked in, passed the note to the waitress, and left before anyone noticed."

They sat staring at the note for five minutes, neither one saying a word as they studied the piece of paper from every angle trying in vain to decipher the handwriting.

"I think I've got it," Hack said. "The first word is 'the.' I'm pretty sure of that."

"Me too," said Decker. "But that doesn't help."

"Okay, how about this?" Hack offered. "The beginning

is Angular August Kayaking. Warming: his december."

Decker gave Hack a doubtful look. "What the hell does that mean?"

"Maybe it's code."

"Maybe it's not even close to what it says. I think you're way off."

Hack slid the note back to Decker. "I don't see you coming up with anything better."

"Yeah? Well, I think I've got it. It says 'The bussing is Angiology Again Kampuchea. Warring: it's dampening.'"

"'That's the best you've got?" Hack laughed.

"I think it's close. Maybe a word or two off."

"A word or two? That makes less sense than my translation. Maybe it's written in Tagalog. That's why we can't read it."

"A good point," Decker said, glancing behind him. "Here comes Pong. Let's see if he can read it."

Pong approached the table and spread several peso notes in front of the sailors. "Gentlemen, the newest additions to my collection," he said, proudly.

"Pesos?" Decker said. "If I knew you were collecting those, I have a few I could've sold you. I'd even do it at the rate of eighteen pesos to a dollar."

Pong laughed and pointed to the bills. "No way, *pare*. Everyone knows the rate is twenty and half pesos. But these are no ordinary pesos. Look closely."

Decker and Hack leaned in to study the bills. There were several denominations ranging from a fifty centavos note to a one hundred peso bill. Printed across the top of each one was the wording "The Japanese Government."

"Occupation currency?" Decker asked.

"*Oo*," said Pong. "The Japanese started printing the

money in 1942. I have a few already in my collection, but this is the first time I have been able to buy notes in such good shape."

"Very interesting," Decker said. "And I've got a note to show you, too." He handed Pong the piece of paper. "Take a look at this. We can't make it out."

Pong studied the writing for a few minutes, then: "It's easy. It says: 'The bellman is August Agent Keypunch. Waving: has depression.'"

"Thanks, Pong," Decker said, exchanging an exasperated look with Hack. "I thought it might be written in Tagalog. Apparently it's not."

"If it is Tagalog, I do not know those words," Pong said, gathering his peso notes. "Sorry I could not be of more help."

"No problem. We'll keep looking at it."

"Can I try," a woman's voice said. Standing behind Decker, he hadn't realized one of Pong's assistants had followed him to the table.

"Sure, go ahead," Decker said. "We're getting nowhere with it."

The girl studied the note with enthusiasm and a smile came across her face. "Okay. I know what it says. My father used to write like this. I was always good at reading his handwriting. It says: 'The busboy is Angelica Against Kangaroo. Warplane: has dungeon.'"

"Thank you, my dear," said Decker, taking the note from the woman. "That is very helpful."

"*Walang anuman*," she said, turning to walk away, looking satisfied that she had broken the code.

"We're wasting our time," said Decker. "Let's go see Rusty. We need to let him know we're back in town. I'm sure he's worried about us and maybe he can make sense out of this."

Ten minutes later, the two sailors were sitting on Rusty's porch. Rusty studied the note for only a few seconds.

"I was worried about this," Rusty said, laying the note on a coffee table in front of him.

"What are you talking about?" Decker asked. "You have any idea what it says? We've been looking at it for an hour and haven't been able to come up with anything."

"I know what it says," Rusty said. "This is interesting."

"What is?" asked Decker, still trying to decipher the handwriting.

"Angelito Agana," said Rusty.

Decker and Hack exchanged glances. "A.A.," they said in unison.

"Chief Fray had those initials written on a piece of paper," Decker explained. "Who is he?"

"Angelito Agana used to work for Mr. Fortuno. I knew him. It has been a long time since I have talked to him. My friend Ducky knows him better. Wish he was here to tell you about Agana. Ducky is in Manila now. He works security for Marcos."

"Agana doesn't work for Fortuno anymore?" Decker asked.

"No, he had disagreement with Mr. Fortuno several years ago. Fortuno accused Agana of stealing money. There is bad blood between them."

"What's Agana doing now?" Decker asked.

"I have asked around about him. I learned he started his own business when Mr. Fortuno kicked him out."

"Black market?"

"*Oo*. And gambling. Agana got friendly with Marcos. The president let him run the casinos on Luzon."

"The president has that power?"

"The government owns the casinos, *pare*. Marcos established the Philippine Amusements and Gaming Corporation in 1977. It is controlled in the Office of the President. Still that way. Ducky told me that Agana once did a favor for the Rolex 12. He got the casinos as part of the deal. Plus Agana's father knew Marcos during WWII. They were part of Ang Mahárlika. Now Agana calls his business by that name."

"The what?" asked Decker.

"Noble warrior," smiled Hack.

Decker and Rusty stared at Hack.

"Lee said the word once," Hack said. "She told me what it meant."

Rusy nodded. "He is right. The Mahárlika. The Noble Warriors. Marcos's guerilla unit. Or that is the story Marcos likes to tell. He claimed it was the best fighting force. Beat the Japanese every time. Marcos says he was the most decorated soldier in the war. But Americans never believed it. Said they never heard of the unit. They said it was a black market operation selling stuff to Japanese."

"Why the nickname for his business?" asked Decker.

Rusty shrugged. "Do not know. Maybe he is trying to impress Marcos. Or to scare people. Make himself sound tough."

"How big is he?" Decker asked.

"Agana? He is real big. The main player in town. He is so powerful that he has broken ties with Marcos."

"It's hard to keep track of who's on whose side,"

Decker said. "So Agana controls all of the black market in Olongapo now?"

"Most of it. Gambling operation, too. There are a few small time operators, but my friends say they are too small for Agana to worry about."

"What kind of things does he deal in?" asked Hack.

"Big stuff. Cigarettes and soap no good anymore. Too many trade agreements between countries have opened up the market. It is different now."

"What kind of big stuff?" Decker asked.

"Material for ships. Aircraft parts. Whoever controls Subic also controls Angeles City."

Hack looked inquiringly at Decker. "Clark Air Base," Decker said.

"Exactly," said Rusty. "It is one area. Mr. Fortuno used to control 80 percent of the black market trade going in and out of Subic and Clark. Now Agana has control. Probably controls more like 90 percent now."

"Where does he send the supplies?" asked Decker. "I don't see any of that stuff around the stores in town."

"You would not see it," said Rusty. "From what I hear, most of the parts goes overseas to other countries."

"What do they do with it?" asked Hack.

"Not sure. They probably use it for their ships and planes," Rusty said.

"We should go talk to Agana," Rusty said, looking at Decker.

"I would advise against that," said Rusty.

"Why? We talked to Mr. Fortuno. That went well. He even helped us in his own way."

Rusty shook his head. "It's a completely different situation."

"How so?"

"Mr. Fortuno is a nice man if you are on his good side."

"What's Agana like?" asked Hack.

"He is different. Agana was always angry about something when I knew him. Like he was pissed off at the world. Never satisfied with his position in life."

Decker stood and paced. "I still think we ought to try to talk with him. See if he knows anything about Chief or Allen Sumner. We can at least stop by his business. Snoop around a little."

"And how do you propose we do that?" asked Hack.

"We can walk in like we're lost," Decker said. "Or we can say we're just curious about the business. Play dumb."

"I don't think we'll have to play if we do that," said Hack.

"He is right," Rusty said, pointing to Hack. "Agana is not a stupid man. Neither are his men. If two American sailors walk in there, they will know you are up to no good."

"Maybe we can go in and ask for Allen Sumner. Or maybe ask for Chief Fray," Decker said. "We can say they're friends of ours and we're looking for them."

"Still not a good idea," Rusty said. "Trust me. I knew Mr. Fortuno would be agreeable. He is retired. But Agana is different."

Decker put his hand on Rusty's shoulder. "I wholeheartedly agree with you, *pare.*" Decker pointed to Hack. "But I'm afraid my friend is determined to pay a visit to the esteemed Mr. Agana."

"The hell I am!" said Hack.

"You can't fool me," said Decker. "I know that look in your eyes. But don't worry, I'll be right behind you when you go in."

Hack shook his head. "I knew you were going to get involved in another trip I'd rather not take." A moment later, he gave in to his friend, but with a caveat. "Alright, I'll go, but we're just going to walk by and take a look around from the sidewalk. I don't even want to pause in front of the business."

"It's a go then," Decker agreed. He turned to Rusty. "Where's Agana's business located?"

Rust drew a crude map and scribbled directions to Agana's on the back of the note from Fortuno.

"Thank you, *pare*," said Decker, motioning with his head to Hack that it was time to go. They stepped off the porch and thanked Rusty for his help.

"By the way," asked Decker, pausing on the sidewalk. "What did Fortuno's note say?"

"That is easy," Rusty said. "It says, '*The business is Angelito Agana Kompanya. Warning: He's dangerous*.'"

CHAPTER TWENTY-SEVEN
1735, WEDNESDAY, FEBRUARY 12

The Marine guard checked their IDs and waved the sailors through the checkpoint at the main gate without saying a word. Decker exhaled loudly as he exited the base. "Another day on the *Harvey* that we survived."

"I was beginning to wonder about you this afternoon," Hack said. "You seemed tense all day."

"I'm dreading talking with Vega tonight," Decker sighed. "She called me on the ship this morning. She invited me over to her place after work."

Hack punched him lightly on the shoulder. "Ah, it's probably nothing. Just wait and see, she'll surprise you."

Decker forced a smile. "Maybe so."

They were half way across the Shit River Bridge when Decker spotted a green Range Rover pull alongside them. He ignored the vehicle, but when the car continued to follow them, Decker turned and realized who it was. "Damn."

"What's wrong?" asked Hack.

"We have company. Let's keep walking."

Hack glanced over Decker's shoulder at the vehicle. "Who is it?"

"It's no one," Decker said. "Don't look at him."

As the two sailors neared the end of the bridge, Inspector Navarro rolled down the passenger side window. "Well, Mr. Decker, how are you this evening? You remember me, right? Inspector Franco Navarro."

"How could I forget," Decker said.

"You have an excellent memory," the inspector smiled.

"You catch the guy who shot at me yet?" asked Decker.

Navarro shook his head. "No, but we know who did it. We're waiting for the right time to make our move."

"I hope you do it soon," said Decker, grabbing Hack by the arm to continue walking.

Navarro edged his vehicle forward to keep pace with the sailors. "Why the rush, gentlemen? Sit with me for a while. We need to have a serious conversation. Man to man."

Decker stared straight ahead. "No thanks. We're in a hurry. Some friends are waiting for us."

"I'm sure the girls can wait," said the inspector. "Get in and let's have a chat. Both of you."

Decker eyed a group of Filipinos milling around the corner of Gordon Avenue half a block away. For a moment he thought about a dash to a trike for a quick getaway through the crowded streets. But when he looked towards the trike stand, he stopped and pulled on Hack's shirt. Three of Navarro's men were blocking the sidewalk. Submitting to the inevitable, the sailors climbed in the vehicle. Decker sat up front, Hack in the back seat.

"I'm glad you decided to join me," Inspector Navarro said. "Trust me, I don't mean to hassle you. I am an honorable cop trying to keep the peace in this fine community."

For a fee, Decker wanted to say, but he knew it would get him into more trouble than it was worth.

"I understand the two of you paid a visit to our most illustrious citizen of Olongapo, Mr. Fortuno."

"How do you know...?" asked Hack.

"Not that my friend is saying we actually did visit him," Decker interrupted.

"Relax, Mr. Decker. There is no crime against visiting someone. We Filipinos are friendly people as you no doubt have learned in your time here. I am just curious what you talked about?"

"I thought he knew a friend of mine," Decker said, unable to come up with a plausible reason why he would be visiting Mr. Fortuno.

"I see," said the Inspector. "I trust it was a nice visit?"

"It was cordial," Decker said. "Turned out he didn't know my friend after all. Case of mistaken identity."

"Well then, there's no need for you to see him again." Navarro turned in his seat so he could also see Hack. "Let me give you guys a warning. Be careful. Watch your step, as you Americans say. People are watching you. This is bigger than you can handle. Don't get involved."

Decker and Hack sat in silence until Navarro waved his hand. "You can go."

The sailors quickly climbed out of the vehicle and stood on the sidewalk as the inspector put the car in gear, squealed the tires, and drove away.

"That was interesting," Decker said as they headed for the trike stand.

"I hope I don't run into him again," Hack added.

"You and me both," Decker said, hailing a trike to take him to Vega's. "Wish me luck. I've been dreading this for several days now."

"Maybe it's not what you think," Hack said. "She's probably been busy with work and hasn't had time to see you."

Decker forced a smile and climbed in the sidecar, appreciating Hack's attempt at comfort. Ten minutes later, the trike stopped in front of a four-story brick building. Decker paid the driver and ambled up the stairs to her third floor apartment.

Vega greeted him at the door in cutoff jeans and a yellow T-shirt tied in a knot at her waist. She kissed him on the cheek and led him inside where they stood in the middle of her sparsely furnished living room. "Hey, thanks for coming over. Sorry I've been hard to find lately. Work and stuff's been crazy. Want something to drink? Have you eaten?"

Decker shook his head "no" and hugged her. "You said you wanted to talk. As you know, I'm not one for small talk when there's business on the table."

Vega squirmed out of the embrace and took Decker by the hand. "Okay then. I've met someone."

Decker folded his arms. "Well, I meet people all the time. In fact, I met my old friend Inspector Navarro this evening."

"What are you talking about?"

"Exactly what I said. Your boss stopped Hack and me outside the gate. We sat in his car and talked over old times."

Vega walked to the refrigerator and opened the door. "Did he have news about the shooting?"

Decker shook his head. "No, he talked to us about Mr. Fortuno."

Vega closed the refrigerator door and frowned. "Fortuno? Why would he talk about that guy with you?"

Decker smiled. "Maybe because Hack and I paid a visit to the Fortuno compound over the weekend."

"Really?" She put her hands on her hips. "Now why would you do that? And, more important, *how* did you do it?

"It was easy. A certain trike driver that we both know used to work for Fortuno many years ago."

"You're kidding. Rusty?"

Decker held up his right hand. "I am not one to name names, but suffice it to say this certain trike driver that we both know set up a meeting with the aforementioned Mr. Fortuno. If you recall, I'm trying to figure out if Kippen's dive—and me getting shot at—is related to the local black market."

Vega walked over to Decker and took hold of both of his hands. "You need to stop this investigation of yours. It's too dangerous."

"I found that out the other night and Rusty has the leg wound to prove it."

"I was so scared when I got there." She looked up at him. "So did Mr. Fortuno actually talk with you?"

"Of course he did."

"Did he give you any help?"

Decker shook his head. "Nope, he was cagey. But he sent us a message after we left his house. We stopped to eat at this little cafe and someone gave the waitress a note to deliver to us."

"What did it say?"

"It mentioned this guy named Angelito Agana with a warning that he's dangerous."

"It was from Mr. Fortuno?"

"I think so. The handwriting was hard to read. We only met the old man and one of his daughters so I assume it was from the old man."

"Which girl did you meet? Olivia or Abbey?"

Decker stood open mouthed. "You know them?"

"I went to high school with Olivia for two years when I came back to the Philippines to live with my father. Then she went to the States to finish her last two years. Somewhere in California I think. She was tall and skinny back then. And very pretty."

"Still is," Decker said. "Tall and skinny anyway," he added. "But I didn't get a good look at her."

Vega dropped his hands and began pacing the room. "It'd be fun to see her again. I still can't believe you went to their house. Don't go near Agana, though. Going to Fortuno's was bad enough, but Agana's a different ball game."

"That's what Rusty said."

"And you should listen to him."

Decker sat in a chair at Vega's kitchen table. "But I digress. You said you met someone."

Vega sat in his lap and crossed her arms. "I did. It's hard for me to tell you this, but I met a guy. We've seen each other a couple times. I know we're just friends now, but I think we should put a hold on your visits. I want to see where this takes me."

Decker put his arm around her waist. "I thought you told me you weren't looking for a relationship?"

"I wasn't really," Vega said, lowering her head. "But I've been thinking lately I might give it a try."

"You can try with me."

She slid her arms around his neck. "You're not the boyfriend type. Don't get me wrong, I like you a lot. You know that. But you're not ready to commit to a serious relationship."

"Maybe I am ready?"

Vega smiled and kissed his forehead. "No you're not. We both know that."

"Well, who is the lucky young man?"

"He's an attorney in town. He works for the city government."

"Ah, I've been torpedoed by a lawyer. Figures."

"It's not like that, Elliott. I've known him for a couple of years. It just sort of happened."

Decker lifted Vega off his lap and stood holding her. "I should be going."

"So soon? Let me make you something to eat?"

Decker shook his head. "Thanks, but I need to go. A long walk back to Magsaysay sounds nice right now."

Vega hugged him tightly. "Sorry about this. I hope we're still friends?"

He kissed her on the top of her head. "Of course."

She smiled and walked with him to her front door. "Hey, listen," she said, taking hold of his hands. "Please don't do any more investigating. I'm sorry I asked you to do it in the first place. I just wanted to get a little information to help me get some respect at work. It was selfish of me."

"I'm glad you told me," Decker said. "But not to worry. I'm being careful. I wasn't sure in the beginning, but I'm now convinced I'm on to something big."

Vega nodded in agreement. "And it's time for you to stay out of it. Let the police handle things. I don't even know if a sailor on the *Harvey* is involved in the black market. It might take us a while, but we'll put a stop to whatever is going on." Vega stood on her tiptoes and kissed him on the lips. "Promise me you're going to stop your investigation?"

Decker walked out the door and turned before descending the stairs. "Bye, Vega. I'll be seeing you. I hope this guy is what you're looking for."

CHAPTER TWENTY-EIGHT
1810, WEDNESDAY, FEBRUARY 12

Hack knocked and heard a woman's voice from within softly call out, "Come in." He pushed open the door and stopped in his tracks at the sight before him. Lee was lying face down on a blanket wearing a red T-shirt and reading a novel. A bath towel was thrown over the arm of the nearby sofa. Angie sat astride Lee's left thigh, massaging her lower back, neither of the women looking up to acknowledge Hack's presence.

Hack smiled at the sight before him. "Looks like I got here at the right time. You always leave your door unlocked like this?"

Lee, eyes still on the book, motioned with her left hand for Hack to sit on the couch. "It was locked. I heard you talking to the trike driver so Angie got up and opened it." She finished reading the page, closed the book, and spoke to the maid. "*Oras na para ihanda ang hapunan.*" Angie got up quietly, smiled at Hack, and hurried to the kitchen.

"I've always been impressed with your Tagalog," Hack said.

Lee turned on her side. "I guess I picked it up easily, but I'm still learning. I think I just asked her to fix dinner.

Not sure if I got it exactly correct, but she understood what I wanted."

Hack looked at Angie in the kitchen and then at Lee. "Must be nice having her here. I didn't know massages were part of her duties?"

"They're not. She worked as a masseuse before I hired her so I let her treat me if she asks. She's taught me how to give them, too. Maybe sometime I'll show you."

Hack smiled at the thought. "Maybe the both of you can show me."

"Don't be a jackass," she said, sitting up and pulling down at the T-shirt to cover her waist.

Hack gazed at Lee's perfectly formed thighs, firm from her workout regimen. "I love you, Leeandra Mansfield."

Lee rolled her eyes knowing where Hack had focused his attention. "Do you say that to every half naked girl you see?"

"No, just to the ones I sleep with."

"Touché, silly goose," said Lee. "Okay then, if you really love me, how about getting me some underwear?"

"What'd you do with the ones you had on?"

"I didn't have any on. I showered and just put on a T-shirt . We were watching TV and Angie mentioned a massage so I took her up on it. They're in the top drawer of my dresser."

"Any particular pair?"

"Doesn't matter. You choose. And throw me my towel."

Hack grabbed the towel but paused before tossing it to her. "You want a bra, too?"

"Are we going out?"

"I wasn't planning on it."

"Then no bra. Just my panties."

Hack flipped the towel to her. "I like the sound of that," he said, walking to the bedroom with one eye on his girlfriend.

He opened the top drawer of her dresser but all he saw was an assortment of neatly folded tops. He thumbed through the clothes looking for underwear and felt something tucked between two shirts. He lifted the top shirt and saw a stack of bills held together by a small binder clip. He quickly counted. Six hundred dollars.

Out of curiosity he opened the next drawer. He found a packet of letters tied together by a bow underneath a pair of jeans. He thumbed through the stack. All were from Lawrence Pinto from the USS *Harvey*, variously postmarked from one year ago to last month.

"Damn," Hack mumbled, annoyed.

"What's taking you so long?" Lee yelled from the living room.

Hack quietly closed the drawer. "I can't find them. You said the top drawer, right?"

"Yes, top drawer of my dresser."

Hack scanned the room. He spotted a five-drawer dresser on the other side of the room near the window. "Oh, I see it. I was looking in the wrong place." Hack walked to the dresser, opened the top drawer, and selected a pair of white cotton panties with pink trim and red hearts printed all over it. He held it up between his thumb and index finger. "This'll do."

Hack walked to the living room, handed Lee her underwear, and then sat on the couch facing her.

"Thank you," she said, extending her legs and slipping on the panties. She sat cross-legged on the floor in front of him and smirked. "Did you get a good look?"

"Not really. You were too fast."

"You need to pay attention next time."

"You should go slower next time."

"I might not be naked next time."

"Do you always walk around nude with Angie here?"

"I wasn't walking around nude. I had a T-shirt on."

Hack sat silent, thinking of the Pinto letters.

"What's wrong with you?" Lee asked.

"I found a bunch of money in your drawer," he said, ignoring the letters he discovered.

"How did you find that?"

"It was in the top drawer of your dresser or what I thought was your dresser."

"That's my vanity, silly goose. A vanity has a mirror."

"I know that now," said Hack. "You think it's safe to have cash like that lying around?"

Lee sat up and stretched her back. "I'm careful. I need cash to pay rent and other bills. I pay Angie in cash, too." Lee crawled to the sofa and sat next to him. "Did you come here straight from the ship?" she asked, changing the subject.

"Sort of," Hack said.

"What do you mean, sort of?"

"I was leaving base with Decker and we got side-tracked. My new best friend, Inspector Navarro, stopped us on the street. We sat in his car and had a nice chat."

"The local police chief?"

Hack nodded. "Yep, he picked us up when we were crossing Shit River. We didn't have a choice. Three of his lieutenants were there to make sure we got in his car."

"Why would he want to talk with you guys?" asked Lee.

"There's something I haven't told you," said Hack. "Decker and I went to see this guy Mr. Fortuno on Saturday. Inspector Navarro knew about it somehow."

Lee cocked her head. "Who's Fortuno?"

"He's an old man who used to run the black market in town. He's someone Decker found out about from his trike driver friend, Rusty."

Lee took hold of Hack's hand. "You need to be careful, sweetie. Don't let Decker talk you into stuff like that. I can't believe you guys are still chasing this inventory thing."

"I know what I'm doing," Hack reassured her. "It just bothers me that Navarro knew about the meeting. We were careful not to be followed. Rusty helped us get there and he didn't notice anything."

"Maybe they weren't following you," said Lee.

"How else would they know we visited?"

"Two ways," Lee said. She extended her left index finger. "One, they could've been watching Mr. Fortuno's house. If he's a shady character, maybe the cops are always keeping an eye on him."

"But we didn't see anyone watching."

"You wouldn't see them. Probably watching from another house. Or maybe it was a spy. You know, some girl working at a *sari sari* store or a trike driver who the police pay for information. Wouldn't take much money. A few pesos here and there can add up for someone like that."

"What's the other way?" Hack asked.

"Perhaps the honorable Captain Navarro is in cahoots with Mr. Fortuno. Think about it. What kind of vehicle does Navarro drive?"

"I think it was a Range Rover," Hack said.

"See what I mean? I'm not sure what he gets paid, but that's a nice vehicle for a public servant in this town. You don't see police officers driving cars like that in the States."

"I guess not," Hack sighed. "I'm not sure what to think anymore."

"What did Navarro want anyway?"

"He warned us not to stick our noses into things."

"He said that?"

"In so many words."

"Well then, you should take his advice."

Hack ran his fingers through Lee's hair. "I'll try to be careful." He paused momentarily. "There's something else. Chief Fray had your name written on a piece paper he kept in his safe."

Lee looked up abruptly. "My name? Why would he write my name?"

"I don't know," Hack shrugged. "He had several names listed and Mansfield was one of them."

"Well, it's a common enough name," Lee said. "It's probably someone else. I hardly know the guy except when he calls or comes by to complain about a shipment."

"I told Decker the same thing, that it's a common name."

"What'd he say about it?" asked Lee.

"Nothing really. But I think it made him suspicious. Vega told us the local cops think someone at the supply depot is in on the black market."

"Well, it's not me! What about him?"

"Who? Decker?"

"Yeah, Decker. He's dragging you into this, but what's

his motive? To help poor Vega?"

"That's not why. She told us not to get involved," he lied.

"Then why is he doing it?"

"I told you, Kippen talked to him about an inventory problem the night he went overboard. I think it freaked Decker."

Lee smirked. "The Honorable Elliott Decker, setting out to right the supposed wrong done to Kippen. Why does he care so much? Just think about it. Was anyone else around when Kippen talked to him?"

"No, Decker said they were alone."

"See what I mean? How do you know what they talked about? Maybe Decker's the one involved in the black market and Kippen confronted him. Maybe he's the one who pushed Kippen."

"That's hardly likely," Hack said, a sliver of doubt coloring his voice.

"Is it? Maybe Decker also found out Chief Fray was on to him. And now he's getting you to do his dirty work to find out what Chief's knows. Maybe Vega's in on it, too. Everyone knows the local cops are corrupt."

"I can't believe she'd be like that," Hack said.

Lee started to say something but, instead sighed and rested her head on Hack's knees. "Let's drop it. I'm tired of talking about it."

Hack massaged Lee's shoulder and was deep in thought when Angie emerged from the kitchen, speaking Tagalog to Lee. The maid smiled at Hack and carried a plate of shrimp and rice to her room.

"She said dinner's ready," Lee translated. "Angie's shy around strangers, especially men. We eat together when we're alone, but she always takes her food to her room when someone's visiting. And before you say anything, no, I don't have men visitors anymore except for you. Before we met, of course a guy would come over once in a while."

"I'm sure Pinto used to make himself at home," said Hack, attempting to stand to go eat.

Lee grabbed his arm and pushed him back on the couch. She waited for Angie to close her door. "I told you before we only went out a couple times. Pinto means nothing to me. What's gotten into you?"

"Nothing," Hack said thinking about the bundle of letters in Lee's drawer and dinner ready in the kitchen. "Don't you want to eat?"

"I'm not hungry," she said, running her hands up and down Hack's legs. "I was surprised to see you tonight. I thought you were going out with Decker."

"I planned to, but I missed you and wanted to see you."

Lee poked Hack in the stomach. "You're a terrible liar."

"You're right," said Hack. "I left base with Decker, but he went to Vega's after our run-in with Navarro." He stroked her hair. "I did miss you, though."

Lee wrinkled her nose. "Whatever the reason, I'm glad you're here instead of out with him. Decker and his little cop girlfriend are going to get you in trouble."

"What's up with you and Vega?" Hack asked. "I thought you got along with her?"

Lee leaned back on her knees and let her hands drift to Hack's waist. "I don't know, just something about her."

Hack laughed nervously. "I doubt if I'll see much of

Vega anymore. I think she's dumping him tonight."

"Really?" Lee said. "I thought she already did, that they were 'just friends'?"

"I don't know what they are," said Hack.

A sly smile formed on Lee's face. "A breakup can be sad, but I'm glad Vega's out of the picture."

"Why's that?"

"She likes you."

"She's never said anything to me like that," Hack said hesitantly. "She doesn't really talk to me that much."

"I've seen the way she looks at you. Remember the time we all went dancing at the Sampaguita Club when we first met? It was so obvious. She had her eyes on you the whole night. She may have been screwing Decker, but her eyes were on my horny goose."

"I didn't notice anything."

"You wouldn't," Lee said. "Guys don't pay attention to that stuff, but girls notice these things. Plus, she's got a big butt and I know you like that."

"I've never noticed that either."

Lee reached up and squeezed Hack's jaw with her right hand. "I told you earlier, you're a terrible liar."

Hack started to respond but Lee put her right index finger to his lips. "Shhh." She stood and gently curled herself on the couch with her head in Hack's lap.

"Want to watch TV?" he asked, grabbing the remote from the end table.

"Okay," she yawned. "I don't know what's on, but maybe there's a movie."

Hack toyed with the remote and paused before turning on the television. "By the way, what did you decide about your orders?

"I was hoping you wouldn't ask."

"I take it you told them 'yes' to Pearl Harbor."

"I did," Lee said softly. "I have to go somewhere so I figured Hawaii was my best option. I've always wanted to visit there and now I'm going to live there. Can you believe it?"

"I don't want to believe it, but I'm sure you'll like it. I'll come visit as often as I can."

Lee squeezed Hack's hand. "I hope so. But I don't know when I'm leaving Subic. I'll get my official orders in a couple weeks. And I hope you can get stationed in Hawaii when you're time's up on the *Harvey*."

"I'll try," he mumbled.

Hack's stomach growled as he flipped through the channels. Soon he detected the rhythmic rise and fall of Lee's breathing. He stared blankly at the television, running his fingers across his girlfriend's cheek. He had a beautiful woman asleep on his lap, but his thoughts wandered first to Pinto's letters, and then to Decker and Vega, and finally to Captain Navarro and his ominous warning: *Watch your step ... people are watching ... this is bigger than you can handle ... don't get involved.*

CHAPTER TWENTY-NINE
1645, THURSDAY, FEBRUARY 20

Decker read the card for the hundredth time. He stood in a phone booth at the end of the pier, staring out the glass door. After five minutes debating with himself, he found the courage to place the call.

"Hello," a woman answered.

"Piper?"

"Yes, who is this?"

"It's me, Decker. Elliott."

"Wow, I didn't expect you to call me, but I'm glad you did. Did you get my card?"

"I did. Thank you for sending it. Sorry it's taken me so long to tell you that. I hope you don't mind me calling."

"Of course not," Piper said. "Every time I drive around base I hope I run into you. Like I told you before, I get lonely up here sometimes. No one to talk to."

"You mentioned that," said Decker. "Well, anyway, I just wanted to say hi. I'd better get back to the ship."

"Hang on," Piper said. "Why don't you come by on Saturday? Bob told me he's going to have to work on the ship all day. I'll tell you about our trip to Hong Kong."

"I don't think that's a good idea," Decker said.

"Don't worry, he'll be gone all day. He works every

Saturday. I'll show you all the stuff I bought."

"I *know* that's not a good idea," Decker said, suddenly regretting he'd called.

"And I still owe you a meal. I want you to stay long enough to eat the next time you visit me."

Decker smiled. "I'll be sure to do that. But I've got ten minutes to go before I leave for the day. I'd better get back to the ship."

"Okay, take care and think about Saturday."

"I will. I definitely will," Decker said, hanging up the phone. He opened the door, walked out of the booth, and rubbed his eyes with both hands. "What am I doing?" he said out loud. "I need to stop thinking about her and take things into my own hands."

He turned back toward the ship, laughing at what he just said.

"Petty Officer Decker, don't tell me the *Harvey's* making you talk to yourself?"

Decker whirled around. The blood drained from his face as he saluted his boss. "No, sir. I was just thinking of something that made me laugh."

Commander Doerr returned the salute. "Well, I'm glad it's not the ship," he said, joining Decker. "So how are things in Supply Support? I know Kippen's death must have been hard for everyone. I know it shocked me."

"We're getting along the best we can, sir."

"Good to hear. I appreciate the work you've been doing. I was telling my wife about that the other night."

Decker's heart pounded in his chest. "Thank you for that, sir."

"And I mean it," said the commander. "When are you

up for promotion? Should be soon, right?"

Decker nodded. "This summer, sir. I take the test in June."

The commander put his hand on Decker's shoulder. "I tell you what. Let's visit about that sometime. I can't today. I have some work I need to do at my desk. But stop by my cabin when you've got a minute and we'll talk about your future."

"I appreciate that, sir. I'll make the time soon."

"In fact, how about coming out to the house for dinner sometime?" said the commander. "Have you ever been out to navy housing? You've probably never had a reason to get out that way."

Decker shook his head. "Uh, no, sir. Never have."

"Well, it's not much, but we like it out there," the commander said. "The neighborhood's surrounded by the jungle. I think you'd like it."

"That sounds nice, sir," Decker said, looking at his watch. "I'd better be going, sir. I'll stop by and visit sometime."

The commander shook hands with Decker. "Please do, Decker. I want to talk about a career in the navy. I always hate to lose good people."

Decker followed the commander up the gangway and then veered aft towards the supply berthing while Suppo walked forward towards the wardroom. Decker met Hack getting changed at his rack.

"What's that worried look for?" asked Hack.

"I think he's on to me."

"Who's on to you?"

"Suppo. I went to the payphone on the pier to call Piper. And before you say anything, I know, it's stupid, but I wanted to say hi to her."

"It *is* stupid. What'd you talk about?"

"She wanted me to visit her on Saturday."

"Are you going to?"

"No, of course not. At least I don't think I will. But then as soon as I hung up, the supply officer walked by."

"Did he hear you talking to her?"

"I don't think so," Decker said. "But we walked together back to the ship. He said he wanted to talk with me sometime soon about my promotion. He even invited me to his house for dinner."

"I didn't think officers were allowed to do that. Isn't that called frater-something?"

"Fraternization," Decker said. "Anyway, it was the *way* he said it. He asked if I'd ever been to navy housing before. Made me think that he suspects something."

"Probably just a coincidence," Hack reasoned. "See, this is what happens when you get involved with a married woman."

"Thanks for the advice, Dad," Decker scowled. "Anyway, let's get out of here. Tonight's the night." He checked his watch. "We can be at Agana's in a half hour if we hurry. I did a little recon work a couple days ago. From the edge of base next to the archery range, I could see across Shit River to the back of Agana's building."

"What did you see?" asked Hack.

"There's a large fence around the place. I saw a forklift unloading stuff from a truck in an adjacent alley. I couldn't tell what was being unloaded, though. That's why we need to take a closer look."

"You sure you were looking at the right building?"

"Positive. I visited the quartermaster shop and studied

a map of Subic and Olongapo."

The two sailors left the ship at 1715 and met Rusty at the trike stand on the corner of Magsaysay and Gordon. Ten minutes later they were on a sidewalk at the east end of Gordon Avenue. The address Rusty gave them turned out to be a storefront in a modern looking building on the south side of the street. A small, nondescript sign read "M. Agana & Co." above the door.

The two sailors stood on the sidewalk and examined the neighborhood. A business half a block down the street from Agana's caught Decker's attention. "Hack, we're in the right spot. Look at that."

"It's a Jollibee," Hack said. "Don't tell me you're hungry?"

"I am, but that's not important now. Remember Chief's note? The mysterious 'j-bee'? It was written next to the initials A. A."

Hack's eyes widened. "Chief must've known it's close to a Jollibee."

Decker smiled. "We're in the right place. We should..."

"This looks familiar to me," Hack interrupted. "I think I've been here before."

"When were you ever out here?"

"The night I jumped in a jeepney when Biff and Dave followed me."

"And you ran into Limpert, right?"

"Yep, and we both got off here."

Decker scrutinized the buildings on either side of the street. "Where was he headed? There's not much out here except businesses."

"I don't know," Hack said. "We got out by the Jollibee. He walked east, but I lost track of him after I went into the restaurant. I guess I was too freaked out about everything to make the connection with Chief's note."

Decker thought for a moment. "Never mind that now. We've found the right place. Let's cross over and head west for two blocks. We'll cross back over to this side of the street at the intersection. We'll blend in the best we can with the foot traffic and walk back up the street and straight into Agana's."

The two sailors headed west in the midst of school kids, business people, and men and women shopping, a scene that stood in stark contrast to the hucksters, street vendors, and drunk sailors on Magsaysay.

At the corner of Gordon and 14th, they crossed the street and turned east. Decker glanced at Hack. "Look at that."

Several women, Decker counted twelve, began filing into Agana's. A few minutes later they exited the building and dispersed onto the sidewalk.

Decker stood silent watching the procession. "That's a lot of foot traffic. Someone must be in there. Let's walk in like we have a purpose. No hesitating at the door."

"I didn't agree to this," Hack protested.

"Just follow me," Decker urged, leading his friend closer to Agana's doorstep.

They exchanged glances mid-stride and took two steps to the entrance. Decker opened the large metal door and walked in as if he had been there many times before. Hack followed one step behind, peeking over his shoulder to look behind him.

"I thought I saw someone following us," Hack said.

"It's just your imagination. Don't let your nerves get to you. Act like we have legitimate business here. Which we do of course."

"No we don't," Hack mumbled.

Decker and Hack stood in a room the size of a small office. Except for an unoccupied service counter against the far wall and a security camera mounted to the ceiling, there were no furniture and decorations to be found. A door that led to the interior of the building was on the other side of the counter.

"It's empty," Hack said. "This is just an entryway. Let's get out of here."

Decker scanned the room. "Let's try the other door. I want to see what's going on back there. Maybe it's a warehouse full of navy parts. Or maybe it leads to the fenced in area." He walked around the counter and jiggled the knob. "It's locked. Damn."

"I don't think we should do that," Hack said, pointing to the camera. "You've seen the place, now let's get out of here before we get caught."

"I wish we could find out what's behind this door," Decker said, continuing to play with the door knob. "Too bad Mo's not here. He can pick any lock."

"Maybe you can ask someone for a key," Hack said.

"Who am I going to ask?"

"These guys," said Hack.

Decker spun around and saw two Filipinos standing in the doorway. A tall man with long, stringy hair tied in a ponytail blocked the exit. A bald, short man stood to his left.

Baldy turned to Ponytail. *"Kaibigan ba sila ni Pinto?"*

Ponytail shrugged. *"Hindi ko alam."*

Decker looked at Hack and mouthed the word "Pinto." He smiled at Ponytail and Baldy. "Is this the medical center? My friend here is in desperate need of help." He put his hand next to his mouth to shield Hack's view. "The clap," he whispered.

Ponytail grimaced. "No doctor here. Get out now," he grunted.

Decker smiled. "No? Oh well, we must have the wrong address. Our mistake." He pointed to his watch. "Hack, my boy, we should get going." He walked over and grabbed Hack by the shoulder and tried to squeeze past Ponytail and Baldy. "Have a nice day, gentlemen."

Ponytail stepped in front of the two sailors and grabbed Decker by the arm. "Not so fast. Who are you guys?"

"Gentlemen, there must be a misunderstanding," Decker said. "We're looking for a medical office. I can prove it if you let go of my arm. I have papers in my pocket."

Ponytail loosened his grip as Decker reached into his back pocket.

"I must've dropped them," Decker said, unable to produce any paperwork. "They're probably behind the counter."

"Stay here. I will look," Baldy said, glaring at Decker as he walked over to the counter. "Nothing is back here."

Ponytail extended his arm to grab Decker, but the sailor was too quick. He shoved Ponytail as hard as he could, sending him stumbling backwards until he tripped over his feet.

Decker and Hack hustled out the door before Ponytail could recover. They glanced to their left towards the Jollibee, then turned and walked to their right amidst Filipinos strolling along the sidewalk.

"That was a close call," said Decker. "We'll be safe on the street with people around."

"The clap?" asked Hack.

"Gonorrhea's the first thing that came to mind."

"And why me? You're the one that should see a doctor." Hack peered over his shoulder at Agana's. "I think Ponytail liked you."

"No, he had his eye on you."

Hack glanced behind him again. "Do you have any idea where we're going?"

"Let's take a right at the corner," Decker said. "We'll walk around to the back of the building. Maybe we'll be able to see what's going on from that vantage point."

"As long as we don't go inside again," Hack said.

"I just want to see what's in back. If we find navy parts stored somewhere, we'll know for sure that Agana's the one involved in the black market. There has to be another way into the place."

Decker and Hack were about a half block from Agana's when Hack once again turned to look behind him. "They're following us," he whispered to Decker.

"You sure?"

Hack glanced behind him. Ponytail and Baldy were closing fast. "Yes."

Before Hack could give another warning, Ponytail struck Decker with a blow to the back of his head, dropping him to the sidewalk with a sudden thud. Hack turned to his right and saw Baldy's fist coming straight for his face. Hack's head snapped back and he fell to his knees just as Baldy kicked him in the stomach sending him down to the sidewalk next to Decker. Coughing and wheezing, he looked up at Ponytail and Baldy looming above them.

"Don't come back here," Ponytail said. "Stay away from Agana's."

Ponytail was about to kick Decker in his ribs, but decided against it when Baldy nudged him and cocked his head toward the cop racing towards the scene. The thugs both turned on their heels and backtracked into Agana's. As soon as they were gone, Hack rolled over on his back and felt his ribs. Decker sat up, woozy from the blow to his head.

"I told you Ponytail liked you," Hack mumbled.

"He has a funny way of showing it." Decker rubbed the back of his head and tried to stand up. "Let's go to Jollibee. I need to sit down for a few minutes before we put Plan B into operation."

"Forget Plan B," Vega said, leaning over them. "Who were those guys?"

CHAPTER THIRTY

Decker squinted and focused on Vega's face. "A couple new friends. I don't think we made a good first impression. I have to say—"

Vega stopped him with a raised hand. "I told you not to visit Agana's. It's way too dangerous." She turned, surveying the crowd of people milling around. "Let's get out of here."

She helped them to their feet and escorted the sailors across the street to a cafe. "I'm in no mood for small talk. Sit down, both of you."

The two sailors complied and found a comfortable seat on a rosewood bench along a far wall. She got bags of ice from the waitress and took a seat across from them. "Here you go," she said, handing them the ice.

"Thanks," they said in unison.

"How did you know we were at Agana's?" asked Decker.

"I ran into Rusty by chance. He was acting weird so I knew something was up. He didn't want to tell me, but I got it out of him." She shook her head. "You're lucky I showed up. Tell me what happened."

Decker spent the next ten minutes detailing the note

from Fortuno, his conversation with Rusty, and their motive for visiting Agana's.

"The Mahárlika, huh?" Vega said, skeptically. "That's just a legend Marcos started in the '60s when he first ran for president. There are plenty of those stories floating around, but I wouldn't believe everything you hear."

"It's a rip-off from Marcos," Decker said. "Agana's father was a buddy of Marcos during the war. Rusty thinks Agana uses the nickname Mahárlika to either get in good with Marcos or to scare people."

"It's still just a name," Vega said. "I don't believe it's some sort of secret society."

"The Rolex 12 sounds believable," added Hack. "We saw Mr. Fortuno wearing a Rolex watch."

"Along with thousands of other people," Vega said. "Just because he has a Rolex doesn't mean he's part of a secret boys' club."

"Then why would Agana's men be so aggressive with us if they have nothing to hide?" asked Decker.

"Because you were trespassing," said Vega.

"They could've just asked us to leave," Hack sighed.

Vega crossed her arms. "You shouldn't have gone in there. I hope now you believe me. What did you expect to find anyway?"

"Something related to the missing navy parts," Decker said. "Proof that Agana's in on the black market."

"And what if you found something?" asked Vega.

Decker looked at Hack and shrugged. "I hadn't thought that far ahead. I wanted to find out what Agana has stored at the back of the building."

"Leave the detective work to the police," Vega said, surveying the building across the street. "What's the inside like?"

"It was empty," said Hack. "Just a waiting area. The door to the inside was locked. We weren't invited in."

Vega raised her eyebrows. "So what do you think is around back? The river runs behind the building."

"I looked from base," Decker said. "He's got a large fence around a piece of property between his building and the river. I bet he's got stuff stored back there."

"I don't know," Vega said, skeptically. "I can't imagine he'd be keeping material out in the open."

"But what if he is?" Decker urged.

"It wouldn't get us anywhere," Vega said. "I couldn't report it to my boss. He'd fire me for snooping around where I shouldn't."

"We don't have to tell anybody," Decker reasoned. "I'm trying to find out what happened to Kippen. I know it's not Agana's men. They weren't on the ship. But if I can prove that someone is dealing in stolen navy parts, I can go to investigators."

Vega stared out the window at Agana's. "If we do this, you guys have to follow my lead. Do as I say at all times. My job is on the line. Got that?"

They both nodded in agreement. Hack rubbed his jaw.

Vega stood and put her hands on her hips. "Don't worry, Hack. I'm in charge now." She turned towards the door. "Follow me. Let's take a left, walk a couple blocks north and double back. We'll take a quick look behind his building and get out of there."

Ten minutes later they were walking along a narrow strip of land that separated the back of the buildings from Shit River. As they approached Agana's building, Vega suddenly stopped. "We've got a problem."

"I think we've got more than one," Decker said.

"True," Vega agreed. "But take a look at the fence."

"I told you it was big."

"It's at least fifteen feet high. Maybe higher."

"Let's turn back," Hack said. "We'll never climb it. It's cinder block with nothing to hold onto."

Vega sized up the obstacle. "It'll be easy. We'll use each other to climb over."

Decker exhaled loudly. "It might be possible. Hack, you be on the bottom."

"Why me? You're taller."

"It has to be you. You're more solid. A perfect anchor."

"I don't care who's on the bottom," Vega said. "I'm on top. I need to be the one that takes a look."

"Okay, it's settled," Decker said. "Hack, you're the anchor. I'll get on your shoulders and lift Vega over the fence."

"She didn't say that," Hack said.

"Come on, guys," Vega urged. "We haven't got all day."

Hack relented and anchored himself bent at the knees with his back against the wall. Decker put his feet on Hack's knees and then climbed onto his shoulders facing the wall. Vega laughed at the sight. "I wish I had my camera," she smiled.

"Hurry up," Hack said, uneasily holding his balance under Decker's weight.

"Okay, okay," Vega said. "But how I am supposed to get up there?"

"Start climbing," begged Hack. "My ribs are hurting."

She easily made it perched on Hack's knees. "Now the hard part," she said. After a few false starts, Vega made it to Hack's shoulders with the help of Decker reaching around with his right hand to pull her up.

"Now I can climb," Vega said. "Stay still."

Vega grabbed Decker's shoulders and shimmied slowly up his back. With a lunge she got her left knee and then her right to his shoulders. Decker took his left hand and slowly pushed her upwards until she grabbed the top of the wall.

"Got it," she whispered. "And get your hand off my ass."

"It's the only thing I can hold onto," Decker protested. "What do you see?"

Vega didn't respond. She kept her attention focused on the scene in front of her. A moment later Decker felt her shift her weight.

"See anything?" asked Decker.

Vega squirmed on his shoulders. "Shit."

"Sorry, my hand slipped."

"It's not that."

"What then?"

"They know we're here."

"Agana's men?"

"Yep, I saw them exit the building. I'm coming down."

Vega slid down Decker's shoulders and jumped to the ground, rolling twice and stopping inches from falling into the river. She sat up and watched as Decker jumped off Hack.

"There were four of them this time," she said. "Let's go back the way we came. It's the shortest distance to the street."

The sailors turned but saw two of Agana's men coming towards them.

"The other direction," Hack yelled.

They turned and stopped in their tracks. Two more Agana henchmen were coming from that direction.

"We're trapped," Hack said. "Maybe we can take two of them but not four."

"Where's your gun?" asked Decker.

"At home. I'm off duty."

"We're trapped."

"We're not trapped," Vega said calmly. "There's a way out."

Decker shook his head, realizing what she had in mind. "Oh no, we're not going there."

"Would you rather stay and fight?" Vega asked.

Decker took a look at the four men closing in on them. "I can't believe I'm going to do this."

"Do what?" asked Hack.

"Last one in is a chicken," yelled Vega as she dived head first into the murky waters of Shit River.

"That, my friend," said Decker, pointing to Vega. "And we'd better follow." He jumped as far as he could into the brown water. Hack followed with a splash.

Three heads bobbed at the surface. Four men stood openmouthed at the shore. "Let's swim for it," Vega urged. "Go south with the current and stay underwater for as long as you can." She put her head underwater and disappeared.

"I'm not doing that," Decker said. "I'll just swim."

A shot fired in his direction changed his mind. The two sailors dove underwater and swam as hard they could. Neither one opened their eyes. After what seemed like minutes, but probably only several seconds, Decker popped his head above water. Hack was already treading water.

A few seconds later Vega appeared clutching a blue plastic five-gallon jug. "I ran into this," she laughed. "Let's float a while and head to shore. I doubt if they followed us. I can't even see Agana's anymore."

Five minutes later the three friends made it to shore with the help of two young women doing laundry on a concrete patch that skirted the river. The sailors didn't know what the girls were saying, but they were sure they were laughing at them. Vega thanked the women for their help and stood dripping wet wringing out her hair. "Let's go to my place and get cleaned up."

They made the eight block walk to Vega's apartment with little conversation. She greeted a group of small boys playing dice near her apartment complex's entrance. "Give me some money," she said to Decker.

"It's all wet," he replied, grabbing his wallet.

"That's okay. How much you got?"

"Two hundred pesos and change."

"That'll do," she said, taking all of his money. She turned to the two boys and spoke something in Tagalog. The boys smiled and ran off down the street.

"What was that for?" asked Decker.

"They're going to buy T-shirt s and shorts for you guys," she said. "And ice cream for themselves. I told them to let their mother know where they're going. They obviously didn't listen. Typical boys." She glared at Decker and Hack.

"So who's first in the shower?" asked Decker.

"Let's flip for it," suggested Hack.

"No way," said Vega. "This is one time when I must say it's ladies first."

The two sailors shrugged and followed Vega through

a side entrance to her apartment complex. They stood in a small courtyard surround by a wooden fence. Vega kicked off her shoes, removed her socks, and pulled her shirttail out of her jeans. "You're not wearing those clothes in my house," she warned. "Strip down out here. No one can see you. But don't take everything off," she added. "I've got neighbors."

Vega and the sailors undressed down to their underwear and piled their clothes in a smelly heap on the patio. "I'll be quick," she said, turning to unlock her door.

Fifteen minutes later she emerged from her apartment freshly showered and holding a plastic trash bag. She wore a clean pair of white shorts, a blue T-shirt, and flip-flops. She had a big blue towel wrapped around her hair on top of her head. "Next," she smiled.

Decker clapped his hands and headed indoors. Vega frowned at Hack. "How does he get to go first?"

"He won the coin toss," Hack said.

"Your coin or his?"

"His. Why?"

Vega shook her head and gave Hack a sympathetic look.

CHAPTER THIRTY-ONE
1840, THURSDAY, FEBRUARY 20

"He'll be in there a half hour at best. And another half hour working on his hair."

"I wish you had another bathroom."

"Me too," Vega said, turning behind her. "The boys are back. Wait here."

Vega returned with two new T-shirt s and shorts. She held the shirts up for Hack to see.

"I'll take the blue one." Hack said.

"Good choice." She handed him the shirt and a pair of light green shorts. "This will actually look nice together. Better than the other pair."

"I wish I could at least put the shorts on," Hack said. "It's a little embarrassing."

"Don't be embarrassed," Vega smiled. She unwrapped the towel off her head and tossed it at Hack. "Put this on if you'd like. I'm done with it."

"Thanks," Hack mumbled as he wrapped it around his waist.

Vega sat on a plastic chair and lowered her head so her wet, frizzy hair draped over her face. Hack leaned against the wall and watched as she brushed lightly until the curls straightened to her satisfaction. A flip of her head sent her long brown hair backwards. She blushed as she opened her eyes and saw Hack watching her. "Sometimes I think about cutting it," she sighed.

"It looks nice long," Hack said.

"Thanks. I like it too, but I'd fit in better at the station if I had it shorter. I'd look more like a man that way."

"I doubt that."

Vega smiled. "I'll take that as a compliment."

"It is."

Vega sat back and let out a sigh. "I know him."

"Who?"

"Agana. My brother worked for him."

"Your brother? Decker never mentioned you having a brother."

"Ato. Antonio. I don't talk about him very often. And I haven't really told Decker everything about him." She eyed Hack. "Can I tell you a secret?"

"Sure."

"It's part of the reason I moved back to the Philippines."

"To take care of him?"

Vega shook her head. "No, to take care of *Tatay*. That's the Tagalog word for 'father'. My brother's eight years older than me. He was taking care of me, but I wish I would've been able to take care of him."

"When did he work for Agana?

"When he was sixteen as soon as he graduated from high school. I know my father was worried about it. He'd write me letters and call me. He'd always try to sound positive but I always knew something was wrong."

"Does he still work for him?"

"I don't know."

"What do you mean you don't know?

"I haven't seen him in two years."

"Is he still in Olongapo?"

"I have no idea. He disappeared a week before Christmas a couple years ago and no one's heard from him since."

"Did you see him much when you moved back with your father?"

"I saw him all the time. We lived together. I was only twelve, but I took care of the house. Our father was sick at the time. Heart problem. Liver infection. Ato made a lot of money. He said he was working for a businessman. But *Tatay* knew he was up to no good. Most Filipinos don't make that kind of money."

"Did you ever meet Agana?"

"Just once. When I was a little older, probably fourteen or fifteen, I followed my brother to work one day."

"A young detective."

Vega smiled. "I guess I was. I wanted to know where he was working. I followed him to the same place we visited today. I walked in and when Ato saw me he got me out of there. But I saw Agana. He didn't speak to me but I got a bad feeling just seeing him."

"How did he get hooked up with Agana?"

"Through basketball."

"Basketball?"

"*Tatay* had big dreams for Ato. He played in high school and two years of college at Far Eastern University near Manila. *Tatay* was so proud of him. Said he was going to be the next Sonny Jaworski."

"Who?"

"Sonny Jaworski. The Michael Jordan of the Philippines."

"It doesn't sound like a Filipino name."

"It's not, but he grew up in Manila. His mom's Ilocano. I think his dad's an American."

"Your brother was that good?"

"I don't think so, but *Tatay* always bragged about him like that. The sad thing is our father died without ever knowing what happened to him."

"Why did he only play two years in college?"

"He hurt his left knee. Ended any hope he had of playing professionally."

"Where does Agana come into the picture?"

"He got a job with the San Miguel Beermen."

"My favorite team name of the Philippine Basketball Association," said Decker as he strode through the doorway wearing a red towel wrapped around his waist. He held out his underwear for Vega to take. "Of course there's stiff competition with the Tanduay Rhum Masters, Great Taste Coffee Makers, and Hills Brothers Coffee Kings."

"I'm not touching those things," she said, holding up the plastic bag. "Put them in here." She sat the bag on the patio and threw him a T-shirt and pair of shorts. "And here's something to wear. I'll let you guys borrow some flip-flops. I've got plenty of old pairs."

Decker held up the yellow T-shirt with prominent red vertical stripes. The words "I've Got Style!" were printed in white across the chest. In his other hand he held up the shorts. One leg was pink. The other orange. A bright blue stripe ran across the bottom. "You're kidding, right?"

"That's what the kids bought."

"My money paid for these things?"

"It was worth every peso," Vega laughed. "It's the irony I love best."

"Very funny," Decker said. "Hey, what did you get?" But Hack was already indoors.

Decker slipped the shorts on under his towel and put on the T-shirt . He looked at his reflection in the glass door and shook his head. "Why were you talking about Philippine basketball? I don't think Hack is much of a fan. Mo's your guy for sports talk."

"I was telling him about my brother."

"Oh."

"And his connection to Agana."

"The same Agana?"

"*Oo.* It's something I've never told you about."

"You've said he worked for a basketball team and then a local businessman. You sure it was Agana?"

"Positive."

"How did he get hooked up with him?"

"Through the basketball team. I think he was some sort of assistant to the coach with the Beermen."

"I still don't understand how that led to Agana."

"It was gambling at first."

"Your brother was involved with gambling?"

"That's what *Tatay* suspected. The government owns the casinos and those close to Marcos probably benefitted the most. Sports betting has become a big-time business since Marcos legalized gambling two years after the PBA formed in '75."

"Rusty told me Agana's father knew Marcos during the war."

"Then we can assume Agana gained access to Marcos through his father."

"But Marcos is out of the picture now," Decker said. "Rusty told me Agana's switched allegiances to Cory Aquino."

"Makes sense," Vega said. "I'm sure he's been playing both sides for a while waiting to see who would win the election. But that doesn't really matter. The problem we have—we, the police—is that he's in business."

"You're right," Decker agreed. "And it's a maze of political relationships that I don't even want to try to figure out." He started to pace around the patio. "So how does Chief Fray fit in?"

"That's your deal. I'm not so sure he's involved. *Someone* is helping Agana from inside the base, but I'm not sure it's someone on the *Harvey*. More likely it's a sailor at the supply depot. Maybe Agana even has some Filipinos working for him inside the base."

Decker folded his arms and looked at a bird flitting in a nearby tree. "Chief had the initials A.A. on a note."

"Could be someone else's initials."

"But he also had "J-Bee" written next to the initials. There's a Jollibee near Agana's."

"And several more Jollibees in Olongapo."

Decker suddenly remembered something that Ponytail had said. "I thought I heard one of Agana's men say the name 'Pinto.'"

Vega laughed. "Now Pinto is involved, too?"

"What does *kaibigan* mean?"

"Friend. Why?"

"I thought I heard that word, too."

Vega began to brush her hair again. "What would be his motive to help Agana? Or any American's motive?"

"Money. It's always about money. Or a woman."

"We can rule out a woman. No need to risk jail time for that in Olongapo. There are plenty to go around."

"Then it's money."

Vega set aside her brush and began to braid her hair. "I doubt if Agana would pay someone that much money."

"You said your brother was getting paid."

"For a Filipino it's a lot, but not to an American. Especially someone of Chief's rank. Plus, there's too much to lose if he gets caught. Significant jail time. No retirement pay. Plenty of reasons not to get involved."

Decker rubbed his chin. "Maybe Agana has something on Chief?"

"Like what?"

"I don't know. But there's a connection. We just need a break."

"A break from what?" asked Hack, emerging from the apartment freshly showered and sporting his new outfit.

"Not a break *from* something," said Decker. "But a break in the case."

"You need to stop investigating," Vega said. "Let the police handle it. I shouldn't have encouraged you guys to snoop around in the first place. And I definitely shouldn't have gone to Agana's with you. I could lose my job."

Decker ignored her. "Hey, you never did say what you saw behind Agana's place. Any Navy parts?"

"Could've been, but I couldn't tell."

"What did it look like?"

"A bunch of crates, but I didn't get a good look at them. I had a hand feeling me up and Agana's men running out the back door towards us. Not much time to look at the surroundings. I read an address on the crates, though."

"Do you remember it?"

"Mahárlika and Co. 228 Palanca St. MM"

"What's the 'MM' stand for?"

"Metro Manila."

"When are we going?"

"*We* are not going," Vega said, firmly. "Let me handle it."

"But you'll need help. Hack and I will be glad to tag along."

"Speak for yourself," Hack countered. "I'm with Vega. She can get along fine without us."

Vega stood and put her hands on her hips. "There are way too many protests going on in Manila after the presidential election. It's not a good place for Americans to be."

"We won't get mixed up in any of that," Decker said. "How are you going to get there?"

"I don't have a day off until Tuesday. Maybe I'll catch a bus."

"What about your boyfriend?"

Vega shrugged. "He works all the time. I'll take a bus."

"I've got a better idea," Decker said. "I happen to be off work that day. A planned vacation day. I'll ask Rusty to drive us. He has a friend with a car and he's mentioned this guy in Manila, Ducky, who maybe can help us." He turned to Hack. "Take the day off, too. We'll run over to Manila in the morning, let Vega take a look around Agana's place, have a quiet lunch, and then be back in Olongapo before dark. It's as simple as that."

"Nothing's ever as simple as you say," Hack said.

"A car ride rather than a crowded bus sounds nice," Vega said. "And having Rusty along would be reassuring." She sat in silence for a minute in obvious contemplation.

She finally stood and eyed the two sailors. "Okay, we can go on Tuesday, but don't wear anything yellow."

"Why not?" asked Hack.

"Cory's supporters have adopted the color. They're all wearing it. Although I support the revolution, I don't want to get caught up in it, especially with you two with me."

"What if someone sees me?" asked Decker, suddenly apprehensive.

"That's what I'm worried about," said Vega.

"I'm not talking about Agana or protestors. I'm talking about these clothes. How am I going to make it back to the ship wearing this outfit?"

Vega couldn't stop giggling. "I'm sure you won't run into anyone you know. And if you do, just tell them it's a new look for you. Maybe it'll catch on."

Decker ignored the comment and focused on Hack's attire. "How did you get those? I should be wearing them. I have my reputation to uphold."

"You showered first."

"That doesn't make any sense."

Hack smiled and put his arm around his friend. "It makes perfect sense, my boy," he said in his best Decker voice.

CHAPTER THIRTY-TWO
0825, TUESDAY, FEBRUARY 25

Rusty downshifted and gripped the wheel of the red Camaro as they sped up the hills along Jose Abad Santos Road north of Olongapo. Hack sat white-knuckled in the front seat as they zoomed past slow-moving cars, jeepneys, and buses, sometimes passing on the right. The trio finally relaxed when Rusty merged onto the North Luzon Expressway in San Fernando, paid the toll, and headed south to Manila. Forty-five minutes later they passed through the Balintawak toll gate and entered the suburb of Caloocan on the northern edge of Manila.

"Don't get on EDSA," Vega warned. "Epifanio de los Santos Avenue," she explained to Decker and Hack. "That's where most of the anti-Marcos demonstrations are taking place. Take Bonifacio into the city."

Rusty nodded and followed Bonifacio and then an array of sidestreets to the corner of Palanca and Plaza Santa Cruz streets. He pulled the car to the side of the street 100 yards north of the intersection. The MacArthur Bridge over the Pasig River loomed in front of them.

Vega studied her map. "We're close. Let's take a left on Palanca and find a parking place."

Rusty spent the next half hour circling the block,

finally locating a spot in an empty dirt lot between two low-rise apartment complexes across the street from the riverfront buildings.

"Let's walk to our left towards the Ayala Bridge," Vega said. "We'll stay on this side of the street and mix in with the pedestrian traffic."

The four friends walked among a growing number of Filipinos filing towards Malacañang Palace, most were wearing yellow, obvious supporters of Cory Aquino. A half block later Vega took Decker by the arm and pushed him into a furniture store. Rusty and Hack followed silently. Vega chatted briefly with a clerk and then pointed with her lips out the window. "Across the street. The blue building. It's the right address."

"I don't see a company name," Hack said.

"I don't either," Vega agreed. "And I don't see any open windows facing the street. They're all covered with blinds. And just the one door to the sidewalk. I'm going to watch the place for a while."

"I am going to Malacañang to find Ducky," Rusty said. "How long you going to be here?"

Vega shrugged. "I'll give it an hour."

"I'll tag along with you," Decker said to Rusty. "I've always wanted to see the presidential palace."

"There is a bank on the corner a block north," Rusty said. "We will meet you in an hour."

Decker glanced at Hack. "You coming with us?"

Hack noticed the determined look on Vega's face. He thought of her brother. "No, go ahead. I'll hang out here and keep Vega company."

"Suit yourself," Decker said, as he and Rusty exited the store. A half block later they drifted out of sight, lost amidst the people and traffic.

For forty-five minutes, Vega's eyes stayed glued on the blue building. Finally, impatiently, she said, "Let's go in there."

"I don't think that's a good idea," Hack said, nervously.

Vega took him by the arm. "There's a travel agency next door to the left. If we run into anyone, we'll tell them we're taking a vacation and must have walked into the wrong building by accident."

"You think they'd buy that?" Hack asked, skeptically.

"Sure they will. I can sell it."

"I don't know about this. Last time it was the clap."

"What?"

"Decker. That's what he told those goons at Agana's. That we were looking for a medical office because I had the clap."

Vega groaned and took Hack's arm. "No clap. I promise. Fifteen minutes max," she added, nudging Hack towards the door. "I want to check what's in there and get out."

Vega and Hack left the furniture store and jaywalked across the busy street, narrowly avoiding honking vehicles. Safely on the opposite sidewalk, Vega motioned with her head towards the door in the middle of the blue building. Hack tried the knob. Bingo.

They stood in a drab vestibule with faded white plaster on the walls. A single naked bulb dangled from the ceiling, providing the only light for a well-worn wooden staircase leading to the second floor. The shiny brass handrail looked like it belonged in a more elegant setting.

Sweat dripped from Hack's forehead. Vega exhaled

loudly and headed up the stairs, motioning for Hack to follow. When he caught up with her on the fifth step, she took hold of his hand, their fingers interlocking. "It's our cover," she whispered. "We're a couple looking for the travel agency."

At the top of the stairs they faced another door. Hack turned the knob. "It's locked."

Vega sized up the obstacle. "The transom window is open. Give me a boost."

Hack hoisted her up with his hands. She opened the window as wide as possible and wedged half her body through the portal. "I'm stuck."

"Suck in your gut," Hack suggested.

"It's not my tummy," Vega laughed. "My rear end is caught."

Hack didn't have a suggestion for that, but could only watch as Vega eventually wiggled herself through the opening, tumbling with a thud on the other side of the door."

"I hope no one heard me," she whimpered, opening the door for Hack.

They entered a long hallway with two doors along the left side. They crept along the passageway, cringing each time the wood floors creaked under their weight. They paused at the first door, listened intently for a few seconds, and tried the knob. Locked. At the second door, Vega got on her knees and listened at the threshold. No sound coming from within. She stood and tried the knob. A sly smile formed on her face as it slowly turned in her hand. They were in.

Six rows of material covered with tarps filled the interior space. The six windows along the far wall were small, letting in only a sliver of light. Hack reached for the switch. Vega stopped him with a gentle slap of his hand. "Someone could see the light under the door," she warned. "Let's look under the tarps."

Hack nodded and tiptoed with Vega to the far end of one of the aisles near a window partially blocked by a large filing cabinet. One drawer hung open. "Check out the parts," Vega said. "I'm going to examine the cabinet."

Hack nodded and lifted one of the tarps. "Look at this," he said, pointing to the military parts stacked to the ceiling. "It looks like one of the storerooms on the *Harvey.*

"Aha," Vega replied, pocketing a slip of paper. She closed the drawer and tiptoed over to Hack. "Any of these navy parts?"

"I think so. But there's not enough light in here."

Vega started to pull more of the tarp from the pallets but a noise in the hallway froze her in place. "Someone's out there," she whispered. "I hope they didn't hear us."

Hack glanced around the room. "Let's hide."

"Where?"

"Under one of the tarps."

But it was too late. The door opened and two men entered the room. One, average height but noticeably chubby, searched the room with squinted eyes. Dressed in a tank top, gym shorts, and flip flops, he walked slowly down one of the aisles. A short, squat man followed close behind. He wore jeans and a red T-shirt , torn at the sleeves and along the collar. A pile of brown, bushy hair was his prominent feature. They stopped midway down the aisle and listened. Vega and Hack stood frozen, holding their breaths.

Satisfied that no one was in the room, the two men turned to leave. They were almost to the door when a small valve, no more than an inch in diameter and three inches in length, fell from an uncovered pallet next to Hack. He flinched.

"*Sino ang nandyan?*" Chubby yelled, slowly walking back down the aisle.

No answer.

"Who's there?" Bushy Hair said, sure that he had seen movement.

Vega nudged Hack. "Follow me," she mouthed, emerging from her hiding place with Hack in tow.

The Filipinos ambled down the aisle. Vega stepped forward three paces until they were standing face to face with Agana's henchmen. "We're looking for a travel agency. We must've gotten the wrong address."

They didn't buy it.

"*Nagsisinungaling ka,*" asked Bushy Hair.

"I'm not lying. It's the truth," Vega replied.

Chubby seized Vega, spun her around, and put his other arm around her throat. She squirmed in pain as one hand crimped her arms behind her back, the other hand squeezed her neck. Bushy Hair grabbed Hack and twisted his arms behind his back.

Chubby tightened his hold on Vega. "You speak Tagalog. Okay, you are looking for a travel agency? *Saan ka pupunta?*"

Vega thought of the first thing that came to mind. The island resort she's always dreamed of visiting. "Boracay," she said, confidently.

The man swiftly covered her mouth with his right hand. "Where you going?" he said to Hack.

"I'm not going anywhere. Your friend has a hold of me."

The grip tightened, Bushy Hair nudging Hack's arms slightly upwards. He let out a cry in pain.

Vega squirmed but Chubby increased the pressure on her jaw. He stared at Hack. "I mean your trip. You are looking for travel agency."

Hack glanced at Vega for help. She pleaded with her eyes for him to say 'Boracay' but he hadn't understood the previous conversation.

Another twist of his arms. "Australia," he muttered.

Chubby laughed and dropped his hand from Vega's mouth, feeling for her back pocket. "Where you from? You have ID on you?"

She struggled against his grip, raising her right leg as high as she could. With all her strength, she lowered the heel of her shoe against his bare toes. Chubby's yell reverberated throughout the room. In a flash, she freed herself from his clutch and spun his body to her left. A karate chop to his throat stunned him. A swift kick to his groin sent him reeling backwards.

Bushy Hair flinched when he saw his friend go down. Hack broke free of his captor, elbowed him in the chest, and rushed towards Vega. Hand in hand they sprinted down the hall, slammed through the stairwell door, and slid down the brass stair rail, each sticking a perfect landing in the foyer.

Hack paused to look behind him. "No time," Vega yelled, leading him out the exit door where the late morning sunlight hit their faces. The sound of footfalls on the stairs behind them gave no time to savor the fresh air.

CHAPTER THIRTY-THREE

Hack and Vega hit the sidewalk running. They were in full stride as they passed the bank on the corner. No words needed to be spoken. Decker and Rusty fell in behind their friends and it was only as the group approached a throng of people two blocks away that they slowed their pace to a brisk walk.

"Why the rush?" Decker asked, breathing heavily.

"We went inside," Vega said. "We found a room where they've stored military parts."

"Navy stuff?"

"I think so, but I couldn't tell," said Hack.

"And then we ran into a little problem," added Vega.

"What was that?" asked Rusty.

"Two men." She glanced behind her. "I don't see them now, but they could be around here somewhere. Let's get lost in the crowd. We can be Cory supporters for a few minutes."

"I knew we should've worn yellow," Decker said.

Vega didn't reply. Another roll of her eyes spoke for her. She led her friends into the hundreds of singing anti-Marcos demonstrators gathering around Malacañang.

"What are they singing?" asked Hack.

"*Bayan Ko*," said Vega. "My Country. It's a patriotic song that Cory supporters have adopted for the revolution."

Vega started to quietly sing. "*Bayan ko, binihag ka, Nasadlak sa dusa.*" The guys smiled in amusement. "Stop it," she said, noticing their smirks. "I'm just trying to fit in." She glanced around her at the protesters. Chubby and Bushy Hair stood six feet from them, separated by several bystanders. Chubby opened the palm of his hand revealing a small switchblade. "Uh oh, let's keep moving."

"Your singing's not that bad," Decker said. "No one's going to kick us out."

"They found us," she yelled, pushing the guys forward until they were inching their way through the crowd along the outer perimeter of the Malacañang Palace grounds.

Decker scanned the crowd behind them. "How many?"

"Two."

"Let's take 'em."

"One's got a knife."

"Keep moving," yelled Decker. "But we're going to run into the river if we keep going this direction."

"Follow me," Rusty yelled, shoving people aside as the group made its way south along the fence line. "Maybe Ducky is still around."

Forty feet from the river, a hand from a Filipino army sergeant reached through a slightly opened gate and pulled Rusty into the palace grounds. The same hand plucked Decker and Hack from the crowd and into the safety of Malacañang property.

The sergeant grabbed Vega's left arm but, half-way in, she suddenly fell backwards, an equally strong hand gripping her right arm.

"You hurt my foot," Chubby bellowed, reaching for her throat with his free hand. "You see how it feels when I…"

Decker sidestepped the sergeant and delivered a right jab to Chubby's eye.

"I guess it's just not your day," Decker quipped as Chubby let go of Vega, reeled backwards, and fell into Bushy Hair, knocking them both to the ground.

The sergeant yanked Vega inside, pushed back a group of protestors, and locked the gate. He led the party across the lawn into a pocket of banyan trees out of sight from both the main house and the protestors.

"Vega and Hack, meet my friend, Ducky," Rusty said. "Thank you, *pare*. That was a close one."

"*Walang anuman*," Ducky replied. "Who were those guys?"

"They work for your old boss," Rusty said. He pointed with his lips to his comrades. "My friends are on the trail of Angelito."

Ducky fixed his eyes on the Filipino cop with obvious skepticism as Rusty filled him in on their snooping in Olongapo and Manila.

A Filipino army major in green camouflage fatigues approached the group at a trot. Ducky sprang to attention and saluted. "It's starting," the major barked to Ducky. He eyed the four people with Ducky, his eyes settling on the Americans. "Are you the ones from the embassy?"

Decker didn't skip a beat. "Yes, sir. We're here waiting." Waiting for what, he had no idea.

"Get to the courtyard," the major said. "It is going to start soon. I do not know what time the other event will happen. If it happens."

"No problem, we've got all day," said Decker, watching the major turn and walk briskly towards the main building.

Vega punched Decker in the arm. "What'd you say that for? It's only 1115 and now we have no way out."

"It sounded like the right thing to say at the time," said Decker. "And I had to protect Ducky."

"Thank you for that," Ducky said. "*Tayo na* to the courtyard. The inauguration is going to start any time now."

"Hey, we're going to witness history," Hack said.

"Maybe more history than you think," Ducky said. "We have received word that Cory had her inauguration a half hour ago at the Filipino Club. The rumor is spreading that the U.S. military is going to come in and take Marcos out of the country sometime soon. That is why the major thought you were from the embassy. We are expecting Americans to help with the process." He looked at the four stunned faces. "Stick with me. At least you're not wearing yellow."

Vega grinned at Decker as they began walking to the courtyard where a few thousand Filipinos had been bussed in to witness Ferdinand Marcos' fourth inauguration as President. For a half hour they ate sandwiches and drank coffee and waited with the rest of the crowd. At 1150 the Marcoses appeared at the balcony, the sixty-eight-year-old president looking frail in his white *barong tagalog*. His wife, Imelda, wearing a snow white *terno*, nervously paced to his immediate right. On the president's left, wearing green military fatigues stood his defiant son Ferdinand, Jr., known to the country by his nickname, Bongbong.

The crowd hushed into a murmur as Chief Justice Ramon Aquino administered the oath of office. The president followed with a twenty-minute speech, mostly inaudible to the crowd below. At its conclusion, the Marcoses waved to their cheering supporters and then retreated into the palace. It was all over in less than thirty minutes. The Philippines had two presidents.

The crowd dispersed as fast as it had assembled. Ducky emerged from the palace and led the group into an interior hall. They found a quiet space in the presidential library, a spacious room with parquet floors and elegant bookcases along the walls. "Wait here," Ducky said. "I will check the perimeter."

Ducky returned with bad news. "No way out now," he said. "Plenty of protestors at the gates. Looks like things are going to explode any minute."

They all took a seat at a table along the north wall. Decker took out his Book of Dates and began writing. Vega put her head on the table. Rusty leaned back in his chair, while Hack folded his arms and sighed. Ducky broke the silence. "Rusty told me about your adventures with Agana," he said softly. "Take his advice and stay away."

"Too late for that," Decker countered. "We're in this too deep."

"He owns the town," Ducky warned. "He's not someone to be messed with."

Vega popped her head up. "What do you mean, he 'owns the town?'"

"He has taken over the entire province from Fortuno. There was a brief power struggle, but with Marcos' protection gone, Agana gained the upper hand. That is why Fortuno retired. It was a forced retirement."

"We know Agana's running the black market," Hack added. "I saw proof of that today."

"It is more than the black market," said Ducky. "He is the new *jueteng* lord of the territory."

"*Jeuteng*?" the American sailors said in unison.

"It's a numbers game," Vega said. "Popular with everyone, rich and poor."

"Can there really be that much money in it?" Decker asked.

"A lot of money," Ducky said. "Billions of pesos a year across the country. Most of it goes into the *jueteng* lords' pockets, but a lot also goes into the pockets of politicians, police chiefs, and district attorneys. Enough money to keep everyone quiet."

"What do you know about Agana's *jueteng* operation?" asked Vega. She handed him the paper she nabbed from Agana's filing cabinet. "I've known for a long time he was involved with gambling, but I thought it was just with casinos."

Ducky studied the document. "This is a *jueteng* work sheet," he said. "No names listed to protect people. Just numbers. The two numbers in columns are the draws. The one circled was probably the one they wanted to win. It is rigged. Everyone knows it. They always pay out to the numbers with the lowest amount of bets. That is how they make so much money."

"Why do people bet on it if it's rigged?" asked Hack.

"Hope," said Rusty. "Especially for poor people. If they bet a peso and win 400, that is a big payday for them. It is part of society."

"He is right," Ducky agreed. "Each territory has a *capitalista*, the one who finances the operation. That is Agana in Olongapo. Or, I should say, it is his son, Angelito Agana Jr., although he goes by his nickname, Lito."

"I didn't know he had a son," Vega said. "How old is he?"

Ducky shrugged. "Lito is probably mid-twenties by now. His father is grooming him to take over someday. Step one is to run the *jueteng* operation."

"What are these numbers?" asked Decker, pointing to a row of letters with numbers written beside each one.

"Those are the *cobradores*. They go out each day and collect bets. They are usually women."

Decker jabbed Hack in the ribs with his elbow. "Those are the women we saw going into Agana's building."

"Probably so," Ducky said. "They report to *cabos* who collect the money and act as salesmen for the operation. The cabos report to a table manager. He runs the day-to-day operation. He reports to the *capitalista*. In Olongapo it is Lito Junior.

"Sounds like a lot of work," Hack sighed. "I can't believe they don't get caught."

Ducky laughed. "Like I said, the *jueteng* lord makes sure everyone is paid off. See these notes," he said, pointing to the bottom of the paper. "It looks like they paid 'N' 10,000 pesos this particular week. Another 10,000 went to 'G' and 5,000 each to 'L' and 'L2'."

"Who are those people?" asked Vega.

"I have no idea," said Ducky. "Maybe names or titles. Who is your police chief?"

"Inspector Navarro," Decker said.

"There you go," Ducky smiled. "Maybe 'N' is Navarro. It makes sense."

"And the district attorney is Antonio Gonzales," Vega whispered.

"The 'L's' could be someone with the same name,

maybe a senior and junior," Ducky added. "Or people with the same job title."

Vega thought for a moment. "I don't know who that could be. I'll have to think about it."

Ducky tapped the note. "This is interesting. Angelito Junior has someone helping to finance the operation. The letter 'P' shows up two times with dollar amounts. It is being paid into the operation rather than outgoing payoffs. Here is one payment for 18,450 pesos on December 27."

Vega snatched the paper from Ducky. "I don't know anyone with the name 'P'," she said, folding the paperwork into her pocket.

"Could be anybody," Ducky shrugged. He stood and put his hands on Rusty's shoulders. "I will go check things."

The hours crept by as the group huddled in the corner of the library. Decker and Hack drifted off to sleep. Vega and Rusty quietly chatted as Ducky came by to check on them from time to time. "Not yet," was all he ever said. "Crowd outside is too big. No one coming or going."

At 2030 all that changed. A hurried group of military personnel passed through the library, oblivious to the strangers lounging in the southeast corner of the spacious hall. Ducky came running by a minute later. "Marcos is leaving," he said, trying to catch his breath. "Helicopters are landing across the river in the presidential park. We need to—"

Ducky stopped talking and snapped to attention. A lean middle-aged Filipino general in full-dress military attire emerged through a door on their left. The rest of the group slowly stood, not sure what was going to happen.

The general turned to Ducky and spoke softly but firmly. "Load the boats. *Bilisan mo.*"

"Yes, sir," Ducky said. "We are on our way."

The man nodded and walked away, heading up a set of stairs and disappearing into one of the many rooms of the palace.

"That was General Ver," Ducky whispered. "Marcos' right hand man. He wants us to take some luggage to the boats waiting to cross the Pasig River. We need to hurry."

Decker saluted. "We've got our orders. And it's our ticket home."

Ducky led the group out of the library and into a passageway lined with paintings of famous Filipinos and historical events. Decker recognized depictions of Lapu-Lapu, Magellan, the Filipino-American War, the great patriot Emilio Aguinaldo, and the Japanese occupation during WWII. He was familiar with some of the former presidents: Osmeña, Quezon, Magsaysay, and, of course, Marcos. He made a mental note to someday find out who else was depicted in the murals.

Heroes Hall buzzed with activity, the mirrored ceilings making it seem even more crowded. Ducky led his new friends to a group of Filipino military men.

Soon the elevator door opened. The president and first lady emerged from the elevator and walked by their luggage.

General Ver followed a step behind. "Get this luggage across the river and into the helicopters coming from the U.S. Embassy grounds," he barked.

The military personnel gave a "yes, sir" in unison, but none of the soldiers was quick to pick up the bags.

President Marcos greeted each soldier, quietly mumbling a 'thank you' to each one. Imelda, openly weeping, shook hands with each person she passed, dabbing her eyes dry with a white handkerchief with her free hand. When she approached Decker and Hack, she paused and said "bless you" quietly to the sailors.

Hack stood speechless.

"It is an unfortunate hour," Decker said, solemnly. "My bosses at the embassy regret that it's come to this."

Vega nudged Decker to quiet him, but it went unnoticed. "Bless you," Imelda said once again and continued her final walk through Malacañang. When the first family left the hall, Ducky pulled Decker and Hack aside. "There's more luggage in the basement," he said. "I need some help."

Vega jumped in front of Decker. "I'm going, too."

"*Sige*," said Ducky. "But we have to be quick." He glanced at Rusty who waved him off, obviously wanting no part in the evening's events.

The trio followed Ducky down a flight of stairs to the basement. Ducky turned on a light. "This is below Imelda's bedroom."

Four pieces of luggage set on the floor at the end of a vestibule.

"Geez, how much clothes do these people need?" Vega said. "I counted eighteen suitcases up in the hall."

Ducky was apparently in no mood for chit chat. "Grab everything. We must hurry."

The sailors grabbed the suitcases, but a screech from Vega halted their progress.

"Check this out," she yelled from a nearby room.

"What is it?" asked Decker, grimacing at the weight of

the luggage. "These are kinda heavy."

"Shoes."

"There's more?" asked Hack.

"I don't think they're planning to take these," Vega said. "You need to see this. It's like a department store in here."

The guys dropped what they were holding and peeked into the spacious room. Hundreds, perhaps thousands, of shoes lined racks along each wall. Several more rows of shoes filled the middle of the room.

Vega sat in a chair and tried on a pair red pumps. "These would go with a dress I have."

"No time for that," Ducky urged. "Let's get moving."

"They're too big for me anyway," Vega shrugged. She hustled from the room and grabbed an oversized bag. "Come on guys, I'm waiting on you."

Ten minutes later they sat in a motor boat crossing the Pasig River, the sound of rowdy protestors filling the night air behind them. The boat tied to a pier on the south bank of the Pasig and the group carried the suitcases to a waiting Sikorsky HH-3E search-and-rescue helicopter courtesy of the American military. The first family had already boarded another chopper that was taking off from the grounds. The U.S. Air Force flight crew member noticed the Americans loading the luggage and grabbed Decker by the arm. "Where are you from?" he yelled over the thumping of the rotor blades.

"The embassy," Decker shouted.

"No you're not!"

Decker started to reply, but it was time to go. The pilot ordered the door closed, the crewman staring at Decker and Hack as the copter lifted off the ground, cleared the trees, and disappeared on its way to Clark Air Base.

Ducky led Rusty and his friends to a side entrance on the west side of the grounds, said good-bye, and watched as they walked away. The group hiked a few blocks south where they crossed the Ayala Bridge and slipped back to their car under the cover of darkness.

They arrived back in Olongapo shortly after midnight, exhausted from their day in Manila. News on the radio told of hundreds of protestors storming the palace grounds, looting what was left of Marcos' extravagance.

"That was fun," Decker said as they reached the Olongapo city limits. "Sounds like we made it out of Manila just in time."

"Speak for yourself," Hack said. "We barely made it back to our car. That's not my idea of fun."

"We made progress," Decker said. "We know the black market operation is a fact."

"We still don't have proof of Chief's involvement," Hack said. "That's the whole reason for this."

"We're close," Decker argued.

"No we're not," Hack countered. He looked at Vega for reassurance.

"You guys need to drop your investigation," Vega said, yawning. "I'm serious this time. Finding out that Agana's involved with gambling and the black market only proves what I've suspected for a long time. I just need to figure out a way to tell my boss about it. And unless you guys suddenly get a lucky break that an American's also involved, there's no reason for you to go any further with it."

"We've just had our break," Decker announced, running up to Hack in the berthing.

"What break?"

"The break in the case."

"I'm heading to Lee's," Hack said. "We can take a break tomorrow."

"No time for that," Decker urged. "Chief is on his way to Agana's."

"How do you know that?"

"I overhead a telephone conversation from the storeroom. I think it was with his wife."

"He said he was going to Agana's?"

"Not exactly. He said he was heading 'there.'"

"'There' could be a lot of places."

"I don't think so. He was secretive about it. He changed the subject when I climbed up the ladder. We need to follow him."

"I'm not doing that again. Plus, Vega told us not to go there again. I'm going to follow her advice this time. And you should, too."

"All we have to do is get to Agana's before Chief. We'll sit in the Jollibee and watch what he does."

"No way," Hack said. "I'm not going near that place again. Next time it might not end so well for us."

"Alright," Decker said, taking a deep breath. "I'm going alone." He strolled out the berthing, determined.

Hack punched his bunk mattress and cursed under his breath.

* * *

Twenty minutes later the sailors sat at the Jollibee in a corner booth facing the window to the street. They ordered hamburgers and fries and ate slowly, patiently watching the building for thirty minutes. No one entered or exited the business.

"Not much activity today," Hack said, fishing several folded pieces of paper from his back pocket.

Decker nodded while eating a French fry. "I doubt if it's a business people routinely visit. Most of the activity probably happens through the back entrance."

"Here you go," Hack announced, tossing the papers on the table.

"What are these?" asked Decker.

"The requisition lists. Against my better judgment, I did a quick inventory of the high priced items yesterday."

Decker studied the papers in front of him. "I take back all the bad things I've said about you."

"I'm thrilled to hear that."

Decker quickly flipped through the documents. "The requisitions from December 24 and January 2 are obviously bogus," he said, pointing to the papers. "The expensive parts never arrived on board. The same with the January 21 list." Decker looked up at Hack. "If your inventory is accurate."

"It's accurate," said Hack.

"Just checking your confidence level," Decker smiled. "The others seem to be legitimate requisitions. All of the parts are on board where they're supposed to be." He handed the papers back to Hack. "Unfortunately, these don't tell us anything new."

"What are you talking about? We have proof that someone on the *Harvey* is illegally ordering parts."

"We've always suspected that," Decker said. "But the lists don't tell us who placed the orders."

Hack folded the papers and placed them back into his pocket. "So what are we going to do?"

Decker stared out the window towards Agana's. "We sit here and wait. Maybe we'll see something."

"We could be here all night."

"Let's give it a few minutes. I have a feeling about this."

"I was afraid you were going to say that," Hack sighed.

They sat at Jollibee for another twenty minutes and were contemplating heading back to base when they noticed a man enter Agana's building. He was Filipino but neither Decker nor Hack got a good look at him.

"That's the first person we've seen go in or out of that place," Hack said, looking at the clock behind the counter. "And it's been nearly forty-five minutes."

"He was a businessman," Decker said. "Not your typical person walking down the street.

"A businessman? He didn't look like it to me. He wasn't wearing a suit."

Decker shook his head. "He wouldn't be. He was wearing a *barong tagalog*, and nice slacks and shoes. That's business attire in the Philippines."

"Let's wait to see if he comes out," Hack said.

Fifteen minutes later the man exited the building, turning right and heading east away from the Jollibee until Decker and Hack could no longer see him.

"I think he got in a car," Decker said, craning his neck to see out the window. "I'm not sure, though. I might've lost sight of him. I saw a car pull up to the sidewalk and pick someone up. I couldn't tell if it was him or not."

Hack sighed. "We've been here about an hour already and only one person went in to Agana's the entire time. At this rate we'll see two more people the rest of the night. I think we're wasting our time."

"Maybe so," said Decker, keeping his eyes on Agana's front door. "And then there's Pinto."

"Pinto? What about him?"

"Remember? I thought I heard Baldy say 'Pinto' the other day."

"I thought I heard that, too," Hack said. "But he was talking too fast and I don't know any Tagalog."

"And he also said *kaibigan* which Vega said means 'friend.' I think he was asking if we were friends of Pinto."

Hack sat back in the booth. "Now you think Pinto's somehow involved?"

"I have no idea. But why would they say his name? And why would they even know the guy?"

"Maybe it's just a coincidence. It could've been a Tagalog word that sounds like Pinto."

"Maybe so," said Decker. "But maybe ... well, I'd better not say."

"Say what?"

"Maybe Pinto *is* involved at some level. We know he has a connection to the supply depot."

Hack sat up. "Don't go there."

"It's just a theory."

Hack paused momentarily before speaking. "She's not involved. I'm sure of it."

"You hesitated," Decker said. "What's going on?"

"It's nothing. I found some money at Lee's a while back."

"What do you mean you found money?"

"I was getting something in her dresser and discovered cash she had hidden underneath some clothes. Six hundred dollars."

"That's interesting," Decker observed. "I wonder if—"

"She said it was for rent and bills," Hack interrupted. "Lee's too honest to get into something like a black market scheme."

"I'm sure you're right," Decker said, taking the final bite of his hamburger. "Forget I said anything."

The two sailors sat in the booth without speaking for five minutes, Decker reflecting on the chain of events of the past few weeks. He finally broke the silence. "Let's get out of here. We'll try again tomorrow."

Decker began to stand when someone across the street caught his eye. "Holy shit!"

Hack turned to look. "What's Chief doing here?"

"We've got him," announced Decker.

"Maybe he's running an errand," Hack countered. "See, he went into that grocery store."

"He could be doing a million things. But the fact is he's walking up the sidewalk towards Agana's."

"So were we," Hack reminded his friend.

"And we came out here because of Chief's conversation I overheard. We're finally getting somewhere. Let's watch him."

"What, exactly, are we going to do if he goes in Agana's?"

"Nothing. We'll just watch him."

"What good will that do?"

"It'll prove that he's involved with Agana. A known black market operator."

"It'll prove nothing," Hack said. "It'll prove that we saw him walk into Agana's, but he could say he walked in there by mistake or even say that it never happened. It'll be our word against his."

"*We'll* know," Decker said. "And then we'll be able to go to someone with the information. It may not be provable in a court martial, but it'll connect this dot for us."

Fifteen minutes later Chief Fray emerged from the store carrying a brown plastic bag. He walked slowly up the street, towering over the Filipino pedestrians in his midst. He slowed almost to a stop at the entrance to Agana's, pausing briefly to examine the door before opening it.

"He's inside," Hack said. "Now what?"

Decker glanced at his watch. "Let's see how long he stays in there."

Chief Fray walked out five minutes later, actively engaged in a conversation with another man.

"There's Ponytail," Decker said. "More proof that Chief's involved."

"It doesn't look like a friendly discussion," said Hack. "They seem to be arguing. I think that's all Ponytail knows how to do."

"Could be a disagreement over a shipment."

"Maybe we should do something."

"Do what?"

"I don't know," said Hack. "What if it turns into a fight?"

"Then we watch the fight. My money's on Chief. He's got at least fifty pounds on the guy."

"At least that," said Hack. "But I'm not so sure he'd win. He's too slow. There's Baldy."

Seeing that he was outnumbered, Chief turned to walk away, retracing his steps towards the grocery store. Baldy and Ponytail started to follow but were held up by a third man that appeared on the sidewalk.

"That could be Agana or his son," Decker said. "We need to follow Chief."

"I'm not going out there now," Hack protested. "They'll see us and it'd be a rerun of our previous encounter."

"I don't see them anymore," Decker said. "They must've gone inside."

Chief walked down the sidewalk obviously angry at something, talking to himself and swinging his arms. At the intersection in front of Jollibee, he flagged a jeepney, hopped in, and headed toward base. Decker and Hack ran out of the restaurant and hailed a trike. Decker handed the driver a hundred pesos and told him to follow the jeepney carrying the big American.

"Don't get too close," Decker advised. "We don't want him to see us."

"I am very good at following people," the driver said. "You stick with me. I am an expert driver."

As they made their way back to base, the driver skillfully kept his trike a safe distance from the jeepney. Two blocks east of Magsaysay, Decker touched the driver's arm to stop. He eased the trike to the sidewalk. "There's your jeepney," the drivers said, pointing with his lips.

"*Salamat*," said Decker, closely watching the people emerging from the back end of the vehicle. Two old women. One old man. A mother with three young kids. Two high school kids. And finally Chief Fray.

"He's going back to base," Decker said.

"Looks like he's headed in that direction," Hack agreed. "Do you want to follow him?"

"I don't think we'll be able to. He'll probably have his car there or his wife will be waiting for him. He doesn't strike me as the type who likes to walk."

They both laughed and watched Chief Fray cross the street between blocks making his way towards the Shit River Bridge. They didn't see, nor did Chief Fray notice, the jeepney barreling down the street. Decker and Hack saw it only after the vehicle zoomed by them. No passengers inside. Just a lone driver.

Chief Fray turned around, but had no time to react. The front end of the jeepney hit him with a force that sent him flying forward, his head bouncing on the pavement, his arms and limbs swinging wildly at his side as if he were a rag doll. The jeepney turned right down an alley and sped away.

Decker and Hack and the trike driver sat stunned. The driver started the engine, but Decker grabbed Hack and pulled him out of the motorcycle. He motioned to the driver to cut the engine.

"What are you doing?" Hack said. "We need to help him!"

"Look who's already there to help," Decker said, pointing to a man kneeling beside Chief Fray's body.

"It's Ponytail," Hack said. "How did he get here?"

"Don't you get it?"

"Get what?"

"This was a set up. That jeepney didn't have any passengers. They always have passengers."

"You think it hit Chief on purpose?"

Decker nodded. "Absolutely. It was going way too fast. I've never seen a jeepney drive like that. They always go slow so they can pick up and drop off people. That's how they make a living. And then as soon as Chief is hit, it disappears and the first person on the scene is one of Agana's goons. A helpful bystander there to provide first aid."

"What's if he's doing more harm than good?" Hack pleaded with Decker.

"I doubt if that's possible. Chief was probably gone by the time his head hit the pavement. That jeepney had to be doing fifty or sixty miles an hour. Chief didn't have a chance."

A crowd of people gathered around Chief Fray's body, the sounds of police and ambulance sirens blared in the background. An ambulance arrived at the scene, followed closely by a green Range Rover.

"It's time to go," Decker said.

"Let's stay and watch the crowd. Maybe we can learn something."

"I just saw Captain Navarro arrive. He's parked on Magsaysay. I can't see him but I know that's his vehicle."

"You've convinced me," said Hack. "Let's get out of here."

Decker paid the trike driver another forty pesos. "Let's go find Mo. We need to talk. Something tells me this may be just the beginning of our investigation."

CHAPTER THIRTY-SIX
1910, THURSDAY, FEBRUARY 27

"Jesus, what the hell happened," Mo said, as Decker and Hack sat at the table. "You look awful."

"Chief's dead," Decker announced.

Mo sat back in disbelief. "Chief Fray? What are you talking about?"

Decker spent the next five minutes telling Mo an abbreviated version of events.

"Tell you what. I'm buying," said Mo, glancing around the bar for an available waitress. "So what were you doing at Agana's this time?"

Decker frowned. "We watched the place for several minutes from a Jollibee."

"And I wanted to leave," interjected Hack. "I should've been more persuasive."

Decker ignored the comment. "We're lucky we stayed. We wouldn't have seen Chief otherwise."

"How long was he in Agana's?" Mo asked.

"Not long, just a few minutes," said Decker. "He ran into the same guys we did the other day."

"Did Fray see you two?"

Decker shook his head. "No, he had no idea we were watching him."

The three sailors sat quietly at their table lost in their own thoughts. When their second round arrived, Hack broke the silence. "I feel bad for the kid. His wife, too. They probably know by now if they were home."

"And we have to tell someone what we've found," Decker added.

"Who?" asked Hack.

"Commander Doerr would be the logical choice. It's Thursday now. Tomorrow will be a zoo on the ship with Chief's death. But Suppo will probably be at work Saturday. I'll talk to him then after things quiet down."

"How do you know he'll be at work on Saturday?" asked Mo.

Decker glanced at Hack. "Because his wife told me. I called her before I left the ship yesterday."

Mo shook his head. "I knew you couldn't leave that alone."

"I *did* leave it alone. She invited me out to her house last Saturday. I told her I'd think about it, but I never showed up. She said that he works most Saturdays."

"You're going to give in eventually if you keep calling her," Hack said. "But that's your problem. I think we ought to wait until Monday and see what people are saying about it."

"We can't sit on this," Decker countered.

"Why not? If we start talking, then people will know what we've been up to."

Decker sat back in his chair. "It's time to bring in the pros. Chief's no longer involved, but Agana's still operating the business."

"Not our concern anymore," Mo said.

"Of course it is," Decker said, staring at Hack. "And

then there's Pinto."

"Pinto?" Mo asked. "What's up with him?"

"Nothing," said Hack. "Decker thought one of Agana's men mentioned Pinto the other day. But the guy was speaking Tagalog and I had no idea what he was saying." He turned to Decker. "It was our concern when our lives were at risk. Or I should say when your life was at risk. Let the navy figure out what's going on with the missing parts."

"That's why I think we should tell someone," said Decker. "Kippen's dead. Our number one suspect is dead and something is bothering me. I can't put my finger on it, but it's nagging me." He saw a familiar face walk into the bar from the back entrance. "Wait, we've got company."

Out of breath, Vega hurried over to the table. "I thought I might find you guys here. I saw you when I got to the scene, but then you disappeared."

"We didn't want to have another chat with your boss," said Hack.

"Smart thinking," Vega said. "I don't think he saw you guys, but, in case he did, you'd better get out of here."

"Let's go to Lee's apartment," Decker said. "You think she'll mind?"

"Yes," Hack said. "But she doesn't stay mad for very long. You coming along, Mo?"

"Might as well," Mo sighed.

"Take the back way," Vega advised.

The three sailors exited Cal Jam out the back door and made their way to the trike stand on Gordon out of sight from the police who were still working the scene of the accident.

Rusty waved to the sailors as they rounded the corner. "What is going on, *pare*? Lots of excitement."

"It's a long story," Decker said. "I'll fill you in on the way."

"Okay," Rusty said, worried. "Where to?"

"Lee's apartment," Hack said, climbing in the sidecar. "It's 501 Jones Street."

Rusty kick started his bike and nodded towards the jeepney accident. "Must've been a bad accident. Too many cops around for my liking."

"That's part of the long story," Decker said, sitting sideways on the bike's seat behind Rusty. He turned to Mo. "I'll ride with Hack. I don't think the bike can take your weight."

"Great," Mo mumbled as he waved to another driver. He started to enter the trike but a hand grabbed his shoulder. Mo turned to see a retired sailor, probably in his 60s, standing to his side.

"Mind if I share a ride?" the old man asked.

"I guess not," said Mo, clearly irritated at the inconvenience.

Decker laughed at Mo and sped away with Hack in Rusty's trike. Ten minutes later Mo trudged up Lee's stairs and entered her apartment.

"What the hell took you so long?" Decker asked.

"Some old retired sailor wanted to ride along. I couldn't say no."

"That's sweet," Lee said. "Looks like you're the only one who didn't get mixed up in all this."

"I was smart enough *not* to go along," Mo said, laughing at the sight before him. Decker was lying sprawled on the couch, Hack slouched in a recliner.

Angie was cleaning in the kitchen, preparing what smelled like pancit and rice.

Mo sat on the floor and turned to Lee. "Did they tell you what happened?"

"They did," Lee said. "They shouldn't have gone there."

"That was Vega's advice," Decker said.

"You should listen to her next time," Lee said. "You guys are going to end up like Chief Fray if you keep snooping around like this."

"I hope I don't end up like that," Mo said.

Lee smiled at Mo. "You're smarter than that, Maurice."

Decker and Hack snickered at hearing Mo's real name. Lee silenced them with a glare.

"No, I mean like that old man that rode in the trike with me. He probably retired here thinking his money would go farther than in the States. Now he's a drunk living paycheck to paycheck. Nothing to show for his twenty years except an old ballcap from the *Zellars* and twenty-three tattoos."

"You counted the tattoos?" Hack asked.

"No, just a guess. He had a lot of them."

"I don't see you living like that." Decker thought for a second. "The hat maybe. And definitely a drunk. But not that many tattoos. Maybe ten or twelve, but not twenty-three."

"Gee, thank you for the confidence."

"Don't listen to him," Lee said. "A guy like that has problems. You see a lot of them around here. Most retired guys don't live like that."

"I know you're right, but it still makes me—"

"Wait." Decker interrupted, sitting up quickly. "What

did you say he was wearing?"

"I didn't."

"Yes you did."

Mo shrugged. "I don't know. He had on an old shirt and jeans. I didn't really look at him too closely. You saw him, too."

"I wasn't paying attention," Decker admitted. "You said he was wearing a hat. What ship was it?"

"*Zellars*. USS *Zellars*. I noticed it because I had a friend with that name in middle school. Tommy Zellars. Skinny little obnoxious kid. Why?"

Decker looked at Hack. "Does the name Zellars ring a bell?"

"No, should it? I don't know many ships' names."

"It's not a ship I've heard of either. But I know it from somewhere."

"If we see the old man again, we'll ask him about it."

Decker paced the room. "I don't care about him. It's the name on his hat that interests me." He walked over to the recliner and tapped Hack's foot. "Where's the copy of the note you got from Chief's safe? The one with the names on it?"

"On the ship. Why?"

"Let's go," Decker said.

"Now? We just got here."

"Yes, now. Come on Mo. You come along, too."

"Do I have to?" Mo protested. "It smells like food's about ready."

"Yes, we're going to need more brain power."

Mo slapped his hands on his knees and stood. "Great. I knew you'd drag me into this sooner or later."

CHAPTER THIRTY-SEVEN
1950, THURSDAY, FEBRUARY 27

"Someone's been in my locker," Hack said. "I'm sure of it. Things have been rearranged."

"How can someone get in there?" Decker asked, skeptically. "It has a lock on it. A combination lock."

"I can't tell you how it happened. All I know is that someone was in here."

"Did you give anyone your combination?" Mo asked.

"No, the only one who knows the combination is Lee. She was with me when I bought it. I set it with her, but she couldn't have come on board and gotten in here."

"Highly unlikely," Decker said. "Which means you're probably mistaken. I suspect you came in drunk one night and messed things up. Happens all the time."

"I haven't been drunk," Hack said. "But I was in my rack late last night and I didn't turn my light on."

"Are the copies still there?"

"No."

"What do you mean, no?"

"I mean they aren't in here. I've never put them in my rack."

Decker looked at Hack, confused. "I thought you said that's where you keep them?"

"Not *in* my rack. Next to it. I just needed to get some money." Hack closed his locker and locked it. "See, the copies are back here." He reached behind his bed and peeled back a small piece of insulation. "I noticed that there's a secret hiding place in the bulkhead if I pull back this insulation. I put the papers in here."

"Smart thinking," said Decker. "Let's have a look."

Hack spread the papers on his mattress. "Here it is," said Decker. "The list of names. Allen Sumner on top. There's Zellars."

"The ship name on the hat the old man was wearing," Mo said.

"Exactly," said Decker. "We were thinking they were people's names. They probably *were* people's names, but I bet they're all ship names and there's only way to find out. Let's go see the Joker."

"Who?" Mo asked.

"The Joker," Hack said. "At the library. Wears make-up that makes her look like the Joker from Batman."

"Do you guys have nicknames for everybody?" Mo laughed.

"Almost everybody," Decker said, leading the three sailors toward the exit. He stopped them near the doorway. "No one's in here. Let's have a look around."

"A look around where?" asked Hack.

"At Pinto's rack," whispered Decker. He turned to Mo. "You can pick a lock, right? You opened my rack when I lost my key a couple months ago."

"I don't like the sound of this," Mo said. "If we get caught, it'll be Captain's Mast."

Decker thought for a moment. "Hack, you be lookout. Stay here at the entrance and yell if anyone comes in."

"What am I going to yell?"

"Reveille," said Decker.

"Reveille?"

"Just say anything," Decker said. "And try to stall them."

"I'll try," Hack said as Decker and Mo walked to Pinto's rack on the port side of the berthing.

Decker watched nervously as Mo took a small tool from his key chain and inserted into the lock. "It's a cheapy," Mo said. "I've about got it." A few seconds later, the pin tumblers opened. "*Voilà*," he announced.

"You're a genius," Decker said. "Now let's have a look." He opened the rack and did a quick scan of the contents. "He's too neat. Everything's folded and stowed like he's in boot camp. Here, hold it open."

Mo held the lid to the rack open as Decker quickly rifled through Pinto's belongings. A sweep of his hand under folded uniforms uncovered several magazines. "Check this out. It could be a clue."

"It's a *Penthouse*," Mo said.

"He's got a stash of them." Decker flipped through the pages to the centerfold, holding it open for Mo to see. "Now those are impressive."

"Good genes," Mo said.

"And a little surgical help," Decker said, returning the magazine to its hiding place. He felt around in another compartment. "Aha, what do we have here?"

"It's a bunch of letters," Mo said. "So what?"

"Look who they're from," Decker whispered.

"Oh," Mo mumbled.

Decker pointed to the postmark dates. "Looks like Lee's been writing Pinto when we've been out to sea.

Most of them are old." Decker held up a blue envelope. "But check this out," he said, opening the contents. "She sent him a birthday card last month." Decker began to read the card when he heard the alarm.

"Hey you guys coming?" Hack yelled from across the berthing. "It's reveille time."

Decker threw the letters and birthday card in the rack as Mo closed the lid and secured the lock. They rounded the corner and saw Hack standing by himself at the door.

"I thought someone came in?" asked Decker.

"Someone did," Hack whispered, pointing to the other side of the berthing. "I don't know his name, but he went to the starboard side."

"You scared the hell out of us," said Decker. "But mission accomplished."

"Did you find anything?" asked Hack.

Decker glanced at Mo. "No, nothing of interest to our task at hand. Some well-hidden magazines that I'd like to borrow from him, but that's all. Let's get out of here."

Ten minutes later, Decker, Hack, and Mo sat at a table in the corner of the library. The Joker eyed them skeptically at first, but resigned herself to the idea that the sailors were, in fact, in the library to do research. Several volumes of Jane's military books were spread out on the table before them.

"Here it is," Decker said. "The USS *Zellars*. The ship was an *Allen M. Sumner* class destroyer. In service from 1944 to 1969. Here are the other names that were on Chief's note. The USS *James Owens*, USS *John Thomason*, USS *Wallace Lind*, USS *Brush*, USS *Stormes*, and USS *Hank*. All built during WWII. And, get this, the *Zellars* was sold to Iran in 1973. It's now the *Babr*. The *Stormes* was also sold to Iran. It's now the *Palang*.

"Are you guys thinking what I'm thinking?" asked Mo.

"That we may have found the missing link to Chief's black market scheme?"

Mo shook his head. "No, it's time for dinner. We left Lee's before the food was ready."

"Is that all you can think about?" Decker said.

"A man has to eat."

"You have a point," Decker agreed. "Come on, Hack. Let's find a Xerox machine and get out of here."

Decker and Hack made copies of the pages that listed information on the ships written in Chief Fray's note. Thirteen ships in all, including a page on the lead destroyer of the class, the USS *Allen M. Sumner*.

They hiked the two blocks to the Spanish Gate cafeteria and found a booth in the back corner away from other people. Hack didn't order anything to eat. Decker ordered a coke. Mo ordered The Battlewagon. A half-pound hamburger. And fries. And a coke. They spread the documents in front of them.

"Okay, here's what we've got," Decker said. "The navy commissioned fifty-eight *Allen M. Sumner*-class destroyers during World War II. Most of the ships were decommissioned in the late 1960s and early '70s. Several were sold to other countries."

"I had no idea we sold our ships," Hack said.

"Happens all the time," Mo said. "I once read that we even built ships specifically for another country. The *Kidd*-class destroyers were built for Iran. The revolution happened before they could take delivery of them."

"It does happen frequently," Decker said, reading

from the documents. "Several of the *Sumner* class ships were sold to foreign countries. Four went to Argentina, two to Venezuela, one to Turkey, two to Korea, four to Brazil, two to Chile, two to Columbia, one to Greece, eleven to Taiwan, and the *Zellars* and *Stormes* to Iran."

"What's this mean?" asked Hack.

"This has to be the end game of the black market," Decker said. "It makes sense. The navy sells the ships to a foreign country. Someone, probably Agana, steals parts from the navy and sells them to the countries. And he had help from someone like Chief Fray."

"Or Pinto," Hack added. "You thought Agana's men mentioned his name."

"Or Pinto," Decker agreed. "They both have, or, in the case of Chief, had access to order parts. But we saw Chief at Agana's, and we know that he was topside the night Kippen went overboard."

"Where was Pinto that night?" Hack asked.

"I have no idea," said Decker. "He was doing his exercises the last I saw of him. I fell asleep and when the man overboard alarm sounded, he wasn't in his rack."

"He could've been topside," Hack argued. "We can't rule him out as a suspect. There's no other reason why Ponytail and Baldy would know his name."

"Don't forget, Chief Fray was also researching these ship names," Decker said, pointing to the list. "We have no proof that Pinto was doing the same."

"Why would Chief do the research?" Mo asked. "If he's involved, then why worry about it?"

"Maybe he initially had no idea where the parts were going," Decker said. "I assume, and, mind you, I'm no expert in the black market, he probably got involved without knowing the details. Just an easy way to make a few bucks selling navy material, stuff that didn't seem valuable to him. Then he got curious."

"Maybe he was having second thoughts about it," Hack added.

"Perhaps," Decker agreed. "Maybe he found out where the parts are going and decided that he no longer wanted to be a part of it. Especially if the parts are going to Iran, which I suspect is where most of the stolen material ends up. That's why I want to tell someone."

"Why don't you follow Pinto like you did Chief?" asked Mo. "Or did you ever think about the possibility that there's more than one person involved?"

"A conspiracy?" Hack said.

Decker leaned back in his chair. "Whatever it is, I think we're in over our heads."

"No kidding," Mo said. "I knew that from day one."

"I have to agree with you," Decker added. "Two people are dead and I came close to being shot. It's getting hot around here, and I'm not talking about the weather."

Hack suddenly held up his hand. "Hang on, guys. Check this out," he said, pointing to a ship in the book.

"The USS *Mansfield*," Mo said. "DD-728. So?

Hack grinned at Decker. "See, I was right. Chief didn't write Lee's name in his list. It was a ship's name. An *Allen M. Sumner* class destroyer."

"Ah, but it doesn't explain the cash you found in her drawer," Decker said. "How do you explain that?"

"What cash?' asked Mo.

Decker pointed to Hack. "Our friend here found cash in Lee's dresser. A few hundred dollars. It seems odd to me. And we know someone's involved at the Supply Depot."

Mo and Decker stared at Hack. "Hey, she said it was for rent and to pay bills. And she doesn't stay in touch with Pinto."

Decker glanced at Mo. "But who pays bills in cash?"

"Hell, I do," Mo grunted. "I don't write many checks for things. It's hard for some Filipinos to cash them so they'd rather have cash. U.S. dollars. Hell, I have cash stashed at my place most of the time, but I'd better not catch you guys snooping around in my dresser."

Decker put a hand on Mo's shoulder. "That's one thing you don't have to worry about, my friend. After all, as our official locksmith, we'd need you to break in."

CHAPTER THIRTY-EIGHT
1320, SATURDAY, MARCH 1

Decker stepped aboard the *Harvey* and had second thoughts. The confidence he'd had the past two days had suddenly vanished. Instead of heading to the commander's stateroom, he decided to take a detour to Supply Support to collect his thoughts.

He walked through the ship ignoring everyone who asked him what he was doing on board on a Saturday with no duty, his mind on the task in front of him. At the door to Supply Support, he hesitated, slowly inserting the key and turning the knob. He took one step into the office and didn't know who was more startled: himself or Ensign Limpert.

The ensign jumped in his chair and quickly tried to cover the computer screen.

"Sorry to scare you, sir," said Decker. "I didn't expect to run into anyone down here."

"Petty Officer Decker," Ensign Limpert said. "What are you doing, um, do you have duty? No you don't. I know that."

"That's what everybody's asking me today," Decker said. "No, sir, no duty today. I came on board to talk with Suppo about something."

"He's been here since, um, I think he came early this morning. He told me, well, I have to go."

"No need to leave," Decker said. "I can let you get back to whatever you were doing."

Ensign Limpert smiled and nervously fumbled with the keyboard. "I, um, it was just … well, I was just playing a game."

"A game?"

"Yes, well, a video game. I don't usually spend my time, you know, I just thought I'd play a while. It's golf."

"I didn't know you play golf, sir. Never have taken up the game myself."

"I don't really play, but, um, I just like to, well, it's just a computer game."

Decker felt the ensign's uneasiness and decided it was time to accomplish the task at hand. "You know what, sir? I'll let you get back to the computer. I want to catch Suppo before he leaves."

Decker walked out of Supply Support and laughed as he remembered Olivia Fortuno's nickname for Limpert, "Ensign *Malata*." He walked forward and up one level to Officer Country. A few paces aft of the wardroom, he stood in front of Commander Doerr's stateroom and put his ear to the grey metal door. He could hear the supply officer busily typing on a keyboard, the sound echoing in the tiny room. He thought about walking away, but forced himself to knock. "Sir, do you have a minute? It's Petty Officer Decker."

"Just a sec," said the commander. "I'll be right there."

Decker waited for two minutes as he heard the commander shuffling papers and tidying his room.

Commander Doerr opened the door a moment later.

"Come on in, Petty Officer Decker. Do you have duty today?"

"No sir," said Decker, looking around the stateroom. The commander was out of uniform, wearing jeans and a dark green polo shirt. Paperwork lay strewn across the floor. The computer, Decker noted, was turned off.

"Well, what brings you to the ship today? It's a weekend. You should be out doing something. Anything but walking around here."

"I plan to, sir. I just wanted to talk with you about something."

"You sound serious. Shut the door and come in and sit down."

Commander Doerr got up and removed books from his bunk. The supply officer sat on the mattress and offered Decker his chair, the only seat in the tiny stateroom. Decker spent the next twenty minutes telling the supply officer about his conversation with Kippen, what he knew about the missing inventory, his suspicions about Chief Fray and possibly Pinto, the black market business in town, and what he had learned about Agana and how it tied together with the missing parts from the *Harvey*.

When Decker finished, the commander stood and paced around the small room.

"This is serious news, Decker," the supply officer said. "Have you or Wilson told anyone else?"

"No, sir," said Decker. "I'm not sure what we have so I wanted to tell you first. The investigator gave me his card and told me to call if I had anything further to tell him. I was thinking about doing that."

"I would advise against that, Decker. Not yet anyway.

Why have you and Wilson been doing this?"

"I became convinced Kippen's death wasn't an accident or suicide."

"Why do you say that?"

"Because of my conversation with him the night be went overboard. Looking back on it, Kippen was worried about missing parts."

Commander Doerr nodded. "Did you tell the investigator about this?"

"I mentioned it, but he apparently didn't think it was a problem."

"Well, I'm glad you came to me," said the commander. "In fact, I know about the missing inventory. The investigator mentioned it to me before he left the ship. It was the first I had heard about it."

"Did you talk to Chief Fray about it?"

"I did and I've been waiting on a report from him. I guess now I won't be receiving that. I've spent the morning gathering Chief's personal effects. It's a difficult part of my job. I've had to do it twice now in a month and it doesn't get easier."

"I'm sure it doesn't, sir."

"Even if he was involved in something like a black market business, it's tough to talk to the wife and children. Between you and me, though, I believe you're right about Chief."

"What about Pinto?" asked Decker.

"I don't think Pinto's involved. Seems unlikely to me. Chief Fray, though, is a different story."

"Why's that, sir?"

"This is top secret, Decker. Got that?"

"Yes, sir. Of course."

"Did you know he was planning to retire in another year?"

Decker shook his head. "No, sir. He never mentioned that to me, but he never really talked about his future plans. It was always about the navy and the ship."

"He used to talk to me about it," the commander said. "He was worried about money. He knew that he had his retirement pension, but he also knew it wouldn't be enough. Especially when he moved back to the States. His kid is still young and he was worried about college and things like that."

"He could always find another career," Decker reasoned.

"That's what I told him. He had enough experience and knew enough people. I told him he'd be able to find a government job, maybe even with the navy, and he'd be fine. I just hope now he had enough insurance."

"I hope so, too, sir." Decker said, standing to leave. "That's all I wanted to talk with you about. I'll let you get back to your work."

"I'm glad you stopped by, Decker. I need to know these things."

"No problem, sir."

"By the way, do you have the business card from the investigator on you? I've misplaced the one he gave me."

"No, sir. I'm not sure where it is. I think I might have it at my friend's place in town. Why?"

"I should be the one to report this. It'll look better coming from the department head. Chain-of-command type of thing."

"I understand, sir. I can bring it in on Monday."

"I tell you what. If you don't mind, can you meet me

tomorrow? I know it's a Sunday, but we can get together on base somewhere. Not on the ship. I need at least one day away from this place."

"Sure, I can meet, sir."

"Okay then, how about we rendezvous at the Spanish Gate, say, around 1100? If you have the time, we'll drive to the navy golf course and have lunch at the club restaurant. I'd do it today but I have to finish inventorying Chief's personal effects. Then I have to go to the supply depot tonight. They just called me. We have some shipments coming in from Clark Air Base that I need to deal with. There are several high priority parts that should be arriving. If they don't show up, I need to be there to expedite them."

"Tomorrow sounds fine, sir," Decker said.

"Great. See you tomorrow at 1100. And don't forget to bring the card. I'll call the investigator tomorrow afternoon."

"I'll bring it, sir," Decker said, exiting the stateroom. He walked forward several frames, emerging from the superstructure on the port side near the torpedo tubes. He leaned over the railing and exhaled, relieved that he had finally told someone about his investigation, but still uneasy about something he couldn't quite put his finger on.

He studied the brown water lapping against the hull, racking his brain for several minutes. Nothing. A quick perusal of his Book of Dates. Zilch. Satisfied that whatever was bothering him was inconsequential, Decker turned and walked to the starboard side, crossing the quarterdeck and leaving the *Harvey* and its problems behind him.

CHAPTER THIRTY-NINE
2015, SATURDAY, MARCH 1

Mo scanned the room, spotted a waitress, and tried valiantly to catch her attention. No luck. He returned to reading his newspaper. "It's going to be a few minutes. Cal Jam's busy tonight."

Decker didn't stop writing in his Book of Dates. "I can wait," he said rather glumly.

"What's with you?" asked Hack.

"Just bothered by something."

"He's been like this all night," said Vega. "Tried to cheer him up, get him to talk, but he keeps writing in his book."

"Something doesn't make sense," Decker said.

"What doesn't?" asked Hack. "Did you talk to the supply officer?"

"I've been trying to get him to tell me for an hour," Mo said, still waving frantically at a waitress across the bar. "They need more wait staff in this place. Now I know why I don't like coming here anymore."

"I talked with Commander Doerr earlier today," Decker finally admitted. "I filled him in on everything we've done."

"Did you mention my name?" asked Hack.

"I may have."

"Thanks."

"You're welcome," Decker said. "He was busy, though. He said he has to go to the supply depot tonight to check on parts, and he wants to meet me for lunch tomorrow."

"On a Sunday? Lucky you," Hack said. He reached into his back pocket and grabbed a wad of folded papers, placing them on the table for everyone to see. "You know what I have here?"

"Please enlighten us," Decker said.

"These papers are copies of the requisition orders and notes from Chief's safe. I no longer need them or want to ever see them or think of them again."

Vega mimicked Hack and removed a copy of the paper she'd picked up at Agana's warehouse in Manila. She waved it in front of her. "Same with me. I obtained this piece of evidence illegally so I haven't been able to show it to Inspector Navarro."

Decker leaned forward and reached for his Book of Dates. Opening it to a blank page, he began to write.

"Here we go again," Hack said.

"I don't want to miss anything," said Decker. "I realized I forgot one important entry for today. I have to note that the four of us went to Cal Jam."

"That's important?" Mo asked.

"Of course it's important."

"If you say so," said Mo. "As for me, all I want to remember is what I do from this point forward tonight."

"I'm with you," Hack said, announcing that he needed to hit the head.

Vega watched Hack make his way to the restroom. She turned her attention to Decker and his Book of

Dates. "What's this?" she asked, grabbing for a slip of paper in the notebook.

Decker stopped her hand as soon as she touched it. "It's nothing, just a list of cities and times."

"Where did you get it?"

"I picked it up from the commander. It's a long story."

"Why'd you keep it?

"Curiosity."

"Let me see," she pleaded, twisting her arm to free herself from his grip. Finally, Decker relented and let go of her hand.

Vega grinned and studied the sheet of paper. A second later, her smile disappeared. Her eyes widened. "It's a gambling sheet. I recognize this from stuff my brother used to keep. Looks like winnings and losings on games."

"Could be basketball," Mo added, taking a peek at the note. "Those are all NBA cities."

"Suppo's not a gambler," Decker said firmly.

"And there's L2-50% on the back," Vega said. "Must be fifty percent of something." She quickly added the numbers on the front. "He won $1,800 on December 27."

"He didn't win anything," Decker countered. "I think it's a list of military times."

Vega picked up her sheet of paper she had grabbed from Agana's filing cabinet in Manila. "Let's see, on December 27 someone by the initial 'P' paid 'L2' an amount of 18,450 pesos."

"Suppo's not a 'P'," said Decker. "He's a 'D' for Doerr. And are you sure it's Agana who was paid? He's an 'A' no matter which name you use."

"Forget the names for now," Vega said. "Step One is to

do the math." She fished a pen out of her purse as Pong ambled towards their table.

"Lady and gentlemen, I hope you are enjoying your evening," Pong said. "We're very busy tonight. Let me take your order."

"Pong, you are a lifesaver," said Decker. "My friend here is becoming very impatient."

"Another round of San Miguels," Mo said, "And a hamburger and a large order of lumpia."

"I will have them out immediately," Pong said. "And I have a note for your friend, Mr. Hack. I saw him here earlier."

Pong handed Decker the note and scurried to take orders at a neighboring table. Decker focused his attention on the copies of the requisition lists. He turned to his notebook and found the date. "Saturday, December 28 - Spent time with Piper Doerr at her house. Moved boxes, etc."

Vega shot Decker a surprised look. "You didn't tell me about that?"

"That's part of the long story," Decker mumbled, avoiding eye contact.

Something about that date gave him pause. He couldn't quite figure out why, but the date stuck in his mind.

"Enjoying the reading?" Hack asked as he returned to the table.

"Something's weird here," Decker said. "Oh, and here's a note for you. Pong came by and handed it to me."

Hack took the piece of paper from Decker and slowly opened it. "It's from Lee. She wants me to call her at work. She says it's important."

"There's a phone behind the bar," Decker said, never looking up from his reading.

"Be right back," Hack said. "And just in time. Look who's here."

Petty Officer Pinto stood in front of the table, smiling broadly. "Where's he going?" he said, pointing to Hack.

"Has to make a phone call," Decker replied. "Don't tell me it's time for your monthly beer?"

"I think it might be," Pinto said, folding his arms and flexing his muscles. "If you don't mind me joining you."

Decker glanced at Mo and shrugged. "Sure, why not? Pull up a chair. Let me warn you, though, it's going to take a while to get a beer tonight."

"In that case, I'm heading to the bar. Be right back."

"Take your time," Mo said out of earshot of Pinto.

Two minutes later, Hack returned to the table, visibly worried. "Lee didn't answer. I called three times. Maybe I should go see her."

"She's a big girl," Decker said. "I'm sure whatever it is can wait."

"Maybe so, but I'd feel better if I went there. She never calls me like this. I want to make sure she's okay and then I'll meet up with you guys later. I'll be back before you finish your beer."

"Why not stick with us tonight," Decker argued. "You can see her when she gets off work. Besides, do you even know where she's working? The depot's a big place to be running around at night."

"I know her duty building," Hack said as he chugged the last third of his beer and scurried out of the bar.

Decker shrugged and returned to reading from his Book of Dates and the requisition lists. "This is weird."

"What do you mean 'weird'?" asked Mo. "It's *your* writing."

Decker looked up with a quizzical expression. "There's something about the dates of a few of these entries. I include in my Book of Dates when certain people go on vacation or are away from the ship."

"That is weird," said Mo. "Strange that you would write that in your book. Who do you keep track of?"

"My supervisors. Chief and the commander. It's always a banner day when they're off the ship."

"Agreed," said Mo. "When my chief's gone, it's like a vacation day."

"Thank you, sir" Decker said. "I'm glad you agree with my methodology."

"But what do vacations have to do with anything?"

"Saturday, December 28," Decker repeated. "You remember that date?"

"Not off the top of my head."

Decker held his notebook in front of Mo, pointing to an entry. "That's the day I went to Mrs. Doerr's house. I believe you'll find that entry right here."

"Why did you go to her house?" asked Vega, visibly annoyed.

"The boxes, remember," Decker said, refusing to meet Vega's eyes. "I just helped her move some stuff to her garage." He put the book in his lap and grabbed the copies of the requisition lists. For the next couple of minutes, he spread the papers on the table and began comparing the papers with entries in the book.

"I knew it," Decker said, continuing to leaf through the papers.

"Knew what?" asked Mo. "Don't tell me you're going

to be like this all night?"

"December 28," Decker said once again. "That's the date I went to Piper's house."

"You told us that already," Vega said, sounding exasperated. She held up her hands. "Now don't bother me. I'm trying to do long division. I wish I'd paid more attention in math class."

"That's not the only important event of December 28," said Decker, holding the book open to the entry for Mo to read. "Chief went on leave to Baguio City the following week."

Mo shrugged. "No big deal about that. He takes time off now and then like we all do."

Decker paused, collecting his thoughts before he spoke again. "That's not the only thing that happened that week. There was a requisition placed on January 2 the week Chief was out of town."

"Maybe Pinto placed the order," Mo said. "Ask him when he comes back."

Decker took hold of Mo's arm. "Don't say anything about it to him."

"Why not?"

"Hack did an inventory of these requisition lists. Three of the orders were fake. The items were never delivered to the ship." Decker picked up the papers. "One of the bogus orders was placed January 2."

"So Chief Fray had help," Mo said. "Or you were wrong about him like I've been saying all along."

Decker took a quick look behind him. "Where'd Pinto go anyway?

"I have no idea," Vega said. "I watched him take off as soon as Hack left. Maybe he—"

"Here is your order," Pong interrupted. "I am so sorry for the delay."

"No problem at all," Mo said, smiling at the extra portions of lumpia piled on the plate.

Pong leaned over the table next to Decker. "Let me show you something," he said. "I bought it in Manila the other day. An M1917 Enfield."

"A what?" asked Decker.

"A rifle, *pare*. It was used by the Philippine army at the start of the war. I bought one in very nice condition. They told me it still works. I would bring it out to show you, but I do not want to scare people."

"This I've got to see," Decker said. He turned to Mo and Vega. "Be right back. Don't drink my beer."

"I'll take good care of it," Mo smiled, winking at Vega.

"I'll bet," Decker said with a laugh and followed Pong through the club to a door behind the bar that led to a narrow hallway. Pong, obviously excited, talked about the rifle until Decker suddenly stopped in front of a set of double doors at the entrance to the kitchen. "What's that sign say? The one on the left."

"Use other door," Pong said. "Some of my employees do not know English too well. They come from the provinces. So I make all signs in Tagalog."

Decker turned to Pong. "My friend, I have to go. I'll be back to look at the rifle later. I promise." Decker ran down the hall and across the club to Mo and Vega's table.

"Mo!" Decker yelled over the noise of the band.

"We have to go!" Decker and Vega said in unison.

Decker cocked his head. "How did you know what I was going to say?"

"You surprised me," Vega said. "The numbers adds

up. We need to find Hack before he gets to the depot."

"Now?" Mo asked. "My food just got here."

"No time for that," said Vega, grabbing him by the arm. "We've got to move fast."

Mo stood, threw his napkin on the table, downed his beer, and belched. "Great."

CHAPTER FORTY
2035, SATURDAY, MARCH 1

Hack jostled his way through the throng of sailors, street walkers, food vendors, and unfortunate Olongapo residents who had to fight their way through similar crowds each day. He walked briskly, wondering what it could be that was so important. *Maybe she just misses me*, he smiled to himself.

Hack thought about taking a trike the short trip to the gate, but decided against it. He knew he didn't have anything smaller than a one hundred peso bill on him. He crossed the bridge and slowed to show his ID to the Marine guard who smartly waved him through. He made a left past the gate and walked towards the taxi stand where Filipino drivers stood in a circle next to their vehicles, talking and smoking and laughing. One man, the driver of the lead car, noticed Hack and threw his cigarette to the ground, stepped on it, and climbed in the driver's side.

Hack was ten feet from the taxi when he first noticed them. "What the hell do you guys want?" he said, showing his irritation.

"We don't want anything," Biff said. "Where you headed?"

"Nowhere," Hack replied, nervously.

"We need a taxi, too," Dave said.

Hack pointed to the line of cars. "There's plenty of them here tonight."

"Maybe we can share one," said Biff.

Hack looked at Biff, standing directly in front of him. Dave was to his right, blocking his path to the taxi. "I don't know who you guys are or what you want with me, but I'm in a hurry. Now get out of my way."

"Come on," Dave said. "It'll be on us."

"No thanks," Hack said as politely as he could under the circumstances. He took two steps toward to the taxis. Biff and Dave closed ranks.

"Let's share a taxi," Dave said. "We want to have a talk."

Hack slumped his shoulders and nodded. "Okay," he said. "But hang on a minute. I need to check how much money I have on me."

Hack reached for his wallet as Biff and Dave relaxed their postures. In one swift motion Hack lunged at Biff, pushing him with all his might. Biff stumbled and fell backwards on the sidewalk, cursing as he hit the pavement. Before Dave could react, Hack turned and kneed him in the ribs, sending him tumbling backwards off the curb against the trunk of a car.

Hack jumped into the waiting taxi. "Suppy depot as quickly as you can!"

"Sure thing, boss," the driver said, stepping on the gas and racing down the street. The taxi arrived at the depot's main entrance in under two minutes.

"Three dollars, forty-eight cents," the driver said.

Hack took out his wallet and thumbed through his

bills. Twenty-eight dollars and a couple hundred pesos.

"Here you go," Hack said, handing the driver all of his money. "Don't tell anyone about my little incident back there. Say you didn't see anything, okay?"

"See what?" the driver said, smiling as Hack closed the door and ran for the entrance of the depot.

CHAPTER FORTY-ONE
2040, SATURDAY, MARCH 1

"What the hell's the rush?" Mo panted, as he lagged behind Decker and Vega jogging towards base. "We'll never catch up with Hack. Let's wait for him to get back from the depot."

"I'll fill you in later," Decker said, urgently.

A half block from the nightclub, Mo grabbed Decker's shoulder to slow his stride. "You're walking too fast," Mo huffed. "Let's get a ride."

"It's only a couple more blocks," said Vega, pointing to the main gate in the distance.

"Then I'll catch up with you," Mo said, struggling to catch his breath.

Decker looked at the night sky, slowly exhaling. "Alright, let's get a trike."

The trio turned left at the corner of Gordon and spotted Rusty standing next to his bike, mingling with the other drivers. He saw Decker and Mo as they approached. "Need a ride, fellas?" he asked, moving to get on his bike.

"Yes, and we're in a hurry," Decker said.

"Sure thing, *pare*," Rusty said, kick starting his bike.

Decker climbed in the sidecar. Vega sat on his lap.

"Get on back," he said, motioning to Mo who sighed and found a spot behind Rusty.

"Where we going?" Rusty asked.

"The base," said Decker.

"It's only a block," Rusty said, nodding in the direction of the gate.

Decker pointed to Mo. "I know, but we had trouble walking fast."

Rusty smiled and put the bike in gear, speeding towards the Shit River Bridge.

Mo leaned into the side car. "Hey, let's stop and get something to eat along the way."

"You just left your dinner at Cal Jam," Decker said, annoyed. "Can this thing going any faster?" he yelled to Rusty.

"Sorry. *Malaki puwet*," Rusty said, tilting his head backwards to point at Mo sitting behind him.

"What did he say?" Mo asked.

"He said you're a fat ass," Vega giggled.

"Great," Mo grunted.

Rusty dropped them off a hundred yards from base. They jogged across the bridge to the main gate, passed through security as quickly as they could, and headed for the taxi stand.

"We still have time to catch up with him," Decker said. "I'm assuming he walked to base."

"I hope so," Mo said, trying desperately to catch his breath as they hurried down the sidewalk. "You sure we can't—"

"Hold up," Decker said, stopping in his tracks at the sight of the taxi stand. "I don't believe it."

"They're taxis," Mo said. "What's not to believe?" He

bent over, hands on his knees and breathing heavily. "I don't see Hack anywhere so let's slow down."

"I know those guys," Decker whispered, pointing to two men in front of them. One was kneeling, cursing. The other was leaning against a car holding the kneeling man's shoulder.

The man standing turned towards the sailors and Vega. "Hey, what's up with your friend?"

"You're Biff and Dave," Decker said.

"Who?"

"Biff and Dave," Decker repeated.

"Who are you talking about?" the younger man said. "We tried to talk to your friend. But he took us by surprise and got us pretty good. Do you know where...?"

"First of all, who are you guys?" Decker interrupted. "If you want anything from us, you'd better tell me who you are and what you want right now."

CHAPTER FORTY-TWO
2052, SATURDAY, MARCH 1

Hack sprinted to the main entrance of Lee's building and tried the door. Locked. He ran to a side entrance on the west side of the building, the door sailors and Filipino workers used as a shortcut to the mess hall and coffee shop. He hesitated at the doorway and turned the knob. It opened effortlessly. The office Lee worked in was located at the south end. A faint light appeared through the windows even with the shades drawn. He made his way cautiously through the dark warehouse to the office door. He knocked loudly, calling her name.

"Hack? Is that you?" asked Lee.

A wave of relief rushed over him as he recognized her voice. He opened the door and Lee came over and hugged him. "Thanks for coming out here. You could've just called."

"I tried," Hack said. "Three times. You said it was important and I got worried."

Lee held him tightly. "It's just something I discovered a little while ago. It got me a little worried. He promised me he'd end it."

"What's wrong?" Hack asked. "And who are you talking about?"

She handed him a computer printout. "Look at this."

Hack studied the document for a moment. "It's a requisition list from my ship. What's the big deal?"

Lee pointed to the date and time. "It's from today, early this afternoon."

"I still don't see what the big deal is," Hack said, puzzled.

Lee handed Hack a folder with previous *Harvey* requisitions. "You asked me to print out *Harvey* requisitions, but I didn't want to help Decker. And I didn't want him to drag you into anything dangerous."

"I remember," Hack nodded.

"But I did it a few hours ago out of curiosity. That's when I saw two requisitions from earlier today and I noticed these parts," Lee said, pointing to several high-priced items listed on the sheet of paper.

"What about them?"

"They were the exact same parts he's, I mean someone on the *Harvey*, has ordered over the past few months. They aren't parts we typically keep in stock. I had to call the manufacturer directly. And they're important enough that the navy tracks who, when, and how many of them are ordered."

"You mean they're classified?"

"Not exactly," Lee said. "But they're sensitive enough that the navy wants to know when they're being used. They're called 'depot level repairable' items. You should know what that means."

"I vaguely remember learning about that in supply school. So what are you saying? We know Chief was probably involved in the black market. I'm sure he placed these orders."

Lee grabbed hold of Hack's arm. "Don't you get it? Chief didn't place the ones today. He died Thursday."

Hack sat back in his chair and looked at the ceiling. "Maybe it *was* Pinto."

"Pinto?" Lee laughed. "Why do you think that?"

"One of Agana's men said his name when Decker and me went there. Or we think we heard him say Pinto. And that's not all."

Lee looked at Hack, worried. "What else?"

"I saw Biff and Dave on my way here. They tried to stop me at the taxi stand by the main gate."

"Who?"

"I don't know who they are. Just two guys who I've seen following me before. I call them Biff and Dave."

"Filipinos?"

Hack shook his head. "No, Americans. I should've told you about them, but I didn't want you to worry."

"Well, I know it wasn't Pinto," Lee said.

"How do you know that?"

"I just do."

"He must be the one," Hack urged. "I have to go tell Decker."

"Hold on," Lee said. "I know it's not Pinto. Trust me."

"You keep saying that. What's going on?"

Lee breathed deeply and let her eyes drift to the floor. "Look, there's nothing going on anymore between Pinto and me. Not that there was ever anything serious. Like I told you, we went out a couple times and that was that. It's not like we hate each other, though. He just wasn't my type. Anyway, he came out here today."

"To see you?" asked Hack.

"Yeah, and I don't know why. He just showed up

around 1300. I was going to eat so he had lunch with me in the cafeteria. He stayed about an hour and then left."

"Why did he come here to see you if nothing's going on?"

Lee shrugged. "I don't know. I don't think he has many friends. He just showed up and I had no idea he was coming here until I saw him. Honest."

Hack reached over and took hold of her hands. "I believe you. I don't like that he did that, but I believe you. But why does that rule out Pinto?"

Lee gave him a peck on the cheek and squeezed his hand, then let go and picked up the *Harvey* requisitions. "See, this first requisition was sent at 0514 Zulu. Then the second one five minutes later at 0519 Zulu."

"I don't know Zulu time," Hack said. "I have no idea what time that is."

"The first one was sent 1314 local time," Lee said. "The second one was 1319. Which means it couldn't have been Pinto. He was having lunch with me."

Hack leaned back in his chair. "Then who sent them?"

Lee looked around the office, her eyes beginning to tear. "He promised me he'd stop."

"You keep saying that. Who are you talking about?"

"It's complicated," Lee said. She grabbed the phone-book on her desk. "Let's call the investigator who you said came to the ship."

"I have no idea what his number is. I lost the business card he gave me." Hack walked over and knelt in front of Lee. "What's going on? You're beginning to scare me."

Lee ignored the question. "Okay, let me call my supervisor. He needs to know about the requisitions anyway."

"You sure it's okay to call him at home?"

"I have before," Lee said. "He doesn't mind if it's important and this is important." She picked up the phone and paused before dialing and turned to Hack. "I also have other news."

"What is it?"

"I got my official orders today. I'm leaving in three months."

Hack stood and kissed her. "Let's not think about it now. We still have three months to be together."

Lee put her hand on Hack's face. "Okay, I just wanted you to be the first to know." She turned to the phone. "Now let me make the call. He'll be interested to know that the *Harvey* ordered two of these parts today. It'll raise some huge red flags."

"It won't raise anything," a voice behind them announced. They turned and saw Commander Doerr standing in the doorway holding a .45 pistol in his right hand. "Put the phone down, Lee, and back away, Wilson. I hate to have to do this. You're good sailors, but I've recently become aware of the black market scheme you're running."

"You're crazy, Bob" Lee said. "Don't point that thing at me."

The commander shook his head. "I have all the evidence. Bogus requisition messages. Lists of missing parts. Eyewitness accounts of your boyfriend visiting known black market operators in Olongapo."

"You'll never get away with it," Hack said. "The police know about you."

"I don't believe you," the commander said. He pointed the barrel of the gun towards the office door. "Now we're going out the back way. Lee, honey, you go first since you know the way. I'll be right behind you with a gun on you guys in case you think of trying anything stupid."

"Honey?" Hack looked at Lee, but she just turned and walked quietly out of the office, leading the trio single file through the maze of pallets and boxes of supplies arranged in orderly rows.

"It's dark in here," Hack said. "I hope you know where we're going."

"I usually have the lights on," Lee whispered.

"Shut up, you two," the commander ordered.

They continued walking through the aisle, cautiously making their way across the deserted warehouse. A few feet from the end of a row of supplies stacked nearly to the ceiling on pallets, the commander stopped abruptly. "Hold up. And be quiet."

They listened intently. Only the sound of a distant crane moving along a pier broke the silence of the warehouse.

"It's just your imagination," Lee whispered. "Or a rat running wild in the building."

The commander exhaled. "You're probably right. Keep walking."

When they reached the end of the aisle, the commander halted in a spot that was lit by pole lights shining through the windows. He pointed the gun directly at Hack. "The way I see it, I have two choices," Suppo said. "One, I could turn you guys in. It will be obvious you were the ones behind the black market business. Who are they going to believe? A commander or junior enlisted sailors? Or, two, I could shoot both of you right now. Either way I'd be in the clear." He pulled a small revolver out of his back pocket. "I'll plant this gun on you. I'll tell the police I knew you were involved. I came here looking for you. You threatened me. 'I had to shoot, sir. It was self defense.' They would all believe me."

Through the dim light, Hack watched as the commander began laughing nervously, dropping the gun to his side. Hack saw an opening. He lunged towards the commander who instinctively put his shoulder into the sailor, knocking him to ground. The commander smiled at Lee and then at Hack on the deck, pointing the gun at Hack's chest, his finger slowly squeezing the trigger. "I told you to cooperate, but you didn't listen."

The instant the flash of explosives erupted from the gun, a large beast shot out from behind the pallets to the left of the commander. Suppo caught a glimpse of the figure in his peripheral vision and flinched a half step to his right. Mo hit the deck with a thud, a perfectly executed belly flop on the concrete pavement.

Vega instinctively sprang into action. She sidestepped Decker and sprinted towards the commander, lunging towards him while he stared at Mo prone on the deck. She drove the full force of her weight into Suppo's left side, sending his weapon careening across the floor.

The commander recovered from the body blow and kneed Vega in the ribs. She dropped to her hands and knees gasping for breath and crawling towards the weapon. Decker sprinted and slid face down across the concrete, desperately reaching for the gun. But Suppo was too quick. He pulled his spare revolver from his pocket a split second before Decker could grab the pistol.

"Don't move," the commander said, slowly standing, surveying the surroundings. He looked at Lee giving first aid to Hack. "Get away from him, sweetheart."

"He needs help!"

"Just back away from him."

Lee inched away, keeping her focus on Hack, while the supply officer aimed his pistol at her.

"Drop the gun," a voice behind the commander ordered.

Suppo wheeled around. He stared at Biff and Dave with their guns drawn.

"Drop it," Biff commanded. "You have no way to escape. The building's surrounded. Put the gun down now!"

A stillness enveloped the warehouse. Everyone waiting on the commander's next move. He started to drop his weapon, but instead turned towards Biff and the Dave, his gun still raised.

Two shots pierced the silence. The supply officer stumbled backwards three steps and fell to the deck with a thud.

Lee rushed to Hack's side, kneeling to begin first aid.

"How's he doing?" Biff asked, removing a small walkie talkie from his pocket to call for an ambulance.

"I put pressure on the bleeding." She lowered her head to Hack's face. "And he's still breathing."

"Okay, good. We'll take over first aid from here. You guys wait in the office," Biff said. "We'll get your friend to the hospital. Don't go anywhere. Don't call anyone. Wait for us."

"Yes, sir," Decker said, standing to look at Lee, Vega, and Mo. The three friends took one last survey of the scene, and then slowly walked down the aisle towards the office. Vega put an arm around a sobbing Lee.

"Looks like it's going to be a long night," Decker said.

Mo shook his head. "Great."

CHAPTER FORTY-THREE
1310, SUNDAY, MARCH 2

She sat on the edge of the bed watching Hack breathe, then reached up and brushed the hair away from his forehead. "Hey, how're you feeling? I hope you can hear me. I wanted to see you before the others get here. I feel really bad about what happened." She leaned down and kissed his forehead.

The sound of Decker's voice in the hallway startled her. Vega jumped from the bed and scurried to a chair a few feet away.

A moment later Decker strolled through the door with Lee and Agent McCoy, a.k.a. Biff, in tow, each one holding a coffee cup. "Hack, don't tell me you have late sleepers again," Decker said, finding a chair at the far end of the bed.

Agent McCoy followed and sat in a chair next to Vega.

Lee walked over and stood next to the bed. She glared at the police officer. "What are you doing here? I thought you said you were going to the head?"

"I *did* use the restroom," Vega said. "But I didn't feel like waiting on you guys to finish eating. I decided to come up here, and the nurse said I could come on in."

Lee sat on the bed next to Hack, watching his body

twitch as he awakened. He slowly opened his eyes, startled that someone was sitting next to him holding his hand.

"Hey, sweetie. How are you feeling?" Lee whispered.

Hack looked up at her and a smile spread across his face. "I'm doing okay." He glanced around the room and focused on Decker. "Where am I?" And then at McCoy. He tried to push himself to a sitting position. "What the hell are you doing here?"

"Hey, don't get up," Decker said. "You're hooked up to all kinds of stuff. You're at the Subic Bay Naval Base Hospital. And this is Special Agent McCoy from the Naval Security and Investigative Command."

"We meet again," McCoy said. "The guy you refer to as 'Dave' is my partner, Reed McGruder. It's nice to have new nicknames. We're usually called Old Mac and Young Mac. He's on the *Harvey* now, but you'll meet him later today."

"How long have you guys been here?" asked Hack. "I woke up this morning and no one was here."

"We've been here all night," Decker said. "We slept, or tried to sleep, in the waiting room. The nurse wouldn't let us visit you until now." He pointed towards the door. "Mo's here, too, but he's working on seconds in the cafeteria. Or maybe it's thirds by now. He was complaining about me not letting him eat for the past three days."

"Food sounds great," Hack said. "Even navy food. You know what?" He looked up at Lee and squeezed her hand. "I just had the best dream. I was sitting with a beautiful girl and she was holding my hand and kissing me. And then I woke up and here you are. It's like my dream came true."

Lee scowled at Vega. "A dream, huh?" She turned back to Hack. "I'm just glad you're awake."

"What happened last night?" Hack asked. "I remember being at Cal Jam and the next thing I know I'm waking up here."

"It's a common response," McCoy said. "I've seen it a lot in trauma victims. You may never remember anything about getting shot."

"It's for the best," Lee said, patting Hack on the hand. "You shouldn't try to remember last night. It was awful."

"But, let me fill you in on a few minor details," Decker said. "As soon as you left Cal Jam, I realized what had been bothering me for the past couple of days. It was the dates."

"The dates?"

"Yes, the dates. I remembered the date December 28."

"Why is that important?"

"It isn't, but the following week Chief Fray was off the ship. As you may remember, someone placed a requisition order on January 2. And thanks to your inventory, we knew those parts never made it to the ship. Based on that information, I realized that it couldn't have been Chief Fray because he couldn't place an order if he wasn't logged into the system. It had to be someone else with access. And then you got the call from Lee, and we followed you. We reached the taxi stand and you were nowhere in sight, but we ran into Special Agents McCoy and McGruder, and long story short, the commander shot you, and McCoy and McGruder shot him. Suppo died this morning."

"How did you know it was the commander?" asked Hack. "We had another suspect or two."

Decker sipped from his coffee. "I didn't at first. It was a hunch I got when I read a sign at Cal Jam."

"A sign? What are you talking about?" asked Hack.

"After you left the club, Pong wanted to show me something in his office. A new WWII rifle he had purchased for his collection. As we were walking through the back of his bar, I saw a set of double doors with a sign in Tagalog that read *Gamitin ang kabilang pinto*. I'd seen the sign a hundred times before, but I never paid attention to it."

"Use other door," said Vega.

"Exactly," said Decker. "That's what Pong told me. *Pinto* is the Tagalog word for 'door'. And then it hit me. We thought Ponytail and Baldy were talking about Petty Officer Pinto, but they were saying, 'Are they friends of Door'. It must've been a nickname they gave Commander Doerr. Then I remembered that Suppo told me he was going to go to the supply depot because some special parts were coming in, and since I'd already told him how much we knew, I deduced he'd start to feel threatened we were getting close. So Mo, Vega, and I tried to catch up with you to warn you." Decker turned to Vega. "And some careful police work also pointed towards the commander."

Vega nodded. "I knew there had to be a reason an American was involved. A good reason. When I saw the slip of paper Decker got from the commander's wife, I knew it was from gambling. The numbers didn't add up until I remembered I was looking at dollars on the commander's sheet of paper and pesos on the paper I got from Agana's. I did the math with the exchange rate and it worked out perfectly. The commander won $1,800 on December 27 betting on basketball games. But half of it, $900, went to Agana to fund his *jueteng* operation. 18,750 pesos. I also remembered Ducky had said Angelito Agana had a son, Lito Junior. I deduced he was the 'L2' on the commander's note. And the 'P' makes sense as the one helping fund the *jueteng* operation. It was 'P' for Pinto, the nickname Decker figured they had for the commander."

"Wow," Hack said, turning to McCoy. "How much did you know?"

"We obviously knew there was a black market operation going on," McCoy said. "We also knew someone on the *Harvey* was coordinating it. We suspected someone at the supply depot was helping, but didn't know who. We'd been following you because it made sense at the time. You were on the *Harvey* and your girlfriend worked at the depot. The only problem in our minds was that you and Petty Officer Mansfield were junior and my bosses believed, correctly as it turned out, that it had to be someone at a higher rank."

"Then why were you still following me if you thought I wasn't the suspect?" asked Hack.

"Two reasons. We thought you might have become involved somehow and we also found out from following you that you were up to something. We didn't know what, but we knew you guys visited Fortuno and Agana." He chuckled. "You seemed to be everywhere we turned. At one point, Reed, or Dave to you, thought you guys might be undertaking some sort of investigation on your own, but dismissed it. Didn't think you had it in you."

Decker leaned back and spread his arms expansively. "Ah, the little guy. Always underestimated."

McCoy laughed. "Don't let it bother you. That's the way we operate."

"Clearly a lack of training on your part." Decker tsk tsked at him. "Maybe we could give you guys a few pointers."

"Yeah right. I'll be sure to send that recommendation up the chain of command and see what they say. I'll sign it 'Biff and Dave.'"

Hack blushed at the mention of the nicknames. "So what's everybody saying on the ship?" Hack asked.

"They can't believe it," said Decker. "The commander was too smart to get involved in something like this."

"Smart, yes, but also someone who needed money," McCoy said.

"I thought officers made a good living," Hack said, reaching for a glass of water.

"They do, but even with an officer's pay, a gambling problem can get you in deep trouble pretty quickly," McCoy said. "When we talked with Mrs. Doerr last night, she told us it started when he was stationed in Nevada. He'd always been a social gambler, betting at casinos or putting money on a game here and there. But something triggered a bigger problem. I'm no psychologist, but I'd say he was addicted. She thought the move to the Philippines would help, but he found the casinos here and continued betting on sporting events."

"Didn't she try to help him?" asked Vega.

McCoy blew on his coffee to cool it. "She said she insisted he get counseling in the States a couple times, but nothing seemed to work. He'd go cold turkey and then she'd notice the bank account dwindling again. And he did all that off the record. Didn't want the navy to know otherwise he'd be a security risk and future promotions would be at stake."

"I'm surprised she stayed with him," said Decker.

McCoy nodded. "He said he worried about her leaving."

"You talked to him before he died?" Lee asked with a quick glance down at Hack.

"He woke up after surgery," McCoy said. "We managed to talk to him for about fifteen minutes before he slipped into a coma. He never recovered."

"What did he say?" asked Hack.

"He was deep in debt. And it's an old story with gamblers. The more they get into debt, the more they want to place that one last bet that will make a killing. He said he tried to quit but he never could shake it. And then he discovered the black market operation going on under his nose when he was stationed at the supply depot. Agana had a guy working for him there."

"And he has since escaped," Vega interjected. "But we know who he is. It's only a matter of time before we track him down."

"The commander confronted Agana's man," McCoy continued. "He told us he planned to turn him in, but, instead, they made a deal. Suppo needed the money and it looked like an easy way to pay off some gambling debts. I'm sure it started out with small stuff, but with a senior supply corps officer in the fold, Agana probably upped the ante. They moved into household items, stereos, televisions, stuff like that. Then it became parts for ships. From what we can tell, most likely going to Iran."

"The ships we read about in the library," Hack said.

Decker nodded. "The very ones."

"Commander Doerr had the seniority to move the kind of material that other countries need," McCoy said. "Circuit cards, valves, radar components. The kinds of things you can't pick up at the local hardware store. And then the commander's gambling problem resurfaced. He got into sports betting at one of Agana's casinos, which turned out to be an easy way for Agana's son to skim the winnings to help fund his *jueteng* empire."

"I can understand, I guess, why Suppo was involved when he was stationed at the supply depot, but why didn't he quit when he transferred to the *Harvey*?" asked Hack.

"Agana threatened him. And then he became desperate. But the commander didn't have the same access and authority anymore to go over to the depot and make things happen. And when he knew Kippen was on to him, he turned to murder." He glanced at Decker. "You almost ended up the same way. He admitted that he tipped off Agana about you. It was one of his men who chased you in the trike."

"I'm glad he was a bad shot," Decker said.

"The commander said he got scared after that," McCoy added. "He convinced Agana to call off the hit on you, said he'd take care of it himself."

"Was that all he said?" asked Lee, glancing at Hack. A glance Vega noticed.

"Yep, he started mumbling something else, then closed his eyes and never woke up."

"I thought sure it was Chief," Hack said, looking at Decker. "You had me convinced. We should've gone to him."

"Easy to say that now," Decker said. "But we had no idea whether he was involved or not. It would've been too risky. Apparently, though, Chief Fray was also conducting his own investigation."

"How did he find out about Agana?" asked Hack.

"From his wife," Vega said. "We talked to her last night. She has a relative involved with Agana. Chief told her about the inventory problem and she guessed it was a black market operation and told him about Agana."

"So it wasn't Pinto either?" Hack asked, not remembering that Lee had told him she'd been having lunch with Pinto when the last orders were placed.

Decker glanced at Lee. "No, he's been ruled out."

"Same with Ensign Limpert," McCoy added. "We had our eyes on Petty Officer Pinto for a short time, but all he ever did was go to the gym. Limpert never left the ship except to visit a family in town. We focused on—"

A nurse entered the room, interrupting the conversation. "Don't stay too long," she said, sternly. "He needs his rest."

"So where does this leave us?" Hack asked, watching the nurse leave the room.

"Needing more coffee," said Decker. "I'll make a cafeteria run and try to get you a cup, too."

"You are a true friend." Hack gave Decker a weak salute.

"Don't thank me yet. I still have to smuggle the contraband past Nurse Ratchet." Decker stood and started for the door.

"Wait," said Vega.

Decker whirled around. "What's up? Want some coffee, too?"

"I do," she said. "But that's not it. I forgot something." She reached into her purse and took out an envelope. "I went with Inspector Navarro to see Mr. Fortuno late last night as part of our investigation. My boss didn't let me sit in on the conversation, but I didn't mind this time. I got to talk with Olivia who I hadn't seen since I was fourteen. She told me she met you guys and we had a good laugh about it."

Decker gave a stiff bow. "I'm glad the both of you could find us humble sailors so entertaining."

"She actually likes you," Vega smiled. "I could tell by the way she talked about you. And she asked me to give you this." She handed Decker the envelope.

He set down his coffee and opened the letter. Everyone sat quietly as he started reading. A few seconds later, a frown came over his face.

"What's it say?" asked Hack.

Decker looked up at Hack with a confused expression. "I have no idea. I can't read her handwriting."

ACKNOWLEDGEMENTS

Thank you to Kristina Makansi, Donna Essner, Lisa Miller, and the entire Blank Slate Press team. Their guidance, support, and editorial skills not only improved the book, but also made the publication process a pleasure.

A special thank-you goes to Donna Swischer for her tireless efforts. She read (and re-read) multiple drafts, discussed story lines with me, and always offered spot-on feedback and suggestions. I could not have written this book without her help. Thanks, too, to Tom and Linda Pratt. Their insightful critiques of early versions of the novel helped shape and improve the plot and characters. Also thank you to Kathleen Hanselmann, Michelle Lahey, and John Lopez for reading the manuscript and providing helpful comments.

Finally, my biggest thank you is to my wife and lifelong Cal Jam partner, Lynn. She has heard me talk about writing a book for many years and always encouraged me to make it happen.

ABOUT THE AUTHOR

Jack Ambraw is the pen name of Eric Ward, a native of the small town of Newton, Illinois. He served eight years in the U.S. Navy, including a two-year assignment on board the USS *Sterett* at Subic Bay, Philippines, the setting for his debut novel. His day job is Vice President for Public Programs at the Linda Hall Library of Science, Engineering & Technology, an independent research library in Kansas City, Missouri. Jack has a B.A. in English from Hawaii Pacific University, an M.L.I.S. from the University of Hawaii, and is a doctoral student in an interdisciplinary Ph.D. program in history and English literature at the University of Missouri-Kansas City. He and his wife Lynn live in the Northland of Kansas City, where he is at work on *Yamashita's Gold*, a second Subic Bay Mystery featuring Elliott Decker and his friends.